LOVE AND BETRAYAL

Angie bolted upright in the bed, her eyes wide and unseeing, and screamed uncontrollable wails, over and over again.

Matt crashed through the door with Buster at his heels, fearing what he'd find. He saw Angie, and in a flash, threw back the netting to get to her. She sat unmoving, her face wet with tears and wrenched in a scream. She was seized by a dream. He dropped to the bed and grasped her upper arms.

"Angie, wake up." He shook her.

The scream in her throat died, but she closed her eyes and gentle moans replaced the earlier hysteria.

"Angie, it's Matt." He spoke gently. "Wake up. You're dreaming."

She opened her eyes and raised her hands in a fighting posture. Slowly, recognition began to surface. She threw her arms around Matt's neck and buried her face there.

"It's okay," he said, over and over again, and rocked her back and forth. "It was only a bad dream." Matt held her tight so that her sniffles were muffled against his body. He could only hope his comfort would keep the dangerous nightmare at bay.

Angie raised her face to Matt's and, like a moth to a flame, his shiver of desire would not be denied. Hungrily, he covered her mouth with his.

BOOK YOUR PLACE ON OUR WEBSITE AND MAKE THE ARABESQUE ROMANCE CONNECTION!

We've created a customized website just for our very special Arabesque readers, where you can get the inside scoop on everything that's going on with Arabesque romance novels.

When you come online, you'll have the exciting opportunity to:

- View covers of upcoming books

- Learn about our future publishing schedule (listed by publication month and author)

- Find out when your favorite authors will be visiting a city near you

- Search for and order backlist books

- Check out author bios and background information

- Send e-mail to your favorite authors

- Join us in weekly chats with authors, readers and other guests

- Get writing guidelines

- AND MUCH MORE!

Visit our website at
http://www.arabesquebooks.com

UNDER A BLUE MOON

SHIRLEY HARRISON

ARABESQUE

BET BOOKS

BET Publications, LLC
www.msbet.com
www.arabesquebooks.com

Although Cave Cay is a fictional islet
Near the Bahaman Out Islands,
There are over a thousand undiscovered,
Uncharted land masses in the Caribbean.
To preserve their natural beauty, steps have been taken
To set up national parks and nature preserves
On many of the more secluded, lush islands.
Your adventure awaits!
—S. Harrison

ARABESQUE BOOKS are published by

BET Publications, LLC
c/o BET BOOKS
One BET Plaza
1900 W Place NE
Washington, D.C. 20018-1211

First Printing: October, 1999

10 9 8 7 6 5 4 3 2 1
Printed in the United States of America

*To the men in my life—my husband, Wilber
and my sons, Joel Rodney and Brian Reggie
(the power of the middle name).
Their support is both considerable and unconditional.*

*I would like to thank:
Rudy Rudolph, the ultimate computer guru,
Dr. Ivan Cazort, Det. Gary Lovett, and my sister,
Brenda Stanley,
willing sources any time of day;
Jan Byrd, who never fails to tell me what she really thinks;
and Barbara Fambrough, my friend, my ear.*

*I am grateful to all of you for your patience,
explanations, and guidance.*

TRUST

While I was sleeping in my bed there, things were happening in this world that directly concerned me—nobody asked me, consulted me—they just went out and did things, and changed my life.

—Lorraine Hansberry
from *Raisin In The Sun*, 1959

CHAPTER ONE

The air hung hot and humid. Angie loved it, was used to it, and had dressed for the occasion of an afternoon of sun worship in Biscayne Bay with her wretched husband.

Her gait slowed as she neared the pier of the bay marina, where a line of boats stood moored in Florida's summer heat. She shielded her sunglass-covered eyes and looked for the sleek cruiser that bore a distinct teal flag—and her name, Angelica.

Before her eyes completed a sweep of the boats, a man waved from the pier and made his way toward her.

Angie sucked in a deep breath and slid the sunglasses from her eyes just enough to make sure it was him. She pushed them back on.

It was him.

While she had avoided her estranged husband's company for the last year, he had managed to avoid the finality of divorce. This arranged meeting, he had promised, was all it would take for him not to contest her petition for divorce. It meant she would be divorced by the weekend.

Of course, Philip was a successful, local attorney, so he could achieve a new procrastination ploy easily enough.

"Hello, Mrs. Manchester," Philip hailed when he got closer.

"Not for long," Angie shot back in a low voice, and regarded him with a sharp stare as she took in his cotton knit polo, linen trousers, and leather woven sandals. A large gold cross around his neck peeked from behind his lapel.

"I heard that," he retorted in good humor.

She arched her brow in disdain at his words. His white teeth gleamed from below a well-groomed mustache, all framed within a smooth, bronzed face. Always proud of his athletic body and good looks, he was a handsome man who turned the heads of women and men alike. Once, she had allowed him to turn hers, but she was no longer under the spell of his manipulative charm.

"Don't forget you agreed to indulge me today in return for my promise." Philip closed in on Angie and let out a sharp wolf whistle, as his gaze traveled over her shoulders bared by her halter top, to the matching long wrap skirt and, finally, down to her sandals, where a thin gold chain encircled one ankle.

Angie pressed her lips together and stifled her rising anger. Still having the devil-may-care attitude, Philip acted as though she didn't know the truth about who and what he really was. She sailed past him and continued toward the boat.

Philip's long strides and lazy laugh easily reached her, and the two now walked together.

"Damn, but you're still a sight to see," he said, his smile broad. "Even your hair . . . you cut it all off." He referred to her dark hair's new cropped style that was no more than an inch or so in length. Large, hoop earrings of hammered gold danced from each ear.

She ignored his comments. "You're up to something

because suddenly, you're reasonable. Are you going to tell me now or surprise me later?''

"When did you get so suspicious?"

Angie caught the glance he darted in her direction, and this time, the old anger, strong as bile, rose into her throat.

"I used to think I didn't have to be."

When Philip declined to return a witty quip, but sighed and pushed his hands into his pockets, Angie experienced a measure of bittersweet triumph. Maybe he had come to understand the consequence of his past actions.

"I only showed up because my attorney and I figured this meeting might get things resolved," she began. "So, I'm here, suspicions intact, for lunch on the boat. That's it."

"Angelica, your attorney's a novice, and was glad to get my help. You should've taken my advice and let me pay for one of the competent firms I recommended." He slipped a hand to her bare back when they reached the boat. "Watch your step."

"Don't patronize me." She skirted away from his hand. "And, don't do that, either. You've lost the privilege."

"That mouth of yours is still pure sass. No matter what's on your mind, I could always count on you to speak it." He dropped his hand and offered her an indulgent smile. "I'll miss that."

Angie shrugged off his smooth words and left him standing there. She moved on sure feet up the steps of the *Angelica* and crossed over its familiar deck.

They both loved the water and the yacht had been their wedding gift from Philip's father, a successful exporter in the northeast. Some of the happiest moments of her short-lived marriage had occurred aboard this beautiful vessel.

Those joyful times, though, couldn't wipe away the memory of the day she'd stumbled onto the unsettling truths that shattered Philip's carefully constructed facade. She had not boarded the *Angelica* since. That had been well over a year ago, and she had done a lot of growing up in that time.

"Despite our problems," she heard Philip say, "I know you love this boat. And, since you won't agree to take anything from me in the settlement, I wanted our last meeting here."

He had masterfully manipulated her emotions once again. Awash in memories, she turned about the deck; but, it could never be enjoyed with the same innocence again, and that single fact sobered her recall.

Out of habit, she reached up to tuck a stray lock of long hair behind her ear, a strand now missing, and spied a table. Linen covered and cozily set for two, it occupied the far corner of the deck, protected from the sun by a striped, teal and white bimini. She stepped in that direction.

"Where's Daniel? Will he navigate?" She turned again, expecting to see Philip's dour, longtime employee. Known to move with a shadow's stealth, the man was creepy and had always made her uncomfortable.

"No, we're alone." Philip joined her near the polished wood rail. "After arranging to spend time with you, I'm sure as hell not sharing you with Daniel."

Philip had leaned in close, as though to draw on their past intimacy, but Angie was defiant and held her ground, unaffected by his presence. Their death knell had long sounded, and she had paid attention.

He pushed off the rail and flipped the engine key in the air. "Why don't you get comfortable and I'll prepare to cast off."

When he walked away, Angie turned into the railing and rested a knee on the padded bench that flanked the side. She closed her eyes and held her head up to catch a wayward breeze that blew across the quiet marina.

"Well, here goes nothing . . . and everything," she muttered to herself. There was no reason to doubt that things wouldn't work out and that the afternoon wouldn't be as painless as her lawyer had predicted. Though trite, today was the first day of the rest of her life.

The engine came to life with a loud hum, and the boat slipped away from the dock. She opened her eyes and looked over the side into the hypnotic ripples that widened in the gray, dusky water near the moorings. As she stood there, she was struck by a mood of skepticism before a dizzying arc of energy passed through her.

An omen? She shuddered in response, and gave herself a tight hug. It was a valiant effort to fight off the chill of doubt that now grasped her.

"Thank God, Matt, it's finally over." Jewel Sinclair gave her son a strong and heartfelt embrace. After a moment, she pressed her hands against his broad, suited chest and pushed away. "Now, you can let it go for good, too."

"It's a start, Mom." Matthew Sinclair squeezed her shoulders before he turned to his lawyer, Albert Foster. "You did a good job, Al. Thanks."

"I told you this would be a slam dunk." He looked at his watch. "I know the press is champing at the bit downstairs to hear the news. Why don't I give them our prepared statement while you slip out the side exit?"

Matt nodded his agreement before the lawyer took his leave.

Only minutes before, the crowd in the small room of the Russell Federal Building had listened in rapt attention to the Board's decision. As they now cleared the room, a steady barrage of hands slapped Matt's back in congratulations. He spoke his gratitude to each well-wisher.

Towering over most of the people in the third floor meeting room in downtown Atlanta, Matt looked beyond his mother and into the face of an older, heavyset woman, who stared back at him. She stood across the room, her features cold and unmoved, and watched the jubilant celebration that surrounded Matt. The old accusations were vivid in her eyes, the animosity rich in her unbowed posture, proof that she would never accept anything except her own twisted version of the truth.

"Jewel is right." The voice belonged to John Parkinson, Matt's mentor, friend, and one of his business partners. "This nightmare is finally over. The last roadblock has been moved so your life can get back on track."

Matt frowned as he looked at John. "Sometimes, I wonder if it'll ever be over." His eyes once again read the anguish captured on the face of the older woman before she turned away and allowed her companions to lead her through the door.

Jewel followed her son's gaze. "We always knew she'd never accept a favorable decision. She's still hurting, and in time, maybe . . ." She drew a deep sigh. "It doesn't matter," she implored. "It's time to heal and move on."

"And, there's no better way than to get out of Dodge," John added in jest. "You are still going to Cave Cay before you jump back into the fire? The office can wait a while longer."

Matt appreciated his friend's attempt to lighten their somber mood and offered the beginnings of a wide smile. "After the way all of you conspired to get me there, do I have a choice?"

John boxed Matt's shoulder. "Hey, don't hand me that. You love that place. It'll do you good to get away from all this crap and spend some time snorkeling and fishing." He held his hands up as though he framed a vision. "Just think, no outside interference from telephones, television, newspapers, or the reporters that go with them." They laughed at the reference to their invaded lives.

"All you have to remember, Matt Sinclair, is that you've never given up and buckled under," Jewel admonished with a finger. "No matter what the odds, you're a fighter;

from the time we were in the projects not far from here
to—"

"I get the point, Mom." He wrapped his arm around
her shoulder and pulled her into his side.

"Hey, that's the spirit," John chimed in.

"When I get back from the island, a new chapter
begins." Matt gave them the thumbs up . . .

It had already started. As he stood on the sand, a spray
of ocean surf splashed against Matt and now pulled him
from the pleasant reverie. That day last week had been a
lucky one for him, and he was equally lucky to have had
family and friends stand by him during the year-long ordeal
that followed Paula's death.

The sun was white bright as he squinted at the mail boat
captain, who continued to carry on a lilting, one-sided
conversation. Out of the corner of his eye Matt saw his
dog, Buster, jump from the boat and splash into the surf.

"I look for you, right here at the shore, after ten days."
The launch captain didn't wait for a response, but tipped
his cap goodbye to Matt. The man's sweat-drenched face,
a leather brown in both texture and color, stretched to
accommodate a wide smile.

Matt returned the captain's goodbye salute with his own
smile and wave. He hefted the last of his bags from the
warm sand and prepared to make his second trek up to
the house on the island. He sharply inhaled a breath of
the sea air and looked up at the clouds that threatened to
produce another of the squalls so common this time of
the year.

He let out a brisk whistle and was quickly joined by
the large, mixed collie breed dog. The launch that had
deposited them on the island skimmed across the calm,
cerulean blue Atlantic, then disappeared around a bend
of boulders.

Within a few minutes, Matt had worked his way across
the sand and past a profusion of flowers and trees that

bordered the stone-pebbled walkway to the house. He set the last of his bags inside the doorway, stepped over them, and looked around to reacquaint himself with the place. Buster pushed his way through, too, and started his own inspection.

"I hope that means you're glad to be here, fella, because this is it." Matt's voice rang with cheerfulness. He felt good, re-energized now that he was on the island. "We're on our own for a while. What do you say to that?"

When the dog performed a nonchalant trot to an adjoining room, Matt laughed out loud.

"It's gonna be a long stay if you keep that attitude. You know, I could've boarded you at the kennel at home."

He looked over the bags stacked at the open door before he headed for them. A thin, dark leather briefcase, with combination locks on the clasps, was set apart from the others.

Matt studied the briefcase a moment before he hefted it into his hands. *What fool would purposely bring a painful reminder of the past to a retreat?* He had asked himself that question ever since he had boarded the plane in Atlanta. He also knew the answer was quite simple: He found a perverse pleasure in the consistent challenge it offered him to get on with his life.

He set the briefcase on an upper shelf of the well-stocked bookcase, then backed away, his eyes still fixed on it.

A rumble of thunder sounded in the distance and caught his attention. Matt turned to the open doorway. A bank of dark clouds gathered on the afternoon horizon. The mailboat captain had warned him that storms come and go quickly, and to keep his eyes peeled for trouble. It seems he had arrived just in time for one of the storms to cool things down.

"Come on, Buster," he called to the errant dog. "Let's see if I can remember how to batten down the hatches."

* * *

"Angelica?"

She raised her eyes and looked across her picked-over lunch. Family and friends never used her full name, except for Philip. He had thought there was a certain incongruity with such a long given name associated with her small frame and headstrong manner; to him, they formed a unique contrast that he perpetuated. Now, it all seemed one of his many pretensions.

They had met during her last year of graduate studies in Washington, D.C., when he was already a rising lawyer attending a university conference, and she was the reckless, hell-bent-for-leather daughter of a privileged family. Only just beginning to glimpse her true self, she had married Philip less than a year later, much to the chagrin of her family. She cringed at her stupidity.

"Care to share your thoughts?" he asked.

She looked down at her hands, bare of jewelry and his wedding ring, and shook her head in wonderment. "I'm trying to find the sense in why you wanted to do this."

He pushed aside his plate and leaned on his elbows. "You wouldn't let me get this close any other way. We should've had kids like you wanted."

"That was before I learned everything, before I left you."

"There's no way we can see our way around this?"

"No, I won't . . . can't live your kind of life," Angie cut in quickly. "I'm no longer that rebellious daughter who married you for the wrong reasons. End of discussion."

"Are you seeing someone else? You're a passionate woman, after all, and it's been a year since you left." He let the innuendo hang in the air.

She glared at him. "Who's fooling who, Philip? I know you've checked on my life so you know everything I've done."

"For your own good."

"Anyway, you're the one who catted around." He did have the good sense to appear uncomfortable at her reminder.

"Things are different. I'm making changes in the business, as well, like I promised."

She regarded him from beneath narrowed brows. "I didn't ask for your promises and we agreed not to rehash the past. I've made up my mind and I don't want pressure from you today. Just lunch." The soft frown on Philip's face became harsh lines. "Should I add fear of you to our list of problems?"

His eyes darted away before they returned and settled easily on her. "No, never that." He gave a deep sigh before he relaxed into the chair. "I wouldn't intentionally harm you."

"Then, let me go," she whispered. When he didn't answer, she spoke in a firm tone. "Philip, what I know stays with me. I told you when I moved out I wouldn't say anything to anyone. All I want is a clean break. I leave with what I brought to the marriage. Financially, I'm doing fine with the jewelry gallery. The shop is beginning to take off. I just want out."

"What about Reed?"

"What about him?" Angie's brother thought even less of Philip than her parent's did, if that was possible.

"He has a way of pushing his way into things that don't concern him."

"Unlike you?"

"It's been a long time since we talked about . . . everything. That's why I had to see you. I don't want anyone to have the slightest clue that you have any information. You know, all you have to do is put this divorce action aside for a while longer, and I can turn this stuff around completely. Maybe, we could even rethink the whole divorce."

"Are you crazy?" she asked, puzzled. "What are you talking about?"

He shrugged. "In a few more months, I can tie up the loose ends and suspicions."

"Only for you. It's too late to protect me, Philip." Her voice rose in anger. "You should've thought about that when you introduced this horror into my life."

"I've apologized for the—"

"Please, stop." Angie shook her head at him. "You apologized because you were found out. It doesn't change how I feel." She looked away. "I need simplicity and normalcy in my life. And you can't give me that. Ever."

"You'll have to keep quiet, no matter what."

"I know that." Her hand brushed her brow as she sighed. "I don't know the details of your dirty secrets, and I don't want to know, either." She peered at him across the table. "Is that why you want this dragged out? Afraid I'll talk to the wrong people?"

He tapped a finger against the tablecloth, as if he had to decide how to respond. "I have to be sure. When you left, you were angry and things got complicated for me. I had to make assurances that you knew nothing. You see, suspicions were raised when I severed ties with some of my clients. A quick divorce on the heels of all that would have caused more interest. So, a long, amicable one"—he raised a brow in Angie's direction—"with well placed rumors on the possibility of a reconciliation was necessary to create the right curiosity."

"You told your clients, or associates, or whatever the hell you call them that we're getting back together?" Her voice was terse.

Ignoring her question, he reached across the table for her hand. "I'm making a slight modification to lunch plans. We're going to spend the rest of the day on the boat. It'll be our last time as a married couple. I want it known that we're still friends and okay with this."

Angie jerked her hand away, but he held fast. "What I

want doesn't matter since we're on the water and you're in control of the engine key, right?"

"You'll be fine. Tonight, you'll leave with my promise not to contest the divorce action, and you'll be free of me. That's all you're interested in, anyway."

His melancholy words washed over her as she succeeded at snatching her hand from his. She sat hard against her chair and turned her sight to the few boats that floated in the distance, their images miraged by the sun. She glanced back at Philip as questions formed.

"Are we being watched?" Her answer was mirrored in his detached expression.

"I can't change what's happened, and I'm sorry about the way you found things out. In time, I would have told you. All I want is one last evening together." His eyes swept her face and revealed, for only a moment, something. Desire?

"You think I'll sleep with you for old time's sake?" Her voice carried a deceptive calm, in spite of his audacity.

He smiled. "Ahh . . . now that would be a gift from the gods. But I know you won't go for that. Spend the rest of the day with me, a ride out on the ocean, away from these other boats, where we can swim and explore the way we used to. We'll eat dinner, enjoy the moonlight, just me and you. Your parting gift to me can be friendship."

"And yours to me will be freedom." Angie pursed her mouth in a frown.

He lifted his brow. "Touché. I'll have you back at your car before midnight, with your pride and independence intact. Congratulations. You win."

It was a reckless decision, to stay with him on the boat. Although Angie wasn't afraid, she no longer knew him— if she ever had—or what he could be up to. And so, she allowed her impetuous nature to make the decision.

"I didn't bring the right clothes."

"Angelica, this is your boat. Remember? I haven't

changed anything. You have drawers of clothes below deck."

She considered his words. What did she have to lose?

"Okay," she said, and looked into his expectant face. "But, by ten, I want this boat headed back to the bay so I can get to the loft. I do have a business to run."

"Deal," he said, with a broad smile. "By the way, I picked up a special dessert. Mamie sent it to you."

She offered a reluctant smile upon hearing the name. Mamie Rutledge owned an enormously popular restaurant that they used to frequent as a couple. "Don't tell me. Her sweet potato pie with whipped cream and nuts?"

His eyes were bright as he laughed. "You remembered."

Angie smiled again. It would be all right, after all. Things would work out.

Later that night, when the sun had disappeared and the night lights of the city and coast were an uneven line across the horizon, Angie lay spent on the deck lounger. She was filled from the rich foods that Philip preferred and exhausted from the swimming and exploring. The canopy of twinkling stars she stared into offered a soothing blanket to her peace of mind.

"I'd forgotten how quiet it can be out here," Angie said from the lounger. She still wore the two-piece bathing suit she'd swum in earlier, its matching, long skirt fastened around her waist.

"I told you to take the boat out whenever you want it," Philip said. He unpacked another meal onto the table from a box he had brought up from the galley.

She turned her head in his direction. "I told you I won't do that." He wore Speedo briefs and a heavy gold cross that swung against his bare chest. "Don't tell me you're putting out more food," she exclaimed. "I'm stuffed."

A sudden flash of bright lights from the port side caught their attention.

"What's that?" Angie sat up and shielded her eyes from the brilliance that gleamed across the black water.

"I don't know," Philip answered, "but it's coming in fast."

He set the box on the table, then rushed to the side railing, Angie behind him.

As the lights drew closer, an engine's drone grew louder.

"What the hell?" Philip shouted. A larger boat came about at a breakneck pace and sped straight for them.

"It's going to hit us," Angie shouted.

Philip barreled into her with a protective hug, and they both tumbled to the deck. The impact with the other boat was a hard, rolling jolt. Not as explosive as Angie expected, its captain must have veered at the last moment. When the engines of the runaway boat were cut, silence ensued.

Philip leapt from the deck floor, pulling Angie with him. Before they could make it to the side and see the damage, two men were already boarding the *Angelica* from the other vessel. One was black, a gold earring sparkling against the shine of his ebony skin. His bright, red and white striped nautical shirt played a gay contrast to what was happening. The other man was white, with a pale complexion and similarly bleached hair. A strange pair, Angie thought, as she stared, petrified.

"What the hell is going on?" Philip yelled as he stepped forward. "You rammed my damn boat."

Angie stood behind Philip's straining figure when she saw the gun. Her mouth dropped open as the black man slowly raised the dark, shiny metal and pointed it at them. To add to the surreal picture, he was missing part of the finger he now gestured at Philip.

"I presume you are Philip Manchester?" The black man's clipped accent was precise and almost polite, incongruous with his actions.

Philip took another step forward that brought Angie with him. "Who wants to know?"

The other man also raised a gun that gave off a menacing click. "You'll find out soon enough." His accent was pure American. "Meanwhile, we're gonna be your guests."

Philip took Angie's hand. This time, she didn't snatch it away. Fear and anger knotted inside her as she came to realize the situation she had stumbled into. Remembering her earlier premonition, she drew a deep, ragged breath and forbade herself to tremble.

CHAPTER TWO

"I'm right behind you, Buster."

Matt raced barefoot across the scorching beach toward the dog's faded barks.

The white sand had already heated up again after another of the sudden afternoon storms. The blazing tropical sun could be hell if a body wasn't used to it, and the water spraying off the ocean waves cooled Matt's bare chest. He kicked through the suds of the breaking surf as it snaked along the deserted shoreline before it finally disappeared behind a wedge of thick, swaying casuarina palms. The dog's barks had become yelps, and they came from that direction.

Within moments, Buster came into view, where he nosed around an overturned gray dinghy that rested haphazardly at the water's edge. The dog emitted a series of gruff barks, then returned his attention to the boat.

"You've found something new, huh?" Matt's run slowed to a lope as he joined the dog.

"Okay, let's see what it is this time." He started to walk

over to Buster's find, but stopped dead in his tracks when he saw what had interested the dog.

"What the hell ... ?" The body of a young boy lay trapped under the overturned boat. Stunned by the sight, Matt swiftly hoisted the light vessel away from the body. Surprise lit his eyes as he realized his error.

"Well, I'll be damned."

It was a body, all right, but it belonged to a woman. He was sure this time.

She wore a bright green bikini. Her long beach skirt lay plastered to her legs by the continuous waves of seawater that washed over her.

Matt dropped to his knees next to her small frame and felt for a pulse, as he studied her face in search of life. Her brown skin had suffered sunburns along her face, shoulders, and upper chest. He found a faint, though rapid, pulse.

"Thank God, you're still alive."

He pressed his ear near her mouth as he watched her chest for a sign of movement, and saw none. With no obvious broken bones, Matt had only a few minutes to revive her from the water trapped in her lungs, and acted swiftly. Buster started to bark.

"Calm down, we're gonna take care of her."

He slipped his arms beneath her inert body and quickly moved her beyond the wet surf, where he stretched her out on the sand. In lightning moves, he pried her mouth open and cleared the air passage before he massaged her chest. Sure enough, seconds later, her body jerked with life as water drained from the corners of her mouth.

The woman's coughs were immediate and spasmodic as Matt flipped her over and rhythmically pressed into her back.

"Come on." He exhorted her between presses. "Cough it up and breathe."

The coughs became violent as more water spewed forward.

"That's it, breathe." Matt continued to massage her back, and offered a silent prayer for her recovery. Finally, the coughs subsided.

Spent from the exertion, the woman took great, heaving breaths as she lay on the sand. Matt rolled her onto her back.

"Are you all right?" He wiped the sand from her cool cheek.

Her eyes were closed, framed by dark brows and long, dark lashes feathered stiff from the seawater. In retrospect, he couldn't believe he had mistaken her for a boy. It wasn't just the abundant breasts held in check by the Lycra suit, or even the shapely legs that gave her away; the entire delicacy of her face and form screamed the fact that she was a woman.

"Let's get you out of the sand." Still on his knees, Matt pulled her up to lean against his chest. As she rested within the circle of his arms, he touched her wet head in a soothing gesture. Her black, short hair was a thick bed of wet curls on top, but straight and soft as down along the back.

"Come on, it's time to wake up. Can you hear me?"

She didn't respond and instead, her head fell against his shoulder. Matt shifted her in his arms so he could look into her face and gently tapped her jaw to rouse her from the somnolent state.

It worked. Her hand raised up to touch her ear. With a wince, she opened her eyes to Matt. He glanced to where she touched, and noticed the dark, dried blood smeared against her temple and matted in the short hair there. Despite that injury, her brown, almond-shaped eyes were clear, but they didn't stay focused on Matt. She looked past him, into the horizon. Matt followed her gaze and saw nothing of importance, just birds in flight over a brilliant blue ocean.

"Are you okay?" His attention turned to her blank stare. "What happened to you?"

The woman didn't struggle, but moved her wavering gaze back to his. Again, she winced, but the hoarse words she whispered were unmistakable.

"Help us."

Her eyes closed as her head lolled back against Matt.

"Help who?" He stared at her. "Come on, don't pass out on me again." Her breathing was shallow and her skin was cold; she was going into shock.

"Oh, hell." He drew her to his chest and stood up. "Let's move, Buster, stat."

He jogged back to the house with the woman cradled in his arms as Buster ambled alongside.

Matt thought of the irony of his situation. He had traveled over six hundred miles to a deserted key in the islands to get away from people in general and his medical practice in particular . . . only to arrive in the nick of time to find a woman in desperate need of a doctor, in need of him. It all seemed a bad twist of fate.

From his seat on top of the coffee table, Matt examined the sleeping woman on the sofa and cursed the fact that he had left his doctor's bag stateside. He'd have to make do with the limited supplies he'd brought to the island and whatever was in the house.

She had said nothing else since her earlier words on the beach. Based on her appearance and general condition, Matt figured her unconscious state stemmed from hypothermia and dehydration due to exposure. Buster finding her when he did was a lucky break. Any more time in the surf, and she would have drowned.

He cleansed her scattered scratches and burns with an antibiotic. What was she doing in the islands, and alone at that? The dinghy's presence suggested she may have abandoned a larger boat, but Matt hadn't seen another boat in the vicinity since the launch dropped him off.

As he coated the cut on her head with an iodine-soaked swab, he observed a number of things about her. Her ears were pierced, yet she wore no jewelry. A petite woman, he figured her to be in her mid-twenties. Even in her battered condition, she was a beauty. There was no mistaking her for a boy. He frowned at the direction of his thoughts.

Buster came up, then dropped to the floor by the sofa. "The lady here probably owes her life to you," Matt said.

He set the swabs on the table with the iodine, and decided to clean her up before he dressed her burns. First, though, he needed to get fluids in her.

It had taken close to an hour to complete that task before Matt moved her and the blanket to the middle of his bed. During his constant tending, she hadn't awakened, her momentary stirrings a gentle reminder that she was in a deep sleep.

With only a slight hesitation, he unclasped her swim top. Carefully, he separated it from her raw and burned skin. Liberated from the nylon prison, her breasts plumped like ripened fruit against the angry burn line above and below them. The dark centers rose to attention as the breeze from the ceiling fan taunted their freedom.

He swallowed hard as he acknowledged the lushness of her body, but he quickly locked on autopilot. It took practice, but it was a simple exercise to summon the bedside manner reserved for patients, though some times were harder than others. He squeezed the warm cloth in the basin of water.

He wiped the sand and grime from her skin as questions about her swirled through his head.

He unhooked the damp beach skirt from her waist and pushed it down her legs to reveal a matching green bikini bottom. She had a few bruises, but overall, the skirt had done a good job of protecting her lower body from the sun, and he observed no new burns.

He rolled her onto her stomach. As his practiced eyes skirted across her smooth back, he found more bruising and sunburns. Further down, where her hips widened to accommodate her firm bottom, he saw something else.

Below her dimpled lower back, she sported a small tattoo. It was a tri-colored butterfly in flight. No larger than an inch across, it peeked out of the bikini suit on her right hip. Matt smiled, amused at the discovery. On top of being beautiful, the lady had an adventurous soul.

He rubbed the aloe plant pulp into her broken and inflamed skin and left her upper body bare to facilitate healing. She'd appreciate the soothing effects of the herbal remedy later on.

When he finished, Matt moved to the other side of the bed and lifted her from the blanket to the clean, cool sheets. The skirt that had pooled at her feet now dragged behind her. He whisked the damp skirt away, then tucked the covers under her arms.

One of her feet remained uncovered and drew his attention. But, it was the fragile gold chain that encircled her slender ankle that held it.

He had missed that piece of jewelry. A tiny gold charm plate on the chain was engraved with something he couldn't quite make out. He bent down to read the tiny script.

It read, simply, *Angie.*

And that's when he saw the silver key hidden from view on the side of her ankle.

Curious, Matt dropped to his knees for a closer look. He raised her foot and stared at the key. A gold chain looped through a silver key? He frowned as he tucked her foot under the covers and pushed up from the floor.

He rubbed his hand across his beard and studied the

woman who'd arrived in such a spectacular manner into his world. *Who are you, and why did you wash up on my beach?*

Water as far as I see . . . The sun . . . It hurts . . . I need water . . . Rain . . . lightning . . . Afraid . . . I'm going to die . . . Afraid of the storm . . . Make it stop . . . The oars . . . Hold them tight . . . Don't lose the oars . . . I'm going to die . . . Alone . . . In the water . . . Help! . . . Is anyone out there? . . . Please, help us . . .

Frightened eyes opened with a jolt from the suffocating nightmare. A soft, white haze met their clouded view before they were allowed to flutter closed again. A buzz of lassitude, seductive and enticing, pervaded her limbs. By instinct, she knew that any sudden move on her part would bring about pain. So, she made a gradual struggle to turn her head on the pillow and coax her eyes to stay open.

She tried focusing on the soft haze, but was unsuccessful. Beyond the billowing white, she saw a dog. It was big, golden, and returned her stare. Strange, but she didn't know what to make of all this. Too tired to think, her eyes drifted closed.

She didn't fight it, but welcomed the oncoming languor that would return her to the sweet world that existed between the conscious and unconscious mind.

Matt peeked through the door of the bedroom again. Angie—that's what he decided he'd call her—lay in the same undisturbed position as she had for the last few hours. She had responded to external stimuli, so he wouldn't worry yet. If she didn't break through her lethargy and wake up on her own soon, though, his worry would start in earnest.

He was intrigued by the mysterious woman. Uncomfortable with the admission, he busied himself in the kitchen. He had not done much else except prowl around the house, afraid to leave her alone in case she needed him. Buster had been just as vigilant. He had given up his corner in the living room and had taken to a new one in the bedroom, the one that faced Angie's bed.

With a bewildered sigh, he leaned on the counter. He hadn't given a woman this much thought in quite some time. She needed him, though, and he wouldn't let her down. Not like he'd done with Paula. He shook his head clear of that private, unwanted memory. He wouldn't—couldn't—let that happen again.

She slowly floated to consciousness, awakened by a powerful thirst for something . . . anything. Her dry tongue darted across even drier lips. She was too tired to open her eyes, too weak to call out. Her head . . . the pounding was relentless.

A cool hand slipped behind her neck as cold metal nudged her sore lips. Next came welcome moisture—sweetened water that rolled onto her tongue. She parted eager lips and hungrily suckled at the liquid.

"Take your time. There's more if you want it."

The deep, smooth voice broke through her torpor and gained her trust. She swallowed the sweet water, then allowed more to trickle into her mouth before she tested her voice.

"Thank you." Her words were a whispered croak.

The firm hand slid out from her neck. As she nestled back into the pillow, her eyes blinked open to focus on the hand's owner.

He was turned away. Intrigued, she studied the rugged profile he presented.

"You had me worried for a while. How are you feeling?"

Through the thick mists that clouded her mind, she concentrated on his words and the rich growl in which they were spoken. Unbidden, she formed a groggy smile. She liked his voice.

"What's your name?" He turned to her.

She blinked to keep him in focus. His black beard curled against brown skin, and his dark hair was low. He had intelligent, deep-set eyes, though they seemed . . . sad. He was also tall, a big man. His shirt hung open and she could see his wide shoulders and chest.

She remembered his question now and it struck her as funny. She thought about it for a moment before her eyes ceased to blink and he became a blur again. She was tired, so she closed her eyes and revisited the dark place that kept both pain and reality at bay.

CHAPTER THREE

Something was wrong. Matt bolted upright in the chair and whipped his head in Angie's direction. She was still asleep. He relaxed as he realized the insistent nudge came from Buster. The dog wanted to go outside.

"Good morning to you, too, fella." Matt squinted into the pristine light that slanted through the open jalousie windows.

He raised his large frame from the hard chair he had folded into last night and stretched out his cramped muscles. Through the night, he had forced sweetened water into Angie's mouth to avoid further dehydration, but she had slept quietly.

Stepping to the bedside, he looked down at her face, with the full mouth, soft and delicate in sleep. Make no mistake, she belonged somewhere, and would be missed by someone.

Matt brushed his fingers across her lips and up her cheek before stopping them to rest against her forehead. No sign of fever, and that meant no infection to deal with.

Buster pranced around Matt's legs, anxious to scamper up the beach after being closed in all night. Part of the island was a protected wildlife sanctuary, and Matt didn't like the idea of Buster wandering into the area with hours of unsupervised time where he could harass the local fauna, or vice versa.

"Okay, okay, I hear you. Sorry I overslept." He turned on his heels and walked through the bedroom to the living room's screen door.

"When you get back, you can eat." He pushed the door wide, before the dog scampered down the steps, stopped a moment to snare a scent in the flowers, then bounded off at a breakneck pace for a destination beyond the house.

Matt stretched as he strode back to Angie. He'd take a shower if she still slept.

He loved the island's solitude and had been hooked from his first visit years ago. Paula, on the other hand, had hated the isolation and had never accompanied him again after that first miserable trip. He hadn't done much to change her mind, either. By that time, their marriage had become a roller coaster ride, and the island his straightaway before the next wild turn on the track.

The island house was open and airy, and had all the amenities necessary for a comfortable stay, no matter what your pleasure or poison. There were running water and toilet facilities, and generators supplied the power. Although it lacked air-conditioning, oversized fans graced the ceilings of all the rooms, and screen doors beckoned the cool evening breezes even as they kept out the pests.

Given his size, Matt preferred the garden shower at the back of the house that flowed into the tidal pool. Ostensibly intended for washing away the sand and salt after sunning and swimming, the open shower and pool had become a bacchanalian treat on the private island.

When he reached the bedroom door, he heard Angie's low groan and quickly strode to her bed. Her eyes were closed, but her parted lips moved in pantomime. She was in the midst of a dream, and by the frown she wore, it disturbed her. He pressed a hand on her brow.

"Angie, wake up. Do you hear me?"

Her groans stopped, but her eyes didn't open.

Matt moved his hand and sat on the edge of the bed. "I want to help you," he coaxed. "You have to wake up first, and tell me what happened."

The response was only silence. He picked up her limp hand with its scattered scratches and stroked it. "C'mon, wake up."

He laid her hand on top of the sheet. As he rose from the bed, her lips began a pantomime.

"Help us."

"Help who, Angie?" He leaned over her, and with his fingers along her jaw, tried to nudge her awake. When her head turned into his hand's warmth, he cradled her face.

What are you doing? The stern reminder came none too soon. He jerked his hand away and moved away from the bed. With a glance thrown to her over his shoulder, he bolted from the room.

Vaguely aware of comfort from others, Angie slipped back into the opaque mist that made up her dream . . .

The stars had turned in and left the sky black. She was alone with the dark sea and rocked precariously in the dinghy as it carried her farther away from the yacht. With each furious thrust the oars made through the black, gentle waves, the dinghy rolled back and forth. Adrift on the water, she had kept the receding lights from the boat in her sight as a guide, until they disappeared.

She began to salivate—a sign that she was about to throw up again—and her stomach lurched with the familiar contractions that preceded the gags. Quickly, she anchored the oars as her lips clamped down over her teeth to contain her building sickness.

She leaned over the dinghy in time for the erupting bile that burned her chest and throat to spew into the ocean. Her stomach had long emptied from the prior wretches.

Fear. It had made her sick on the boat, and now out here. Her weight to one side made the dinghy pitch dangerously, reminding her that her fear had to take second place to survival. She couldn't afford to lose either her seat or the oars at this point. She had to keep moving.

She scrambled aft on the little boat and, cupping a hand into the briny water, splashed some onto her face. As she fell back in the small space, exhausted, she pressed her clenched fist against her mouth to suppress a scream.

Only a few hours before, she had wondered at the peace and comfort the sky had offered the ocean she loved. Now, both were necessary evils she had to overcome if she were to get help before they discovered her missing. I can do this. I will do it.

She sat up and willed her stomach to remain calm awhile longer, then reclaimed the oars from their rack. No other boats were around in the inky black. Had she ventured too far? The only sounds were the intermittent splashes of sea life in the water and her own heart beating at triple pace.

She maneuvered the oars into place, as a prayer flowed from her lips. "God, please help us. Give me the strength to survive." Then she nervously hummed out loud as she paddled toward help . . .

Matt sat at the dining room table and looked over the newspaper clippings that were spread out in their normal ritual fashion. He set his eyes to each taunting headline, then moved on to the next. With each successive read, his anger became harder. Then, as always, before he completed reading them all, he shuffled them into an uneven stack and stuffed them back in the briefcase.

It still pained him to read the accusations, insinuations, and gossip, even after the bittersweet victory of a favorable decision from the State Medical Board. Why hadn't Paula kept her promise? Why hadn't he been able to see it had been a promise made by a sick woman? While his colleagues and the community showered him with good-deed accolades, he had ignored her downward spiral.

He stood up to replace the briefcase on the shelf and chastised himself. *Is this how you close the past and plan your future? You can't even read a few cheap articles without sinking into a pit of guilt. Deal with it, man. No amount of what-ifs will bring her back. She's dead. Dead.*

He pushed his hands deep into the pockets of his khaki shorts and paced across the room to the large, open window. The sun sat high in the sky as a tireless Buster chased low-flying egrets in the waves. He swallowed the bitter truth that no matter how accepting his world had been of his high-minded deeds, or how definitive the Board's decision, he couldn't shake a simple fact: he had killed Paula.

Wesley Palmer sat on his screened patio at his Miami home and leafed through the morning paper. He smiled absently at his wife's voice coming from inside the kitchen.

"I know I put the number in here somewhere." Madeleine Palmer rummaged through yet another kitchen drawer in search of an elusive business card that carried her son's new pager number.

"Maddy . . . honey, call him when he gets in tonight. He won't believe it's you sending a message, anyway. In all the time he's had the thing, you've never used it before."

"Nothing has been this important. Anyway, he keeps it on him all the time and I don't want my message sitting on his voice mail." Her voice trailed off, signaling she'd moved her search to another room.

He looked up and sighed. He laid the newspaper down and went inside to find his wife. She was on her knees in the living room as she riffled through the drawers at the lamp table.

"I know it's here somewhere." She dropped her hands

to her lap and raised worried eyes to her husband. "Don't you dare come in here and tell me our daughter is a grown woman and can change her plans without informing us."

"I won't." A thick strand of Maddy's peppered gray hair had come undone from her usually neat bun, a sure sign that her fingers had combed away the pins over worry for their youngest child. In times like these, the urge was strong to protect her from this kind of anxiety.

"She's headstrong, and you know that," he continued. "She's been that way ever since she refused to scream in that delivery room twenty-seven years ago."

"You think she's all right, then?" Her face turned hopeful.

He joined his wife on the floor and took both of her hands into his. "Of course she is." When he saw the doubt continue to lurk in her features, he added, "We're only doing what parents always do." He smiled. "We're making sure."

He released her hands to gather a packet of the papers from the drawer. "The more hands searching, the better. We'll find the number, okay?"

Maddy leaned into him and placed a kiss against his clean-shaven cheek. "Thank you, honey."

The aches rose in rhythmic waves from her body and woke her up from sleep's delicious escape. Her numbed eyes adjusted to the dim room. Beyond the fact that she lay in a bed, she didn't know where she was. Groggy and disoriented, she tried to raise up, but her arms wouldn't cooperate. Turning to her side, she used her elbow to leverage her sluggish weight.

As she tried to lift her upper body, a large dog came to the bed's edge. Netting separated them and she couldn't gauge the animal's mood. Had she seen a dog earlier? She wasn't sure of much, except that her head throbbed, and the pain peaked in direct proportion to the angle at which she rose from the bed.

"Is anyone here?" Her words and voice seemed disembodied. The dog continued to watch her in silence.

"Finally, you're awake."

She turned her pounding head in the direction of the heavy voice. A tall man had entered the doorway and made his way to her. She blinked at his fast-approaching figure. Who was he? Where was she? It hurt to try and assimilate answers. She closed her eyes and lowered her chin to her chest to get her bearings.

Within seconds, she opened them again and, surprised, found herself staring down at her own bared breasts. The white sheet had dropped and settled around her waist.

Shock blanketed her already muddled thoughts as she jerked her head up, only to meet the eyes of the man who tied back the netting.

In an automatic reaction, she crossed her arms over her chest. No longer supported by her arms, she dropped back onto the bed and pillow with a grunt and grimace of pain.

"Hey, take it easy." He leaned over the bed.

"Where are my clothes and who . . . who are you? Where am I?" The questions flowed in quick succession. Her eyes lit over the man who did the same to her. A growth of beard covered his lower face, but it was his dark eyes beneath heavy brows that held her. She remembered his stare. From where?

When he reached down, she strained from his touch, but he only pulled the sheet up.

"I think she'll survive, Buster." A smile began to soften the hard planes on his face.

Her vision blurred again as she darted a look at the dog she supposed was Buster. The dog offered a wide yawn from the bedside before he sat back on his haunches.

"Hello, Angie. Welcome back. I'm Matt Sinclair." His tone had become firm, his smile gone.

As he pulled a chair up to the bed and sat down, Angie digested her situation as she waited for him to speak again.

"Buster found you washed up on the shore, near the other end of the island. You were in bad shape at the time, so I brought you here, to recuperate. You've been sleeping the whole time, and you had me worried."

She tried to focus on Matt, whose blurred image threatened to duplicate, and attempted to understand his words. "What do you mean 'found me'?"

"Well, both you and your dinghy were pretty battered. I figured you were in some kind of a boating accident, but no one's shown up looking for you, yet."

She shook her head against the pillow, confused; but, her eyes remained locked with his. "How long have I been here?" She managed to keep the panic from her voice.

"Since early yesterday. We found you right after a bad squall blew through."

A tumble of disjointed thoughts assailed her achy head. She needed to think—it almost hurt too much to do that. Her memory had become pieces of cobweb caught in a difficult wind, and she couldn't catch the pieces quick enough to make any sense of this. Who did this man say he was? Was she in danger?

"Where am I?" She marveled at her own husky whisper.

"You're in my house. I brought you here—"

She shook her head, frustrated by his answer. "No, no, I mean the location. Where are we?"

"Cave Cay. It's a small private islet in the Atlantic." When she didn't respond, his dark brows slanted into a frown. "Geographically, we're located in the Out Islands."

She barely heard his last words as she concentrated on the earlier ones. Her heart began to pound louder than her head. She pushed against her elbows and tried to raise up on one hand while she held the sheet in place with the other.

"How do you know my name?" Her hoarse voice trembled and carried a panic that reached to the tips of her toes.

Matt tilted his head at her as he spoke. "The name was engraved on your gold ankle chain. I just assumed . . ." He stopped when her eyes grew wide and her low moan pierced the air.

She no longer listened, no longer felt her sore body, nor the ache from her head. Deep, dark terror caught hold in her chest, and she began to hyperventilate. Her eyes darted about as her head came up from the pillow in a counterpoint to her heaving chest.

Matt lunged from the chair to grasp her arms. "Angie, calm down. I want you to take deep, even breaths," he urged. "Gently now, take deep breaths."

She began to shake between the bursts of breath as her eyes searched Matt's face. "Where's the chain?" she gasped. "I want to see it."

"Okay, okay. I'll get it. First, though, you have to calm down. Is that clear?"

His forceful voice elicited her nod and she obeyed. Under his calming instructions, she reined in her panic, and the stress abated.

Matt's dark eyes bored into her. "Now, what was that all about?"

"You said you'd show me the gold chain," she whispered.

He sighed and released her. "All right." He reached over to the nightstand and picked up the short, gold chain. A silver key dangled from it. The jewelry's sparkle under the light was mesmerizing, and caught her stare.

"This was around your ankle." He brought it close to her face.

She reached out cautiously, and he slipped the chain onto her fingers.

A warning sounded in her head and she braced herself for what she would see when she held the jewelry aloft in the light. She saw the engraved plate between the gold links. *Angie.* She stared at the small, silver key as the noise in her head grew. With each studied concentration, it became an overwhelming force. Her fingers pressed convulsively into her temples, the gold chain forgotten as it fell to the bed.

Matt reached for the gold amid the covers. "Something's wrong."

"What's going on here?" she demanded.

In a surprising show of strength, she dug her feet into the mattress for balance and pushed herself up, only to discover that she was naked under the covers. Her fear was now joined with suspicion, and she wrapped herself tighter in the white sheet.

"Who are you?" She barked the question at Matt. "You say you found me on the beach. How do I know that? I want to talk with someone else . . . someone besides you." Her confusion had turned her rapid-fire words into a babble.

She repeated her demands as Matt leaned in closer. She had gathered into a tight crouch, wrapped in the sheet, her back pressed into the headboard.

"Angie . . ." Matt said her name low and held two fingers up to her. "How many fingers do you see? Can you concentrate? Is your vision blurred?"

"I just want to see someone else." She choked back a frightened cry and shook her head at him. "And, don't come any closer to me. I mean it."

"I don't mean you any harm. My God, I'm trying to help you. Your head hurts, doesn't it?"

No longer able to control her colliding emotions, she let out a loud sob. Her head bobbed in an automatic response as tears began to stream down her face.

"Something happened to you out there, Angie. I understand."

"No, you don't." She pressed her hand over her face. "How can you when I don't know what to believe."

"Why don't you start at the beginning and tell me what brought you here."

Trembling from wretchedness, she drew a loud, ragged breath before she dropped her hand and looked at Matt. "You don't understand."

"Then make me."

The disturbing revelation that had hovered over her since she first woke up in his presence had taken hold and wouldn't let go. Finally, she openly acknowledged it.

"I don't know how that chain got on my ankle. I don't know how I came to be here, and . . ." Her lips trembled uncontrollably as she finished. ". . . I don't even know who I am."

CHAPTER FOUR

Matt shifted Angie in his arms before he nudged the bathroom door wide open. She was an unyielding bundle, still swaddled in the bedsheets she wouldn't relinquish.

"Are you sure you want to do this?" He walked deeper into the room. At her nod, he allowed her to stand without his support.

When she swayed, he moved behind her. "I knew it. You're too weak to be up."

"I'll be okay," she whispered, and slowly stepped away.

"The water's already in the tub, and I found a pack of scented soaps in the closet."

The lavender-scented heat that rose from the tub confirmed his find. Angie closed her eyes before she rested her head against the wall.

"Do you need my help with anything?"

She recognized the concern in his voice, but she craved a moment alone to think through this, so she waited for him to leave.

"The towels are next to the sink," he said, before adding, "Oh, I almost forgot."

As his footsteps retreated, she opened her eyes and blinked at the bright, white room, its only bow to color a wide tapestry in primary colors that depicted a moonlit beach. Adjusting the bedsheet tucked under her arms, she stared at the bold fabric yarns that filled the long wall opposite her.

Matt's steps returned. She jerked her head in that direction, almost tripping on the sheet that flowed loosely to her feet, when he filled the doorway.

The strong light in the small room revealed him as both taller and broader than she had realized. His wide shoulders strained against the fabric as he raised something in his hand.

She met his gaze, and thought she saw a flash of pity.

"I brought you one of my shirts," his deep voice apologized. "If you have to wear anything, it should be loose so air can circulate around the burns—"

His words stemmed at the lift of her brow. He hung the shirt on a hook behind the door and turned back to her. "While you freshen up, I'll get something for you to eat. Soup is about all you should have right now."

Angie's continued silence was an unscalable wall, and Matt seemed to know it.

"Everything'll work out." He backed from the room. "I'll be right outside if you need me." He pulled the door closed behind him.

She crossed over to the door and clicked the simple lock. Though the tears had ceased their trail down her face, her misery had simply turned inward, and she drowned in the deluge. A shudder flowed through her as she sank to the edge of the bathtub and contemplated her loss. She tucked an imaginary strand of hair behind her ear, and her hand fell to the short hair at her nape. Reveling in this surprise discovery, she ran her hand over her short locks.

I don't know what I look like. With a hint of trepidation, she rose from the tub and walked to the mirror. She blinked, again and again, at the face that stared back at her. *Who am I?*

Matt stood at the kitchen sink and glanced over his shoulder before he poured the hot chicken broth into a cup. He had suspected something was wrong when he witnessed her unreasonable fear and suspicion. Shock and denial was just the beginning.

She had looked vulnerable and pitiable as she stood in the bathroom. And what had he done to soothe her fear? He'd suggested she'd be better off wearing no clothes. He shook his head. What in hell had he been thinking?

He liked her voice. He had been surprised to hear such a sultry voice come from her slight frame. It reminded him of the dark, smoky jazz clubs he used to frequent in more pleasant times, before the troubles began with Paula. He frowned and closed off that direction of thoughts.

He picked up two capsules from the counter and broke them open. Their powdery contents cascaded into the steamy broth. He stirred the soup until all traces of the powder disappeared. Angie's memory was gone, that was clear. In her current state, it was reasonable to expect that she'd be agitated and distrustful. In order to heal, her mind and body needed rest. She couldn't do it for herself in her highly excitable state.

He took the sedative-laced soup to the bedroom on a tray.

Angie hadn't returned to the rumpled bed after her bath, but sat rigid and upright in the chair facing it. The sheet she had cocooned herself in earlier was gone. It had been replaced with Matt's cotton shirt, which easily reached her knees. Her stony face glistened clean and her arms were braced in a haughty attitude.

"Here's the broth I promised. It'll help you regain your strength."

His bare legs pressed into hers when he sat on the edge of the bed. When he passed the tray to her lap, their gazes crossed briefly before she eyed the steaming soup.

"Thank you. It's chicken. I could smell it from the tub." She balanced the tray on her lap before lifting the cup to her lips with unsteady hands.

"That's a good sign." She was talking to him again.

When her brows raised in question, he explained. "You're remembering things automatically, like how to talk, care for yourself, . . . chickens." He smiled at his joke. "You'll remember other facts imbedded in your subconscious too, like math, how to read and write, that kind of thing."

"Because I know two and two equals four, that's a good sign?"

"Yes," he said. "It could take weeks before we know the extent of the loss. Of course, your full memory could return before then."

She lowered the cup and ran her tongue over her mouth. "My lips are sore."

Matt studied her mouth, moist from the soup. "I put a balm on them while you slept. You can do that now."

She lifted her arm, covered to the elbow by the big shirt. "I have scratches and sunburns, too." Her gaze returned to his. "But, you know that."

He nodded his head as he rested his hands on his knees. "First, can we agree to call you Angie?"

"It's as good as anything else." She took another greedy sip of the broth. "Tell me all you know about me. How badly was I hurt?"

Matt knew that soon the medication would relax her, and he could check for further medical problems.

"You suffered at least one hard blow to your head that broke the skin." He paused when she raised her hand to touch the cut on her head. "Based on the bruises you're wearing, you were bounced around pretty good out there."

Angie listened quietly as Matt continued.

"Initially, seawater was in your lungs, and blocked your breathing. The waves washing over you probably did that just before Buster found you. You seem to have come through it okay. Lucky for us, you don't have a fever or signs of breathing problems."

She finished off the broth while Matt ticked off her problems. "None of your sunburns are serious. The blisters are healing nicely, and will take a few days to disappear. I kept them salved so you wouldn't feel any discomfort." Matt cleared his throat. "That's why I took your clothes off. To, um, let your skin breathe."

Angie quirked a suspicious brow at him again—he had become used to that particular gesture of hers—and shifted in her chair.

"The last thing we need is for you to get an infection in this climate. All in all, with a little time, you should be good as new."

"Except for the fact that I don't know who I am." She paused a moment as she wiped her hand across her mouth. "I saw my face in the bathroom mirror and it was, like, I was seeing it for the first time."

Matt looked into her almond-sloped eyes framed within her oval face. Black, short locks covered her head with the shorter wisps sticking out on the sides. She was a beauty—an exotic hothouse flower. He frowned at his too-keen observations.

"You look fine." He made the understatement in a rush, and crossed his arms. "We don't know what you survived out there, but things could've been worse."

"And they aren't now?" She slammed the cup to the tray. "I didn't know the face that looked back at me."

He tried to allay her frustration. "It'll come back to you."

She grabbed her head. "I don't feel good, either. My head is sort of fuzzy. My stomach is queasy."

"You'll have headaches off and on for a while, too. The dizziness and nausea come from dehydration and should end soon. Maybe you can try solid foods tomorrow."

In an ungainly move, she stood and grazed against Matt's legs as she pressed the tray into his hands. "You keep acting like everything is all right. Well, it's not. What if my memory doesn't come back? What then?" She wound her way behind the chair.

Matt heard the panic in her voice. "Selective memory loss can last for as little as a few hours," he suggested. "It could all come back at any time."

"But, what if it doesn't?" She trained her eyes on him. "You seem sure about what will happen. What are you, anyway, a doctor?"

He paused before he answered. "Yes."

Her eyes narrowed on his solemn face. "You're not kidding, are you?"

He gave her a grudging smile. "Is that so hard to believe?"

"I don't know what to believe."

"All right, then, take it on my word." Under Angie's watchful eye, Matt got up from the bed and set the tray on the nightstand. He turned back to her, with arms crossed as he leaned against the dresser. "I am a real doctor."

"If what you say is true, I should thank you."

"Buster is your hero."

Angie looked at the dog and reached a hand out to him. Buster sniffed, then licked her hand. She jerked it back as Matt laughed.

"He found you before he alerted me. The rest is history. And, it looks like he's pretty taken with you, too." Matt motioned her back to the chair. "Please, sit back down, and let me see if I can figure out how serious a concussion you suffered. I can answer your questions, too."

She went back to the chair and crossed her arms. Matt reclaimed his seat in front of her.

"Why are you on an island?"

"A vacation of sorts," he responded. "Follow my finger." He waved it back and forth before her face. "Good," he announced. "Your pupils are the same size. I'm going to ask a few questions—"

"No, I'm not finished with mine. Where is everyone else? Are you here alone?" She rubbed her arms anxiously. "Maybe someone else around here knows something about me . . ." Her words drifted off when his head shook in denial.

"You're on a private little island, Angie. It's owned by my medical partnership. The problem is, the boat that dropped me off won't return for a little over a week."

She slowly lowered her arms. "No one else is here? What about a boat?"

"Just the dinghy you washed up in, but it's no longer seaworthy. There aren't any communications lines for phones, television, or radio. We keep a CB radio around, but only during the tourist season. We're the only people here."

As her stare turned incredulous, a surge of sympathy rose up in Matt. "This part of the island is leased out during the winter season for income," he explained. "The other half is a protected natural wildlife sanctuary."

"Wildlife?"

He nodded. "Animals natural to the area, like sea turtles, parrots, and a few other varieties that reside deep in the interior." When her expression grew discouraged, Matt quelled the strong urge to pull her into his arms and offer unconditional comfort. "You don't have any images, anything of how you came to wash up on the beach?"

She touched the bruise near her ear. "Where are my clothes? Did I carry any identification?"

"I'm afraid you only wore a bathing suit and a beach skirt. They're in the garden drying. The gold chain that was around your ankle is our best clue."

"I don't recall owning it at all." She massaged her temple in a slow circular motion. "I try to think, and there's no connection."

"Tell me what is there?"

She swayed in the chair. "When I try to remember and hold onto a picture in my head, a black wall comes down, like a curtain, and crushes the thought. It hurts like hell."

"I wish we could get you to a hospital, run some tests, and treat you properly. That's not possible right now." He leaned toward her. "You should rest. You've stirred around for a while now, and your body needs to recover."

"No." She rose from the chair, then grabbed its arms for support. "Where are my clothes?"

Matt also stood. The smell of her scented soap was a luxury that washed over him. "Not so fast." He caught her waist and pressed her back into the chair. The medicine had taken effect. "Take it easy for another twenty-four hours." He recognized her look of determination, and dug in with his own. "Don't you know that if you press yourself too soon, you won't help your condition?"

"I've got to find some answers." Her words were firm. "I feel as though I'm supposed to be doing something. I've got to get out of here."

"Maybe you did have trouble on the water. You said 'help us' when I found you."

Her eyes narrowed. "I have to remember . . . and soon. I'll see for myself if anyone else is around." Again, she tried rising from the chair, but lost her balance and slumped back down.

"You won't get far today," Matt said as he pulled her into his arms. "I gave you something to keep you calm."

"You . . . drugged . . . me." Her words slurred and her fight disappeared as she became complacent in his arms.

"I'm sorry for doing it, Angie." He laid her on the bed-sheets.

She didn't move as she absently slurred a half-hearted warning. "I won't trust you next time."

"It's for your own good." He pulled the sheet over her. "In the morning, you'll awake and feel better." Maybe her attitude will have improved, too, he smiled.

Matt didn't get a response because she had drifted off to sleep. He took the tray and cup to the kitchen with Buster at his heels.

When he returned to her side, her features were relaxed, but her mouth moved in sleep, as though she conversed with some distant dream weaver. As he studied her, a sound flowed from her lips and broke through the peaceful room.

"Reee . . ."

She made the odd, whistling sound again, and then she was silent. Matt frowned. He'd tell her about it later.

"With a little encouragement, of course I'll stay." Florrie whispered the words across her glass of wine.

The lights were low and the seduction scene that Reed Palmer had worked hard to create in his Coral Gables living room unfolded like the plan it was.

"How else will you get a chance to sample the mean breakfast I can put together?" he asked. The flight attendant he had met last weekend on his layover at Kennedy in New York was succumbing to his insistence on schedule. She had agreed to look him up on her next stopover in Miami. Now, they relaxed on oversized cushions on the floor of his high-rise condo.

"You'd do that for me?" she cooed.

"In a heartbeat, because I know you'll be worth every bit of the trouble."

He leaned over and, cupping her head, pulled her pouty red lips to his. What followed was a deep, searching kiss that left no misunderstanding of his intentions.

The evening was headed to a perfect ending for Reed until the pager in his pocket started to vibrate.

"Damn," he whispered, before he pulled away from the velvety-soft woman. "Got to be more careful."

"What's going on?" Florrie asked as she straightened up.

"My pager. I dropped it in my pocket earlier, and forgot it was there."

"Just shut it off." She gave him a look that offered a reward if he did.

"You read my mind."

He pulled the beeper out just as it started to vibrate again. "Someone's pretty anxious to aggravate me this evening." Curious, he looked at the number that lit up the screen.

"Cut it off," Florrie demanded in a purr. "We're losing our moment."

"Oh no, that won't happen," he said as he leapt to his feet. "I'll leave it in the bedroom and be right back. Don't you move, sweetheart." He bent over and kissed her upturned lips.

A few long strides and Reed was in his bedroom. He threw the door shut behind him before he went to the phone. He punched in his parent's number. Strange. It had been his mother's code on the pager screen, but she barely knew how they operated. He tossed the pager onto the bed. The phone rang three times before his mother's voice answered.

"Hello?"

"Mom? It's Reed." He tried to make light of his concern. "Congratulations on using the beeper."

She offered no preamble. "Your dad and I are worried about Angie."

"What's she done this time?" Reed's voice was rife with humor.

"It's serious. Two days ago she planned to have dinner with us to celebrate, she said, but she wouldn't tell us what the occasion was. When she didn't show up, I called her at home and at the shop. She wasn't at either place."

"I wouldn't worry. Fran probably knows where she is." Reed was confident that Francenia DeSantis, shop manager for Angie's jewelry design business, had the answers his mother needed.

"Fran called me because Angie didn't show up at the shop. You know they're working on that big jewelry order and Angie hadn't planned to be out."

Reed still wasn't convinced there was a problem. "Did you go to the loft?"

"Yes, and her car isn't there."

"She probably went away for a long weekend with a friend and simply forget to tell you." He offered his mother assurance that she needed. "That's all it is." He looked at his watch. The lovely Florrie waited for him. He would kick Angie's butt for worrying their mother and causing this interruption.

"Your dad says the same thing, but I know Angie. She may be headstrong about some things, but she would never arrange an engagement with us, then disappear with no explanation. It all seems strange to me."

That was Mom, all right. You had to work hard to get her reassured. "Okay. Tomorrow, I'll track down where she's gone."

"Thank you, Reed."

He eyed his watch again. "I'll call you then. And, don't worry about Angie. Dad's right—she'll be fine."

They exchanged goodbyes before he hung up the phone. He took a quick look in the mirror, then strode back out into the living room.

"I'm sorry, Florrie, but I had to make one call. That's it for the interruptions, though . . ."

His voice trailed off when he saw that she was gone. The obvious sign was the door slightly ajar from her exit.

Reed walked over to close it. On his way to the sofa, he flicked on the full bank of house lights, then doused the candles that flickered on the coffee table. He dropped onto the sofa and touched the nearby remote control, which killed the piped-in sound from the stereo. He glanced at his watch. It shouldn't take Florrie too long to cool off and return.

While he waited, he scooped up a few of the grapes that chilled nearby and dropped them, one at a time, into his mouth as he wondered what Angie was up to this time.

CHAPTER FIVE

Her lungs burned for air beneath the briny sea. Her fingers clawed at the watery space as her body undulated in a frenetic attempt to elude her pursuers. She had to move, keep moving, just a few seconds more . . .

As Angie made the desperate break through the water's surface, she broke free of her dream world and re-entered the dark room's safety.

Her eyes opened wide as she gulped in the sweet, dry air. Having escaped the dream's grasp, she was not convinced the danger was gone, and her body shivered with the fear that she'd be transported again.

She released the panic as her surroundings became familiar. She knew this strange house and the stranger who cared for her, but she hadn't a clue as to who she was.

Angie shook off the fear and ignored the pain as she rolled onto her side. Who was she? The images that had played out in her head neither explained nor answered that question. She shuddered, unable to control her wave of trembles.

The dream images had been intense. Some came in mysterious flashes; others, like the drowning, linked to become powerful, oppressive nightmares. She pressed her fingers against her throbbing head and tried to latch onto a vision, any vision. The faint, steady pulse in her temples threatened to crescendo. She had asked Matt for help on the beach. Besides her memory loss, was that the reason she felt restless and unsure?

Matt unsettled her for reasons she couldn't name. She turned onto her back, the dull stings from the sunburns an uncomfortable reminder of his earlier familiarity. She drew in a deep breath as she raised herself up in the center of the bed, then sat back on her legs. The soft shirt shifted against her skin. Its provocative caress reminded her that she wore nothing underneath. Another reminder of his familiarity.

She peered beyond the gossamer netting, her eyes and ears keened. She didn't see Matt or the dog—the only sounds were her own labored breathing's competition with the creak and hum of the overhead fan.

Angie pushed aside the net. Across the room, open jalousie windows revealed the dark outside. How long had she slept this time? Questions swirled around her head in a dizzying rush. She shook her head to clear the fog.

Other people were around. Of course, she reasoned, and she'd find them before it was too late. She blinked at that unbidden thought. Too late for what? After all, she didn't know Matt. She could be a kidnap victim, drugged so she wouldn't know how she got here. But, that didn't explain her total lack of recall.

As her imagination took control, the panic returned to her chest. *Breathe in deep, and remain calm.* She used Matt's earlier mantra, and now regained control. Her name was Angie. No magic lights, nothing, when she said the name. How would she find her way back to her life and family if she didn't recognize her own name? Family—the word brought on an odd comfort. She had to get out of here and find help. First, she needed a weapon.

She touched her feet to the cool floor. Her moves brought on a wave of dizziness that caused her to pause. Gradually, she pushed away from the bed, then crept across the dimmed room.

Almost at the doorway, she met Buster. She cast a suspicious glance at the dog as he came to her. With his tail in a full wag, he sniffed at her hand.

She silently willed the dog not to bark. He didn't. He settled in front of her and sat back on his haunches. Angie stroked the top of his large head.

"Nice dog," she whispered. "Nice dog."

Obedient, he seemed content to sit there. After a final pat, she moved past him to the doorway and peeked into the living room. A single lamp's gentle radiance broke up the darkness. Matt rested with his head on the end of the sofa and his arms crossed over his bare chest.

Angie's stare roamed the expanse of his hard, athletic physique, which lay clad only in a pair of gym shorts. Her gaze stopped when she reached his feet, crossed and relaxed at the opposite end. Their arches were as powerfully defined as the rest of his body. She drew in a deep breath before turning her head to break her stare. He was asleep. This might be her only chance to leave.

Angie backed up and tripped over Buster.

"Ohhh . . ." Too late, the sound rushed past her lips. She held her breath as she looked back toward Matt. He didn't move. With a sigh, she turned to chastise the hovering dog.

"Keep out of my way," she whispered harshly, and moved to the dresser in the dark bedroom.

She opened the drawers and methodically searched for something that could be used as a weapon. She didn't dare look beyond this room for fear she'd wake Matt. An unhappy grunt was all she mustered as drawer after drawer brought no luck. When she moved her search to the night stand, her fortune changed.

"Scissors," she gleefully whispered to Buster, who'd followed her around the room. "Now, for some clothes."

She returned to the dresser where she found another pair of the gym shorts Matt seemed to favor.

"These will have to do," she muttered, and sat on the edge of the bed to pull on the gaping shorts. As she tightened the drawstring to her waist, she considered how she'd get past Matt and through the front door.

The ache in her head had grown monstrous. It was a simple nuisance, though, when compared to the adrenaline-induced power that surged through her body. She was about to take control of some part of her fate.

She made a survey of the room, desperate to find an escape. As she studied the window, the solution came in a flash. A smile creased her sore face before she moved to the window.

The long jalousie windows opened and closed with a handle crank built into the casing. Angie didn't question how she knew to bend back the metal grips attached to the ends of the glass to slip out the pane. With the scissors as a tool, she removed the lowest panes to allow enough space for her to squeeze through.

Buster mewled while Angie used the chair to climb onto the sill.

"Quiet," she scolded. "You'll wake up Matt." She pushed once, twice, before the screen fell to the ground.

She used her reserve of strength to swing her legs up, then through the opening, the pain almost forgotten as euphoric freedom blanketed her. From her seat on the sill, she turned one last time to the dog.

"If what your master said is true, thank you for finding me and saving my life."

She grimaced in pain as she rotated onto her stomach

and inched backwards through the opening, before she dropped almost a full story into the flower garden below.

Reed stretched his naked body across the king-sized bed and switched on the phone's ringer. He was caught by surprise at its sudden ring.

"This had better be good," he muttered to the offending phone before he grabbed it. "Yeah?"

"Reed?"

"Mom? What are you doing calling so early?" He hauled himself up in the bed and pulled the sheet over his lap.

"I couldn't sleep. I wanted to talk with you before you left the house."

"I had planned to call you later."

"This won't take long." Silence hummed across the line. "Did I wake you?"

Reed smiled. "No, you didn't. So, what do you want to talk about?"

"Make sure you go by the shop and speak with Fran."

"I thought you did that already."

"Well, I remembered Angie mentioning an appointment with her lawyer. I believe it had to do with Philip."

Reed frowned at his brother-in-law's name. "I wonder why? Don't tell me he's trying to contest her divorce at the last minute."

"Fran is with Angie every day, and may know something that'll help. I'm sure she'll speak more freely with you."

"Okay, I'll talk with her." As an afterthought, he added, "Listen, Mom. Don't worry about Angie."

"You think I'm overreacting, don't you? I know your sister's impetuous and . . . and strong-willed, but she's considerate and loving and knows that disappearing would cause me worry."

"You're right. She wouldn't go off like that. I still don't think anything's wrong. But, don't worry; I'll find out."

When he gained his mother's lukewarm promise, he replaced the phone, then leapt from the bed. He strode to the bathroom, where the shrill sound of water grew louder. Clouds of steam rushed to meet him when he opened the door. He advanced, unerringly, toward the shower stall and slid open the frosted glass door to reveal a sudsy, inviting Florrie.

Reed stepped into the shower amidst her peals of unsuppressed laughter. With his arms wrapped lustily about her waist, he made the most of what remained of his morning.

Tired, and with her spirits doused, Angie meandered across the sand, no longer in any particular hurry. She avoided the tangle of dark woods that ran parallel with the shoreline to travel the more open space of the beach.

The sun had begun a bright wash of the horizon, and she followed the shimmer it streaked along the breaking waves. Earlier, she had been sure that she would encounter other people, other houses, something that would bolster her resolve to help herself.

There had been nothing else, though—just the unchanged landscape of thick, menacing woods to one side of her, odd birds that cackled and swooped above, and an ocean of loud, laughing waves that mocked and jested her every step on the other side. Everything worked against her.

Angie kicked at the sticky sand as tears trickled down her cheeks. A few steps later, her first bitter sob escaped. She dropped to her knees, then sank to the warm sand in self-pity. Hunger and weakness permeated her bones.

"Maybe I shouldn't have left," she reasoned out loud. "I had to do something, though. I couldn't just lay there without trying to find some answers."

She raised her head and cried out in anger, "What do I do now?" Another sob rose from her throat as she looked toward the dark forest that rose steadily to a green peak in the distance.

Angie wiped her face with her shirttail and let sand mix with her tears. Her gaze returned to the forest as her resolve built again with the kernel of an idea. Maybe all wasn't lost.

She would go through the woods. It's possible, she reasoned, that she'd find a shortcut to the other side of the island. Someone with a boat would help her and she'd solve the unanswered riddles that pummeled her head.

Renewed, she rolled to her feet. For the first time, as the sun warmed her face, she saw how bright the morning had become. She stumbled across the shifting sand to the pine-strewn pathway that led into the woods.

At the forest's edge, her courage flagged, and she swallowed hard. Although dawn had broken on the beach, darkness still lurked beyond the huge palm fronds that greeted her. She looked over her shoulder and down the beach one last time, gripped the scissors in her hand, then pushed past the fronds into the daunting shadows.

Through a fog of exhaustion, Matt could hear sharp barks and agitated nail clicks against the floor. Buster wanted to get out of the house for his morning run. When the noise continued unabated, Matt gave up on sleep, and swung his feet to the floor.

"Okay, okay." He pleaded with the prancing dog for silence. "You're gonna wake up Angie." He stood and stretched as a great yawn pulled at his face, while Buster fidgeted from side to side.

Matt had slept through the night. The fact that Angie had done the same spoke well for her full recovery. He'd check on her after he let Buster out.

He walked to the front door, but Buster didn't follow.

In fact, the dog ran the opposite way, to the bedroom. Puzzled, Matt scratched his head.

"Come on, fella."

The dog darted from the bedroom, barking as he advanced on Matt. He then turned and raced back to the bedroom.

Buster wanted to be followed.

Matt strode to the bedroom, just in time to see the dog leap onto the chair at the window and rest his forelegs on the sill.

"What the hell . . ." He muttered as he looked around.

He didn't need to search the house to confirm that Angie had left.

"Damn." He looked out the window, across the surf, and down the beach. Only the crash of waves sounded in the early morning's quiet. Matt rubbed at his beard as he looked down on the crushed flowers below. So much for the delicate creature theory. What in hell did she plan to do in her condition or expect to find?

Then, Matt remembered the trouble that could find her, and spoke it out loud.

"The sanctuary."

Twigs, rocks, leaves, and pine needles littered the forest floor. With each step, Angie's soft soles were assaulted. The original path she'd started on was no longer marked and had deteriorated to such a level that it couldn't be distinguished from the rest of the forest.

Light filtered through the overhead trees and foliage. Though the trees offered some protection from the sultry heat, it wasn't complete, and she wiped her forehead with her dirty hand. A pesky buzz sounded past her ear, and she slapped at her damp neck. The burns on her shoulders stung, and she could no longer ignore the hunger that ate at her belly. If she didn't find someone soon, she'd have to give up.

The inclining terrain had become rocky. Up ahead, the trickle of water managed to trigger her thirst. Hopeful, she willed her legs to move toward the water.

The trees thinned amidst a number of flat, marbleized stones scattered in a haphazard manner about the clearing. Some stacked to form a rugged facade that resembled a hill. Her gait, plodding now, soon delivered her to the odd shaped rocks.

Tired, she leaned against them to catch her breath, then walked along their perimeter. She could still hear the stream's gurgle and surmised the source lay somewhere beyond the rocks.

Angie ran her hand along the cool, even rock surface, fascinated by the oasis of forms and flowers in the middle of the woods. "They're beautiful," she muttered.

She continued to study the flowers and natural formations in the growing light, enchanted by their display of discordant beauty. Unhampered by canopies of jungle growth, the exotic blossoms were profuse around the rock formations. As she moved along the stone hill, she came to a rock alcove, where she leaned into the craggy opening.

Splashing water. Her ears cocked at the sound.

Her weight shifted as she stepped onto the smooth, though damp, slanted floor that formed the hill's mouth. Too late, her feet shot out from under her and she toppled onto her butt with a thud and a gasp.

Then, feet first, she slid into the slick, wet incline that took her through the gaping hole in the stone mountain.

Angie screamed.

CHAPTER SIX

"Angie . . . Angie!"

Matt's desperate shouts punctuated the air. He stopped to catch his breath after the hard run across the soft sand. Angie's tracks had been easy to follow on the beach, but the trail now turned toward the heavy woods where Buster nosed around.

Hunched over, Matt surveyed the stretch of land and water in hopes that she'd appear.

"Where the hell are you?" He yelled out his frustration. As he watched the dog sniff around, then disappear into the woods, Matt slowly straightened, his fears ignited. She had gone into the nature preserve area after all. Damn, but she was one determined woman.

He clenched his teeth and followed Buster's lead into the woods. He stayed along the marked trails as he called out Angie's name. But, as time passed without sight of her, his emotions grew conflicted. Anger and fear took turns at the helm. A myriad of wildlife lived here, from innocuous flashy birds to dangerous wild boars. He was in no mood to traverse the entire compound for a woman who cared so little about her health and safety that she'd leave his protection for this.

The fact that he was angry didn't stop his worrying, though. The sooner he found her, and brought her back to safety, the better he'd feel.

After what seemed an interminable time, excited barks sounded ahead. Buster had found something. Or trouble. Or both. He sped off to the discovery.

Angie's fall released her unbridled panic. At the end of her short, wild roll down the chute of stone, she dropped from its rough-hewn edge into a darkly lit pool of water about a foot deep, the air forced from her lungs.

Icy fear roiled through her veins as her bruised body sloshed valiantly in the water to regain a footing. To compound her anxiety, she had lost the scissors in the fall. In desperation, she glided her fingers through the silt on the bottom of the pool. She sank her teeth into her lip and tried not to think about what she touched. It didn't matter. The scissors were lost.

She wiped her hands across her shirt and wrinkled her nose as a pungent odor assailed her nostrils. For the first time, her nervous gaze darted to her surroundings. *Where am I?*

The light, murky and filtered, came from a narrow passageway that led from this—cave.

She had dropped into a cave. At that realization, she turned to observe its shadowy walls. The steady drip of water in the background broke the unearthly quiet.

Angie looked up at the thin stream of light that spilled from the opening. Her gaze traveled across the high, craggy ceiling and the ominous, black shadows that hid between the stalactites. This place spooked her. She drew in another breath of the acrid air as a shiver ran along her spine. She wouldn't leave this place the way she arrived—that was a guarantee.

She turned to the passageway. Maybe that was her way out. She trudged through the standing water, which lowered as she got closer to the tunnel. The rough cave floor was slick with sludge. Although she ached, she moved steadily, for fear that she would be too tired to start again.

Then, she heard faint barks.

"Buster?" She whispered the dog's name in disbelief before she strained to hear above the water trickle. This time the succession of barks were louder. They came from the hole she had fallen through.

"Angie, are you down there? Angie?"

Matt. Her heart did a crazy leap at his faint voice.

"Yes," she called out. "It's me." She waded back through the water to get closer to his voice. Her relief was palpable. "I fell through a hole in the rocks."

"Are you okay? Did you hurt yourself?" His words now came from right above her.

"Just b-b-bruised," Angie stammered. "Can you get me out of here?" Her eyes remained trained on the ceiling far above, but the rocks blocked Matt from her view.

"Why didn't you rest like I told you? This was a crazy stunt, you know." He rushed the words in a terse voice. "I wake up and you're gone, and without a word to me. I've been worried out of my mind over what could have happened."

Angie responded with sharp indignance. "I'm stuck in this hole and you're upset because I didn't do as I was told?" However, the attitude lasted only a moment. She was inexplicably relieved to see him and that big dog. And grateful.

"Matt, I'm . . . I'm sorry."

"No, I'm the one," he quickly interrupted with his own apology. "You're right. This isn't the time for that. I was just worried out of my head about you, that's all."

"I couldn't lie there helpless, with so many questions in my head. It didn't feel right for me. I had to find out for myself if what you said was true and if anyone else was around."

When he didn't respond, it set off Angie's alarms. "Matt, are you still up there?"

"Yes. I'm trying to figure out how to get you out. Look around, these caves can be tricky. Do you see anything that might look like an exit?"

"There's a passageway here, sort of like a tunnel, but I don't know where it leads."

"Good," Matt said. "I'll see if I can find an entrance behind the waterfall."

"I can hear the water in here. In fact, I'm standing in water now."

"That's the run-off from the falls. Walk through the tunnel, and talk loud so I can track you. When you reach the end, call out. If it dead ends or leads deeper underground, come back to this spot. Understand?"

"Yes." She didn't want to end their connection and desolation cloaked her shoulders. "You aren't leaving me, are you?"

A light chuckle floated down to her. "After what I've gone through to find you, I promise I won't. Now, go."

A nervous tremor lurched its way through her before she hugged her arms to her chest and stepped through the groundwater to the passageway. She entered the tunnel, then carefully felt her way along the narrow, curved path. As instructed, she repeatedly yelled Matt's name as she inched forward.

Soon, the passageway widened into another cavern, and Angie's spirits lifted. However, she quickly discovered there was no exit in the chamber.

"Matt," she called. "Can you hear me?"

Buster barked just as Matt's muffled voice came from

the rock wall opposite her. She sidled closer when she heard a grating noise.

"What are you doing?"

"Watch out." As he spoke, dust, sand, and small rocks scuttled down from the crevices.

She jumped away from the falling debris, then craned her neck to look up. Matt had moved aside the rocks to widen an opening at the top of the wall. Finally, she could see him as he knelt on the ground and looked into the ten foot drop.

"It's good to see you again." A wide grin covered his face.

She relished the sight of him as she blossomed with unexpected comfort. Undone by her own traitorous emotions, she harshly questioned them. Had her doubts dissipated so easily, like her memory?

"Aren't you happy to see me, too?"

As he talked, he pulled his shirt over his head and tossed it aside. He now worked to undo his belt.

"Not happy enough to get undressed for the occasion, as you obviously are."

"There you go again." His heavy voice was tinged with impatience. ". . . Thinking the worst of me when I'm trying to help."

"I fail to see the humor when I'm stuck down here. Did you figure a way to get me out?"

"I'm going to pull you up."

"How?"

He held up the shirt and belt. "I want you to grab hold of the belt I've looped through my shirt and I'll hoist you up. Okay?"

Heat raced to her face when she realized she had doubted his motives. She offered a vigorous nod to his question.

"I know you're tired, but I can do it with your help."

More afraid of the claustrophobic cave than the pain

from using her remaining strength, she resolved to get out as the belt snaked above her head. Angie pulled in a deep breath and jumped to grab hold of the belt with both hands.

Her body lifted off the ground and, in a slow swing, bumped the wall. On the next swing, she had better control and used her feet to cushion the bump. With her teeth gritted, she walked the stone wall as Matt pulled her to him.

Before long, his hand grabbed hers. Her stomach was tight from the anticipation. Another pull with a grunt, and he had her other hand. As her face scrubbed through the dirt opening, she squeezed her eyes and mouth shut. When her shoulders broke through, he slid a hand under her arm, then pulled her clear of the cave.

Angie fell against Matt's chest, exhausted yet relieved. With his arms wrapped around her, they both sank to the ground.

"Are you okay?" He voiced his concern between heavy breaths.

"Uh-huh." Angie closed her eyes as she held onto him, and luxuriated in her senses: hair-roughened bare skin, sweaty and warm against her face, the steady drum of his heartbeat, and the taste of clean air. His hand caressed her back and caused havoc to her insides. She didn't want him to stop.

A cold nudge and wet hair broke into her reverie. She opened her eyes to Buster, who proceeded to lick her face.

"Oh, goodness." Her hands pushed out to ward off the exuberant animal, all reality restored.

Matt straightened up, too, though he still held Angie as he cautioned Buster with an order. "Sit, sit."

Aware that Matt studied her, she pulled out of his reluctant release. Shakily, she retreated to a plot of grass a few feet away, and lifted her gaze to meet his.

He cleared his throat. "Let's get back to the house."

Angie's brows narrowed at his arrogant tone.

"What I mean is, you need food and . . ." His words petered out as he took in her dirt-caked face and wet clothes. She barely held her eyes open.

He bounded to his feet to pick up his discarded shirt and belt. Then, without warning, he reached down and gathered her into his arms. She didn't protest, but acceded to his strength by laying her head against his shoulder.

"You and Buster keep finding me." Her voice was a small whisper. "Thank you." She shifted so she could look into his face. "I guess you'll say I shouldn't wander off without one of you with me."

"Would it help?" At her defeated expression, he became serious. "No, you shouldn't, but I'm just glad you're safe." He smiled before he settled her back in his arms.

He and Buster picked their way back through the trees and flowers to start the walk home, but he didn't mind. An inner contentment swirled within him—a peace he hadn't experienced for some time. Right now, he wouldn't question the source. He would simply savor it as an unexpected blessing.

Reed stepped around the middle wall that separated Angie's office from her jewelry workshop, where upbeat music blared from a sound system to fill the airy room. Angie had transformed the edgy, marked-for-destruction warehouse into an upstairs loft apartment where she lived, and a downstairs workshop where she designed and created jewelry from natural materials.

The transformed warehouse was spacious, with long worktables occupied by jeans-clad artisans, who worked with Angie's designs. He immediately recognized Francenia DeSantis, Angie's Cuban-born manager of everything that related to the shop. She was bent over one of the tables with an acetylene torch in her hands and a mask over her head.

As he drew nearer, she looked up. Setting the torch aside, she pulled the mask from her tangled dark hair and grinned broadly.

"*Caramba!* You rascal," she yelled above the music, lapsing as she often did into her native Spanish. She threw her gloved hands around him. "What bad wind blew you back into town?"

He returned the warm hug, then set her from him. He wore a grin as well. "I haven't seen you in months. Isn't that reason enough?"

"Yeah, I wish. You're looking for Angie, no? She's not back. Your Mama came by the other day looking for her, too."

"Any idea why she hasn't returned to work?"

She dropped her gloves on the table. "Come to the office and we'll talk." She led him across the cement floor and, as she pulled the door behind him, turned off the music.

"Mom told me about your conversation."

"I only called her because it wasn't like Angie not to show up without an explanation. I shouldn't have called her, huh? That's why you're here?"

"You think she could be on a quick vacation?"

Fran walked behind the desk and dropped into the chair. "If she is, she deserves one, don't you think? She's done nothing but work hard getting this business off the ground over the last year. And, the divorce, wasn't it final this past weekend?"

Reed sat in the other chair in the office and rubbed his chin. "Yeah. Do you know anyone she would go off on a vacation with?"

She threw her arms up in defeat. "She left here Thursday morning after a call from her attorney, and she was in good spirits. She told me to lock up. That sounds like a vacation to me. What else could the answer be? She should live a little for a change, anyway. I shouldn't have worried your Mama."

"It still doesn't make sense." He leaned on the desk. "No one sees her the first weekend of her divorce, no one knows who she'd take on an unannounced trip. Is something going on I don't know about since I was here last time?"

Fran's expression became worried. "It's just that . . . it's not like Angie to leave us hanging, not with that big jewelry order we received." Her voice grew heavy with concern. "We're in the middle of working it now, but our craftsmen need Angie's guidance, and they're beginning to wonder what's going on. And payroll—if she doesn't return soon, I may have to shut down the shop."

"Has she said anything, been seeing anyone suspicious?"

Fran stared at him. "No. She was relieved that the divorce would soon be final. Her attorney called almost every day."

"Mom mentioned they had a meeting. Do you know his name?"

"No, but his card is in here." She pulled open the middle desk drawer and quickly searched its contents. "Here it is," she said, and offered the card to Reed.

He took the card and gave it a cursory glance. "J. Madison & Associates," he said, before he dropped it into his pocket.

"Do you think the lawyer can help?"

"We'll see." He stood and walked to the door. "Oh, if payroll becomes a problem, make sure you talk with me. Dad and I'll work out something until Angie gets back." He winked at her smile and left.

"Matt, we can talk now."

Angie stood at the bathroom door, dwarfed in another

of his shirts. Although her head and body ached, at least she was clean and dry. And safe, thanks to Matt.

From his seat on the sofa, he turned, surprised by her appearance. He pressed papers he had been reading into the side cushions before he nimbly stood to join her.

"You're feeling better?"

"I'm okay." She spoke quickly as she sat stiffly on the opposite end of the sofa. Matt reclaimed his seat as she drew a deep breath.

He had also cleaned up and changed into shorts and a shirt that hung open to expose his chest. Her curious gaze strayed to his shoulders outlined against the fabric, and dropped to the thick muscles of his outstretched legs, where she lingered a moment. She looked up, to see that he observed her similarly.

She swallowed hard, momentarily struck by a bout of embarrassment, and brushed her hand across her short, wet hair.

He smiled before handing her one of the mugs from the tray on the coffee table.

"Here. More hot soup."

Angie reached out for the cup. When her fingers briefly entangled with his, the unexpected touch was like a spark, and it pleased her. She met his stare as though in agreement on that thought.

She sniffed at the column of steam to hide her flush. "Just soup, right?"

Matt held up his hand. "Scout's honor." He reached for her cup. "Do you want me to try it first?"

She shook her head. "Maybe it's time for me to trust you. You've rescued me, twice now." She took a gingerly sip from the hot brew.

"I don't usually charge the first time. However, if you make it a habit, I'll have to start."

His attempt at levity worked, and Angie visibly relaxed. He leaned back on the sofa and quietly observed her. He knew nothing of her, but was taken by her compelling manner. She'd been a heady experience so far, and every fiber of his being warned him to tread carefully.

As she sipped the broth, her scrubbed face refused to reveal the turmoil he knew resided within. Even in her state, he noticed her every move was one of assured style. She may not know her identity, but grace and self-esteem were part of her character.

"Let's talk," he ventured.

She lowered the cup. "The reality of my situation is, I don't know who I am or where I'm from. I have to do something."

"Have you remembered anything yet?"

Angie shook her head slowly before she answered, "No."

"You've talked and mumbled a few times in your sleep, like you were dreaming. Do you recall any of it?"

Angie frowned. "What did I say?"

"You said 'help us' again last night. You made a funny sound, too." He watched Angie's eyes lower in thought. "I figured you were snoring." When her eyes darted to him, he laughed. "I'm kidding."

She shook her head at him as she made a small smile. "They don't mean anything."

"What about your dreams?" he urged. "They could be important."

"They're more like nightmares."

"Tell me what you can."

"When I wake up, I can sense I've been dreaming, but I can't recall them." She frowned as she tried to explain. "All I get are disjointed pictures of things . . . the ocean, a boat, nothing I recognize as my past. When I try to figure it out, the pain in my head takes over."

"Sounds like post-traumatic stress. Maybe you were severely traumatized out on the water, and don't want to remember. Your mind is protecting you at all costs."

"When I woke up this morning, I was drowning in my

nightmare." She stared past Matt. "Now that I think about it, it was more like being chased."

"Could you tell who was after you?"

She shook her head and leveled her stare on him. "What's odd is, I wasn't worried about drowning. I was afraid I'd be caught and I couldn't let that happen." She raised her brows at her words. "That's the energy I get from the pictures in my head. Dread. Fear. Of what, I don't know."

Matt reached over to the tray, and from under a napkin, revealed the gold anklet with the silver key attached.

"We do know one thing. This chain gave us a name, and maybe it will tell us more." He turned it in his hand so they both could see it. "It's strange to have a functional looking silver key on a delicate gold chain. It unlocks something."

"What?"

He sighed. "I suspect only you know that, but it was put on your ankle for a reason." He shifted on the sofa and turned so he could face her. "Let me see your feet."

She looked at him, puzzled. "Why?"

"I want to see what condition they're in after your trek through the woods." He reached down to grasp her ankle. "I also think you should wear this chain."

She stiffened away from his hand. "No. I don't feel any kind of connection when I touch the thing, anyway." She crossed her arms against her chest.

"Listen, Angie." He leaned in close to her, and stared into the depths of her eyes. Had he noticed their beauty before? "We both know the chances of it not belonging to you are slim to none."

She looked down at her bare feet and the angry welts that swelled across their tops. As she lifted her foot, Matt tore his gaze from her face to grasp her calves and swing her legs onto the sofa before him.

He let out a light whistle of concern as he studied her

feet. "You've got quite a few cuts here. The good news is they're mostly superficial."

Angie sat in an awkward silence against the cushion, again stunned at her reaction to his touch, electric to her exposed legs. With each probe of his fingers, the pleasant sensation in the pit of her stomach increased.

"There were sharp rocks on the cave floor," she managed to mutter and break the pregnant silence.

"Now you know why this island is called Cave Cay. The inner forest is dotted with caves of all shapes and sizes. Stick to the pathways in the sanctuary and you'll be safe." He darted a curious glance at her. "Didn't you see the posted signs?"

"No. It was dark at first. The caves have a funny smell. The air burned my nose."

Matt stopped long enough to give Angie a lopsided grin. "That was guano."

"Guano?"

His grin grew wider. "I'll tell you about it sometime."

"Tell me about your island. How did you get it?"

He massaged ointment into the tender flesh on her foot. "Initially, my partners and I bought it as an investment."

"An entire island? Isn't that expensive?"

"It's not that big, but that was a problem. So, we partnered with a few wildlife groups and used government grants to set up the sanctuary and made improvements to make money."

"How does it make money?" She leaned her head against the cushions and enjoyed the massage from Matt's hands.

"To keep costs down, tourists bring in income eight months out of the year, and the partners share private use the other four."

As he talked, Angie studied him. Her eyes swept over his smooth brown skin and high cheekbones. His low beard's shadow gave him a mysterious aura that was pleasing. He was a handsome man, a kind and gentle one. Even as she gathered the thought, she pushed it aside.

"Let me guess," she said. "Unlucky you had me wash up during your private time."

"I'm feeling pretty lucky." He looked up at her. "I'm thankful nothing worse than a few scratches resulted from your little stunt."

"Nothing worse?" She frowned. "When I fell into that hole, I panicked. And, I'm not usually taken to panic attacks."

Matt stopped massaging her foot and looked up. "You're not?"

The unconscious blurt had startled Angie. "Why did I say that?"

"You didn't think about it. Free association. I'll have to play a game of it with you. Who you are is still inside, and your subconscious hasn't forgotten that personality. It's your conscious thought that suffers the memory loss."

He returned his attention to her feet. "Everything here will heal. I'll give them a little help with an antibiotic."

"What about you? Do you always vacation alone on your cave-filled island?"

"I'm not alone right now, am I?" He didn't raise his head. "And, there's more here than caves. I get the impression you don't like what you've seen."

"I've only spent time in your bedroom and a cave."

He raised his eyes to meet hers and smiled. "Then you've experienced both reasons to come here."

"Pardon?" She raised her brow at him.

"That's how we advertise this place . . . come to our island and discover hidden passions nestled in an exotic paradise."

Angie hadn't missed his meaning and let the warmth from his gaze caress her face, her curiosity in him all the more aroused.

"So, which works for you, passion or paradise?" she asked with a straight face.

His warm fingers encircled her ankle to raise it from the sofa. "These days, the paradise part works fine."

When she saw the gold chain in his hand, she moved to jerk her foot away, but he held tight. A look from him, and she relaxed again. He lay the gold chain against her skin and caught it up with his fingers to clasp the lock. His hand slid to her heel before he lowered her foot to the sofa.

"You should keep it on." He gave her a stern look. "Study it, touch it. It might help you remember."

"Matt, from the things I've said, the way you found me," she mused as she fingered the anklet, "they mean I wasn't alone on the water. That's why I feel this urgency to do something . . . to get help. But, for what?" She slowly raised her head. "What am I going to do?" She slowly raised her eyes to his, and caught the glimpse of sadness that lurked behind his dark eyes.

"I wouldn't be surprised if someone were trying to find you right now."

The tall, granite professional building sat on prime commercial real estate on the corner of Las Olas Boulevard in Fort Lauderdale. Reed pushed through the revolving door and found himself in a lobby that resembled an upscale suburban mall. He crossed to the elevators behind the information desk.

He slid his hand to the inside pocket of his suit coat and revealed the business card with Angie's attorney's name printed in gold relief. J. Madison & Associates. No other names, only a suite address on the twelfth floor. He replaced it and stepped onto the elevator.

Earlier, at the workshop, he had listened to Fran's theory, but he knew his sister better than that. Sure, Angie had the strong and expected temperament of a talented artisan, and had mercurial moods, but she would have told him her plans if they involved an extended stay, even if it meant leaving a phone message. Never one to suppress her displeasure, she'd have left another message that chewed him out for being unavailable.

He smiled as he thought about their troubled start that began with a child's jealousy upon her surprise birth into the family. Reed's parents had been his, alone, for six years, and he didn't want to share them with the tiny, red-faced baby. He had taken on his duties as an older brother seriously, though. Soon, they had forged a devoted filial relationship that continued to this day.

He suspected he was the only person who knew the extent of her troubles with that bastard she'd married, Philip Manchester. He also knew how desperate Angie was to end the marriage, which Philip threatened on more than one occasion to drag out for all its worth. Pride wouldn't let her ask her big brother for help—not after all the trouble her insistence at going through with the marriage had caused the family.

The elevator chime at the twelfth floor interrupted his thoughts. The doors slid open, and he stepped off, then turned toward Suite 1250, as directed by the posted sign.

The hall was clear except for a woman near the other end. She was bent over a doorknob while her gym bag hung from her shoulder. Dressed in gray sweat shorts, a tank top, and sneakers, her hair sagged from the weight of her crooked chignon. He strolled toward the woman, amused at the way her dark tendrils danced to the bob of her head as she forcibly rattled a key in the door lock.

Reed continued on in a leisurely stride. Side glances at the other door numbers in his path prompted his curiosity. The door the woman wrestled with was the suite he sought. As he drew nearer, his brows rose in explicit appreciation of the nicely rounded butt pointed his way. *Nice legs, too. Very nice legs.*

"Do you need any help?" he offered, when he reached her.

"I've almost got it." She spoke the words firmly, though she didn't look up. "It sticks sometimes."

She struggled with the knob on the single, frosted glass door adorned with simple white lettering that announced the firm. It wasn't what Reed had expected in this building. In fact, the other offices along the corridor paraded extravagances like double-door entrances, brass ornaments, and glass inserts that allowed peeks into their plush, planned elegance.

Finally, her key slid from the lock. She let out a sigh of relief as she straightened and turned from the door.

"See, it just takes a little know-how." She shifted her gym bag on her shoulder and pocketed the key before she raised her head.

Reed was confronted by sloe-shaped eyes in an arresting face, chestnut-brown skin, and a wide mouth. He blinked to recall the reason for his visit.

"I phoned earlier and your voice message said this office didn't close until five o'clock."

She clutched the gym bag and didn't give him a second look as she sauntered past in all her long-legged elegance. "The office closed at three today. We'll open in the morning at eight."

Reed tamped down his irritation at her lack of concern that he could be a prospective client. From the way things looked, the firm needed the business. He turned to follow her lean, swaying hips down the hall and to the elevator.

"Are any associates still around that I can talk to—?"

"I'm sorry," she cut in. "It's already past three and I'm late for my boxing class. It would have been a good idea to arrange an appointment." She reached the elevator bay and jammed her finger against the large call button. "Why don't you phone for one tomorrow?"

Reed sucked in a deep breath. Not known for his patience, he tried to muster a shard of it now and retain his civility.

"I called Mr. Madison around noon to arrange a meeting today. Your voice mail said the office would remain open until five o'clock. Now, I want to talk to someone."

When the elevator made a silent arrival, Reed looked from it to the woman. His frowning stare dared her to move, and she didn't. Unoccupied, the elevator's doors closed, then stole away as quietly as it had arrived.

"Our office is small, and sometimes we find ourselves—," she gave him a hostile stare before she finished, "—understaffed."

"Are you one of Mr. Madison's associates?" He didn't wait for her answer. "Good. I'll get to the point. My sister had an appointment with someone in your firm last week. All I want to do is speak with the lawyer handling her case. A phone number will do and I'll call them at home." His voice brooked no argument.

The woman pulled the sagging gym bag from her shoulder before letting it drop to the floor. "You are pushy, aren't you?"

Reed didn't budge, but continued to glare at her.

She sighed and propped her hand on a rounded hip. "All right, you win. Is it too much to ask your sister's name, or will I have to divine that bit of information?"

Reed ignored her pointed sarcasm. "It's Angelica Palmer Manchester."

A sudden, unexpected smile lit the woman's face. "You're Angie's brother? Oh, my goodness." She stuck her hand out in a belated greeting. "She's spoken of you before. I'm Jillian Madison."

In a clarity of vision, Reed peered at her. "You're the Jill she talks about from college?"

She nodded as her grin grew wider.

Reed clasped her outstretched hand. "Funny," he said. "I don't remember you ever coming to the house."

"You were always traveling on business in those days."

"This must mean . . . you're J. Madison?"

"I am," she proudly announced.

"And I'm Reed Palmer. Sorry I presumed so much at the beginning."

"Actually," she said with a gentle laugh, "I'm the entire firm, except for a paralegal and secretary. You know how it is when you're starting out. You have to think big." She drew her hand from his. "Tell me, why are you trying to find information about Angie? You can't ask her for what you need?"

"That's the problem." Reed pressed his hand into his temple before he let out a deep sigh. "My parents and I are worried about her because she hasn't been seen for almost four days."

"Four days ago?" Her eyes narrowed as she looked away in thought. "That would've been Thursday . . ." She jerked her head up to Reed. Her once pleasant expression was now clouded with uneasiness as she finished her sentence.

". . . The day she met with her husband."

CHAPTER SEVEN

"She what?"

"She met with Philip Manchester, her husband—"

"I know who he is, damn it." Reed's voice was the one now riddled with sarcasm. "What was she doing with him after she'd avoided him for all these months? Hell, their divorce would've been final this week."

When Jillian's forehead wrinkled, his suspicions were raised. As she turned away, he knew something was wrong.

"You're not giving away a confidence by talking with me." His brazen baritone sailed through the elevator corridor.

Slowly, she turned back to meet his stare. "Angie was afraid he'd file a motion to put off the inevitable. You know how desperate she was for this marriage to end."

"Well?" he broke in to the uncomfortable silence.

"We received an oral proposal directly from Mr. Manchester. He wouldn't contest the petition in the final days if Angie agreed to meet with him, privately. On Thursday."

"And she believed him?" Reed turned and stalked across the lobby.

"No, I did," was Jillian's curt response. "Given our tenuous position, his wasn't a bad suggestion, so I got Angie to warm to his idea." She followed his pacing figure. "Surely, you don't think he has something to do with—"

"I don't trust Philip any farther than I can throw him, and with my little finger, at that." He stopped before turning in front of her. "Tell me about this meeting he wanted."

When she hesitated, he ranted out his anger. "You sent my sister—your client and supposed best friend—out to meet with that man, and you don't know any details?"

She looked back toward her office, clearly upset over his words. "I . . . I can get the file and—"

"Then, I suggest you cancel your plans for the rest of the day so we can figure out what the hell happened on Thursday." He strode ahead of her, back to the office.

The pain's bite was ferocious, and Angie's head throbbed in its unrelenting vise. Somewhere deep inside, even in a fitful sleep, she had come to know what to expect from the intense explosions—colorful visions of nonsequential pictures—that danced their torment in her head. She thrashed against the cushions as she slipped further into another nightmare that accompanied her agony and framed her fear . . .

"You want me, not her. I'll go aboard your boat."

Angie heard the plea on her behalf before she was pulled behind the man's back.

"No." The black man with the gold earring spoke the word precisely and raised a hand, one that boasted a shortened digit, to signal his white-haired partner. "We both stay here with both of you. And we wait. Together."

"You know them, don't you?" Angie forced the accusation at

her companion while her focus remained on the two dangerous-looking men and the equally dangerous-looking guns they held.

He also kept the men in his sight. "I'm sorry, Angelica. I didn't want you involved in this."

"Answer me," she demanded again from between clenched teeth. "Do you know these people?"

When he sighed, she turned her stare from the men and glared at him. Her eyes narrowed with suspicion when he placed his hands on her shoulders.

"They're waiting for Nick Magellan—"

"Show some respect when you speak his name." The black man was positioned near the stern. His wide sneer gave him the look of an evil African deity.

Angie's lips thinned from both the knowledge and anger that the name imparted. She twisted from under his hands. "That bastard. I thought you didn't work for him anymore. Why does he want you now?"

The white-haired man advanced on her with his mouth curled in a snarl. "We don't need any lip from you. Shut up, stay cool, or I can do it for you."

He came at her with the angry words, his pale skin a ghostly white under the summer moonlit sky. He was a horrific apparition that spurred a childlike fright in Angie, like some Halloween witchery gone awry. She gasped as she stumbled backwards.

"Leave her alone," he shouted.

When Angie heard the order, she broke free of the fantasy. Too late, the white-haired man's gun hand came up. As it chopped down on her friend, he anticipated the blow and deflected it with his forearm. In an instant, the two arm-locked men twisted in a contest across the deck.

"No, no," she screamed, seconds before the gunshot . . .

Angie slowly opened her eyes. She stared into the living room's quiet solitude, interrupted only by her own heart's furious beat. She pushed herself up and tried to recall the dream that languished in her subconscious. Or, as Matt had suggested, maybe she didn't want to remember. White and black images, a name. That's right. A name had been said. What was it? Pieces of images and names. What did it all mean?

She rubbed her hand across her face and realized her headache had decreased considerably since she and Matt had sat here earlier. She liked him, and she liked what she saw in his eyes when he looked at her. Trust was no longer an issue between them. Both he and his dog were her protectors, and she could never repay them for all they'd done on her behalf.

The screen door revealed a burgeoning dusk. She didn't see Matt or Buster.

Angie swung her feet to the floor, and the gold metal shifted against her ankle. She grimaced at the chain's feather touch, a tangible reminder of what she had lost. She would get through these days on the island, but how? Too many questions swirled through her head. Impatient for answers, she could at least get acquainted with her surroundings.

Angie rose from the sofa before she tested her balance. In a slow turn, she took in the spacious room filled with blond woods and Caribbean folk art.

Eventually, her attention returned to the overstuffed sofa and the spot Matt had occupied at the other end . . . and the folded sheets of paper that peeked out from behind the cushion.

Interested, she cocked a brow, but moved, instead, toward an intricately carved bookcase. Hardback books, mostly reference volumes, lined the shelves. She also spied a leather briefcase resting on the uppermost one, guarded by two carved figurines.

She ran her hand along the well-bound spines of the books, even as she found her attention drawn back to the sofa and the sheaf of intriguing papers pushed into its side.

With a glance to the door, Angie treaded the few steps

to the sofa and the papers that would satisfy her growing curiosity.

"I'll put them away for Matt," she promised aloud, and to no one in particular.

"What did they say this time?" Reed circled Jillian's small, neat office like a caged bull. With his hands deep in his pockets, he watched her hang up the phone.

Jillian sighed and slumped back in the big chair behind her antique desk. "They'll get back to me."

"That's not good enough. We don't have time—" He stopped when, in a huff, she shot up from her chair.

"It's late, okay?" Her voice was rife with frustration. "We have to give them time to find the answers we want."

"They can't answer a simple question like, where is the bastard?"

She rested her palms on the desktop and answered in measured words. "Mr. Manchester didn't tell his lawyers about his plan to meet with Angie. They've always followed his lead on how he wanted his divorce handled, anyway."

"What about his law partners? You talked with them. They should know where he is."

Jillian moved around the desk. "Just back off for a minute, okay?" she snapped. "I need a moment to think." With her hands cradling her hips, she started her own pace around the room.

"I hear you," Reed grudgingly conceded the point to her, but blocked her path so they stood toe to toe. "I'm sorry if I'm not being civil, but under the circumstances, I don't have that luxury, and I'm sure as hell not that patient, either."

"That's obvious. But, hey, she's my friend, and I'm also worried—more than you realize." Jillian tried to sidestep around Reed, but he blocked the attempt.

"It's been four days since my sister met with a man she

desperately wanted out of her life, and from what you're saying, and by the way you're avoiding my eyes, I have reason to worry."

"I know." With those words, she moved to the window, where dusk had settled on the landscape.

Reed started to respond, but held back. Instead, he studied her. She flexed her arms, one at a time, to relieve the stress. She was an exceptionally fine-looking woman, one who easily drew stares. Under different conditions, he'd have already wrangled a late dinner promise from her. Unfortunately, she'd turned out to be the inept lawyer who'd allowed his sister to walk into jeopardy. That would be hard to forgive.

He joined her at the window. "What else do you know that you're not saying?"

She turned to meet his steady gaze. "Philip wasn't in his office." She cleared her throat. "What you don't know is that I was transferred to his assistant when I asked about a bogus appointment. She told me he didn't have any appointments on his book. In fact, she was sure I was mistaken because he had purposely cleared his calendar.

Reed frowned. "Why?"

"Philip started his vacation on Thursday."

Matt sat at the tiled cement table anchored in the middle of the garden and drew the towel across his wet back. When Angie had nodded off to sleep on the sofa, he had used the opportunity to take a long, hard swim. She should be waking up soon. Next to him lay her sun-dried bikini and beach skirt. He grabbed up the pieces of bright green material and crushed the softness in his hands.

So much for the swim that was supposed to drown the pictures of Angie that paraded in his head . . . erotic thoughts he had no right to imagine or consider under the circumstances. While he knew his limits, he had a feeling she could test every one of them. She was too . . . everything.

She had no memory of her past while he, on the other hand, was trying hard as hell to forget his. So, how were they to live together for a week? He rubbed his hand across his thickening beard. He had seen amnesia cases like hers. He was sure her past was only temporarily lost; unlike his, forever etched in stark relief.

Matt frowned at his somber thoughts. It did him no good to have her here. Not now, and not when she'd ask him the inevitable questions that would result in the same conclusions. She would be no different from all the others that had passed his way and wanted an explanation for the inexplicable.

He pressed his fingers against his eyes and remembered, with crystal clarity, the parade of indignities heaped on him during that year.

With some effort, Matt left the foreboding gloom of his dark memories and opened his eyes to the profusion of plants that flourished in the yard like a lush Eden.

There was a certain enjoyment in being free of the accusation shackles; yet, a certain melancholy lingered from the entire experience. Had he truly forgotten what it was like to trust and love unconditionally?

He slung the towel across his shoulders and, adjusting his swim trunks, walked to the herb garden at the corner of the house. No more swimming naked unless he could talk his guest into joining in the fun. He smiled at that picture. Probably not a good talking point. He reached down in the patch of aloe plants and broke off a few of the long, fat spears. Angie could use them later.

He reached the front of the house and, through the screen door, saw her standing in the middle of the room with her back to him. When he pulled the door open, she turned, surprise evident on her face.

What a picture she made. In the span of a few seconds,

Matt experienced an unbidden appreciation for her shapely legs and the lushness that formed her fragile frame. Though she might resemble one, she was no tender flower. When it came to temperament, she had already shown a definite lean toward volatility.

"I thought you'd still be asleep," he said as he paused at the step.

"You never mentioned you had a wife."

Angie's unexpected words had the force of a sledgehammer to Matt's chest. Then, his gaze dropped to her hands. His brows knitted into a scowl when he recognized the coroner's report he had pushed into the sofa. *Damn!* He had forgotten to return it to the briefcase.

"What are you doing with that?" he demanded, and propelled himself into the room as the screen door banged loudly behind him.

Angie raised curious eyes to his. "It says you found her and she died in your arms."

CHAPTER EIGHT

Matt was furious.

His mouth had tightened into a grim line when he mutely snatched the papers she held out to him. And as quickly as it took to make the angry move, he regretted it when he saw the stricken look in her eyes that didn't avoid his.

"These are private papers," he snapped, "And none of your business."

"I . . . I only just found them on the sofa. I didn't know what they were, and I didn't read them." Her eyes defiantly held his. "At least, not beyond the headings."

He dropped the plants and bathing suit on the sofa and, like a restless predator, stalked away to the bookcase, where he reached up to snatch down the briefcase.

"I don't want you snooping around while you're here. If you follow a few rules, we can get through this next week."

"A few rules?" She breathed out an indignant huff as she came up behind him. "Don't be so buttoned-up. It's just the two of us, and I didn't snoop. You left them out. And, if they're that private, you should have been more careful."

Matt threw her a terse glance. "I'm beginning to believe you'd find a way to do what you want no matter how careful I am."

"What is your problem?" Her lips thinned with irritation. "Why is your wife's death so secretive?"

Did she ever give up? He slammed the briefcase down with the papers inside as his anger rose again. "My personal life isn't for discussion. It's closed to you and everyone else."

"Be glad you have one to close," she retorted. "I should be so lucky. Don't forget, I didn't choose to be on your personal island. If I could, you know I'd gladly leave."

A great sigh escaped Matt at the quiet anguish in her words. The crash of the screen door alerted him as he replaced the briefcase. When he turned, she was already out the door.

"Damn," he muttered, and headed after her. "This is great. Just great."

He stuck his head out the door and saw her with Buster at the end of the walk. He strode to them down the stone pathway.

Angie looked up from petting the dog's head, acutely aware that Matt closed the distance between them. She inhaled a deep breath and watched as he approached. She had not intended to invade his privacy, but the few lines of the report she had unknowingly skimmed had been compelling, and now she was curious to learn more about his wife. What had happened?

She had been both taken aback by his anger and hurt by his pejorative attitude—particularly in view of their afternoon truce, and especially after she'd noticed how he'd looked at her when he didn't think she watched. Strange, but she was flattered by his attention.

When Matt reached her, he unfurled the towel from his neck and looped it over his bare shoulder.

"Angie . . ." He shifted his weight on the sand. "I—"

"It'll be dark soon," she cut in. "Take me to the spot where you and Buster found me."

Surprise crossed his features at her change of subject, and he openly paused to study her. "Sure. If that's what you want."

"Come with us, Buster." She motioned to the dog as she joined Matt's leisurely stride across the dry sand to the shoreline.

"Back at the house . . ." Once again, Matt grasped for the right words. His deep voice rang out over the crashing surf. "I'm sorry I snapped at you."

"I understand. She was your wife and I'm sure you love and miss her a lot." Angie darted a glance at him as his dark brows slanted in a frown. "How long has it been since her death?"

After an almost imperceptible pause, he answered. "A year. You didn't see the date while you were reading?"

She smiled at him. "I guess I deserved that. In the future, I'll avoid the urge to pick up after you."

"I make no apology for being a private person, but no damage was done, and I probably did overreact."

"Do you have children?"

He looked at her, clearly astonished that she continued with the questions. "No."

But, she bravely pressed on, ignoring her earlier vow to respect his privacy. "The report mentioned her death—"

"Angie . . ."

She sighed. "I know. The subject is off limits."

"I thought I made that clear."

A long silence ensued. Neither said anything as they reached the shoreline and walked barefoot through the sudsy waves. Buster frolicked ahead of them with the sea-birds.

"Since I'm the one with the memory problems," she said, giving him a sidelong glance, "shouldn't you keep the conversation going?"

He shrugged his shoulders. "All right, what do you want to talk about? World events, politics, the weather?"

Angie knew what she wanted and made a capricious suggestion. "Tell me something that's not off limits. For instance, why'd you come here alone? You're a doctor. Aren't you supposed to like people?"

He swung his head around to her, a dazzling smile played across his face. "Now you're beginning to sound like my mother."

"I do? What would she say?"

Matt mimicked a chiding voice. "For heaven's sake, get out there and meet new people." They both laughed out loud. "Actually," he said, "I enjoy solitude, always have. That's why I love it here so much."

As Angie sidestepped a swollen wave, she stumbled into Matt. With an expert hand, he caught her into his side and swung her above the splashing water, out of harm's way.

"Hey, be careful," he said, as he steadied her on her feet again. "You're still not a hundred percent."

She gave a soft laugh at his concern, though she couldn't deny so easily the spark his touch seemed to draw from her. "I don't think I'll have to worry. I've seen you in action, and you're strong and fit enough for the both of us."

He shrugged dismissively before he released her and continued the leisurely walk through the ebbing waves.

Her eyes searched his face for a moment. "I embarrassed you, didn't I? I can see it in that tight jaw of yours."

Matt promptly chuckled as he returned her stare. "You're going to take some getting used to."

"With your size and strength, I'll bet you're into sports, right?"

"I guess. That's how I paid for college. Football."

"And medical school?"

He laughed. "Emory University in Atlanta. They didn't have a football team, though. I had to pay for that with good grades and scholarships."

"So, why are you here alone?"

He looked at her, genuinely confused.

"You've got ten fingers and ten toes, you're intelligent, a successful professional—," she darted a glance at him, "—and reasonably pleasing to look at. So, I find it hard to believe you didn't have anyone to join you on this trip."

"You're talking female companionship, right, and in your humble opinion?" he teased.

At her amused nod, he said, "So, if we had known each other, and had I asked, would you have come with me?"

She tossed her head disapprovingly. "You wouldn't have asked because I seem to be the curious type and not one of your Southern Belles in Atlanta. Like you said, you're a closed book." She watched as Matt did a double take at her comment.

"Do you always say what's on your mind?" At her raised brows, he was apologetic. "I keep reminding you of your memory loss by saying the wrong things."

They continued down the beach amid the roar of the waves and Buster's barks at the complacent birds.

"Don't tiptoe around that. I think I enjoyed forgetting about it, even if only for a while. Maybe my personality is to be direct and honest about things." She clasped her hands behind her back and considered the possibility. "That's good, right?"

"Within reason," Matt said and inclined his head toward her. "Don't forget curious and impulsive."

"I'm impulsive? When?"

He shook his head at her incredulity. "What do you call jumping out of a second story window and then dropping into a cave?"

"That was survival instinct, pure and simple. I thought long and hard about what I was doing before I left your house."

"Did you think at least that long before you got the tattoo?"

"Tattoo?" Angie slowed and gave Matt's knowing smile a quizzical look.

"Where?" She stopped in her tracks, not quite convinced. "I didn't see one this afternoon when I bathed."

Matt walked on past her and looked straight ahead. "It's high on your left hip, just below your back."

Angie touched her hip in disbelief. Matt had bathed her naked body when she was ill, and she'd felt no shame at his actions. Now, clothed and conscious, that same thought brought heat to her face. Right now, he knew her more intimately than she knew herself. She raised her shirt, and tried turning to view the mark. Unsuccessful, she dropped the shirt back in place and jogged to catch up with him.

His brows arched mischievously as he asked, "Did you find it?"

"I can look for it later." She fell in step with him. "You never answered my question about why you're here."

"I wanted to think, so I came alone—on purpose. What better place than here with no distractions." He grinned at Angie. "Present company excluded."

His smile disarmed her and created a pleasant warmth within. "Think about what?"

"Everything. Life, my career, the future."

"So, I did interrupt your peace?" When he didn't respond, she took an abrupt step forward and stopped him. "It may not seem like I appreciate it, but I'm glad it was you and Buster who found and helped me."

"Things always happen for a reason."

Matt's words brought on an unexpected shudder that whisked across her body. Shivering, she reached out to steady herself on his arm.

He pulled her close and rubbed her bare arms. "Hey, what is it? You have goose bumps."

"I'm not sure," she muttered, confused about the source of her agitation. "I had a flash of memory, and then it . . . it disappeared."

Matt jerked the towel from his shoulder and cloaked her with it. "I wonder what brought that on?" As she shivered, he pulled her into his embrace and rubbed her back. "Tell me about it."

"There's nothing to tell, it was just a feeling, really." She pushed off his chest. "Are we far from the spot where you found me?"

"Not too far. Come on." With his arm at her back, he led her farther down the beach, where they walked together in individual thought.

"We knew Jill had started a local practice, but we didn't know she was Angie's attorney. I suspect Angie wanted it that way. Always independent." Maddy Palmer balanced a cup of tea with both hands while she sat curled up in a chair in the softly lit den.

"Her being the attorney surprised me, too." Reed studied his mother as she alternately relaxed, then tightened with anxiety. She shouldn't be worried like this.

He turned back to his sentry position at the wide bay window that looked out onto the manicured lawn bathed in the evening shadows. "At least she has the integrity to have a conscience for her part in all of this."

"You told her it's not her fault, didn't you?"

"I agreed with her that she probably offered bad legal advice."

"Reed," Mrs. Palmer chided.

"Well, she did talk Angie into a bad situation."

At that moment, headlights careened across the dark front yard and flashed brilliance through the window, briefly illuminating the room. Reed recognized his father's car before he moved to sit on the chair opposite his mother.

"Anyway, she won't hear from Philip's lawyers before tomorrow," he said. "When we can show Angie didn't willingly take off with him, we'll file an official missing person's report."

"Why do we have to prove anything?" Maddy set the cup and saucer on the table.

"She's a grown woman. They were still married when she disappeared, and there's no sign of violence. The police could think she left voluntarily or had a change of mind about a divorce." He shifted forward in the chair. "That's where Jillian can help."

"She can explain to the police their real relationship."

"Exactly."

The front door opened to the security system's familiar, high-pitched warning beeps. They both looked through the doorway and into the foyer as Wesley Palmer's tall figure entered the room. In his sixties, his frame didn't carry an extra pound of fat. His usually calm and urbane face was drawn, and he exchanged a weary glance with his son before he bent to kiss his wife's cheek.

"I was beginning to worry, Dad. Where'd you go after we talked?" Reed's words were accompanied by a concerned frown when he saw the exhaustion etched in his father's face.

"I rode around for a while," he replied. "I went out to the marina, thinking I might see or find something you missed earlier."

"And, did you?" Maddy watched her husband clasp their son's shoulder, an empathetic gesture, then approach the bay window and take his turn as guard.

"Her car's not there, and neither is the one that Philip usually drives." Wesley drew his hand across his graying head. "The *Angelica* isn't in her slip, either. So, I'm figuring, how can that be? I checked with the harbormaster and found out that the boat left on Thursday, but no one knows for sure who or how many were aboard."

"That's about what I learned," Reed added.

Maddy reached for her cup. "I have to keep believing that things happen for a reason."

"You always say that," Reed said as he smiled at his mother. "Of course, Angie always teases you about it."

"She understands, though. We have to hold onto our faith to see through these times."

"Angie was always with us before," Wesley offered.

"In that case, maybe this particular trial is meant for the three of us." She rose from the chair to join her husband at the window. "Or possibly Angie, alone."

"That's an interesting take on things," Reed said, curious for her explanation.

She smiled. "You know, when Angie told me she had decided to divorce Philip, she was devastated as well as embarrassed. She had a lot to prove to us when she entered that impulsive marriage, and never wanted things to come to this kind of end."

"You're right, Mom. She took a big step when she left him."

"Later," Maddy continued, "we both cried, then prayed, but not about failure. It was because she had managed to come through a miserable trial she hadn't realized she had the stamina to maneuver, much less survive."

Wesley's voice cracked. "She's learned a life lesson and a lot about herself from that bad marriage."

Maddy turned to slip her arms around her husband's waist. "That's why I believe in fate. You just have to sort the sense from the clutter. She'll be back with us. I know it."

"If Philip has caused Angie more pain, I'll strangle him with my bare hands." Wesley's words were spoken matter-of-factly, before he returned his wife's hug.

Reed looked at his parents and was thankful once again.

In the most difficult of times, his mother's unwavering faith in God and family held them together; his father was the steady rock of reason that seldom became unbalanced. He, on the other hand, relied on the tangible. That was why his normally sensible father would never get a chance to act on his threat—Reed would handle that bastard, Philip, this time.

With what he knew of Philip and his business ties, he was sure of the circumstances that could put Angie in danger, but it was premature to share that information with his parents.

Also, he wasn't sure what form the threat to his sister had taken. First things first, though. He had to locate Philip, who in turn would reveal Angie's whereabouts.

"You were trapped under your dinghy over here." Matt stooped to the sand where the small boat had beached a few days before.

"Where is it now?" Angie slowly circled the spot located near a copse of low-swaying casuarina palms.

"I dragged it to the house and stored it in the backyard. It's no longer seaworthy. The oars are gone and there was nothing in it."

"And that's it?" Her shoulders slumped under the towel. "Whomever I used to be died, and Angie was reborn on this spot, a clean slate."

"You're that same person, only you can't claim her experiences right now. They'll come back to you."

Angie dropped to the sand. Daylight had passed and the dusky sky had begun to turn the white sand into sparkling jewels. She curled her legs beneath her, oblivious to the warm waves that crept in with the rising tide, trapped as she was in a wall of despair. She welcomed Buster's familiarity when he trotted to her side.

She absently stroked the dog's damp coat, dismay her

downbeat, cognizant of the headache that had returned with the vengeance of steel drums. "Do you think I have a family waiting for me?"

Matt joined them and dropped to one knee on the damp sand. "I'm sure you do." He looked out over the ocean and shared her view of the setting sun, an intense, orange orb partially hidden below the horizon. "A mother and father, maybe even a husband and child."

She smiled at the suggestion. "That would be nice. Children. I don't think I'm married or have kids, though." She turned to Matt. "I'd always feel that kind of connection. I know I would." She shook her head as she looked at her hands, free of jewelry. "That would be horrible, don't you think, to love someone so deeply, then lose them through no fault of your own?"

"No matter the reason or fault, love lost is always a tragedy."

She jerked her eyes back to meet his. "You've suffered the loss of your wife."

"I was thinking more in terms of your family's loss of you. Temporary loss, that is."

His quiet compliment beat a warm trail through Angie. She held her hands up. "I didn't wear a wedding ring when you found me, did I?"

"True, but that doesn't mean anything." Matt sprang up from where he stooped on the sand. The conversation had turned and he was uncomfortable with the direction of his thoughts. He held his hand out to her. "You look tired after your first full day of adventure. Why don't we head back to the house? I have a treat for you tonight."

"Oh?" She let him take her hand to stand.

"To make up for your bad start in the caves, I thought I'd let you try shrimp with your soup tonight. Let's hope you don't have any allergies."

When she stood, Matt's stare was drawn to her backside. The shirt was saturated with seawater and clung to her hips like a second skin, leaving little to his already overworked imagination. As she dusted the sand from her shirt, his rapid glance flowed over her, from head to toe. "You also need a wardrobe."

"Are you running out of shirts? I can use my bathing suit and skirt, too."

Matt scratched his head as he gave her slight body another raking gaze. "I was thinking of something a little less . . . distracting."

When she became aware of his scrutiny, she looked down at her wet shirt. "All right, I'll leave it to you to find something appropriate." She tilted her head and gave his healthy torso, covered only by black swim trunks, a likewise study. "Do I get to do the same with you?"

Matt grinned at her quick wit. "We'll figure something out."

She touched her hand to her temple. "That headache I had earlier is back. I feel a little tired after all."

She let out a gasp of surprise when, without warning, Matt scooped her into his arms.

"I can walk," she said, though she made no attempt to lose her seat in his arms.

"And, I can tell you're in pain. See, you just squinted."

"Maybe I'm nearsighted and wear glasses."

Matt threw his head back and laughed out loud. "Yeah, and maybe you're a comedian, too. You can walk the beach another night. For now, let's not push your recovery."

"Okay," she agreed, and settled comfortably in his arms. "There is one thing you didn't tell me."

"Oh? What's that?"

"What does my tattoo look like?"

Matt grinned once again at her unabashed manner. "It's a colorful butterfly, with wings spread wide. Quite tastefully done."

She craned her head to look into his face. "Do you like it?"

Without hesitation, his voice laced with humor, he replied, "Yes, I do."

Once again, bright lights lit up the Palmers' bay window as another car pulled into the front drive.

"Are we expecting anyone?" Wesley called the question out to Maddy, who had gone to the kitchen to complete dinner.

Reed was in the den with his father and hung up the phone he had been using.

"I'll see who it is." He walked to the foyer and reached the door just as the bell rang. He opened it to Jillian. Surprised to see the other, Reed recovered first.

His eyes roamed expertly over her figure, taking notice of the changes she'd made in her appearance. Her dark hair was free from the chignon and fell in thick curls against her neck. She had also abandoned the gray sweats and, instead, wore a soft white blouse under her navy business suit.

"What are you doing here?"

"I came to see your parents. I want them to know I'm here to help locate Angie." She threw an expectant look past him into the foyer. "Are they home?"

"This isn't the best time for a visit."

"Please," she whispered. "I have to speak with them."

"Who is it?" Maddy's voice floated from the rear of the house.

"Jillian Madison," she called out, and boldly pushed past Reed as Mr. Palmer entered the foyer.

"She won't be staying," Reed explained, and resignedly closed the door.

His father smiled. "Nonsense. It's been ages since you've stopped by, Jillian."

"At least a year, I'm afraid. And, please, call me Jill."

She walked into his friendly hug. "I hate that we're meeting under these circumstances."

"Jill . . ." Mrs. Palmer swept in with her arms spread wide and also received a warm hug from the young woman. "You're still as lovely as ever. Reed told us you were Angie's attorney. We had no idea before tonight."

As the others retired to chairs in the den, Reed brought up the rear, curious about his parents' obvious affection for Angie's friend. He'd also noticed that she had yet to extend to him the honor of calling her Jill.

"I feel I'm to blame for what's happened." She shook her head when the elder Palmers protested her words. "Please, I was the one who suggested she meet with Philip alone."

"Sweetheart," Mrs. Palmer began, "we know about that. But, Angie usually does what she wants."

"She listened to your advice," Mr. Palmer added, "but, the decision was hers alone. My girl has an independent streak, and though it lands her in trouble, I'm proud I raised her that way."

"I'm going to help find out what happened," Jillian said.

"That's not entirely true." Reed had listened to their exchange from his spot near the wall. Now, he moved away to perch on the back of the sofa near Jillian. "I haven't come up with a working plan yet."

She ignored his reticence. "I've already made a few calls in the capacity of Angie's attorney. We should have more details by tomorrow that could shed light on what's happened."

"If anything comes of the calls," Reed added, "I'll act on the info in the morning."

"Actually . . ." she twisted in her chair so she could shoot a cold stare his way, ". . . I was thinking it might be better to get all our info at one time and analyze our situation."

"What about the Coast Guard?" Mrs. Palmer looked

from Reed to Jillian. "Shouldn't they be notified to look for the *Angelica*?"

"Yes."

"No," Reed interjected behind Jillian. "We don't want to tip our hand until we have proof that the boat is missing or we suspect foul play." This time, with the power of his stare, he offered her his own cold reproof.

Wesley Palmer exchanged a confused shrug with his wife before he looked to Reed and Jillian. "So, the two of you plan on working together on this?"

Matt stacked the ointments on the tray for Angie's rub. Dinner had been accomplished with only a few awkward moments and minimal damage. For the moment, she seemed to have put aside her preoccupation with his past, and that was fine with him.

Looking around for Buster, he realized the dog must be in the bedroom. Buster had taken to Angie as though she were his own pup. He believed Angie returned the affection. He picked up the tray and headed for her door. The quick rap he gave it was unanswered, so he slowly pushed it open as he called her name.

He entered the room and set the tray on the table. The netting was tied back from the bed, where she lay curled in the middle of the white oasis of linen, turned on her side, away from him. She was asleep, her breaths deep and even. The sleeveless T-shirt she used as a nightshirt was twisted at her midriff, as were the covers.

Out of the corner of his eye, Matt saw Buster leave his new post in the room and join him near the bed. Angie stirred, as though she felt their presence, and mumbled unintelligibly. She then turned onto her back, still asleep.

Matt frowned at the picture she made. The suggested curves beneath the shirt and covers affected him much more than he cared to admit, and reminded him of the light flirtation they'd both engaged in earlier on the beach. He felt her brow. It was still cool. He pulled the sheet across her body before untying the netting.

He glanced once more in her direction before he doused the lights. With Buster in tow, he closed the door behind them.

Angie had entered REM sleep, and allowed the powerful force of her dreams to take over . . .

I can't breathe, I can't breathe. Facedown on the floor, with her hands bound behind her, she used her tongue and lips to leverage the rolled bandanna away from her nose in order to get more air. Try harder, she exhorted herself. There!

She pulled in a deep draft of the warm sea air before she dropped her head back to the floor. It was pitch dark below deck, where she had been left in the narrow space between the bunks. The boat was not moving, so the men must still be topside.

Footsteps. Someone was coming. Her panic controlled, she braced herself for whatever was next. The door creaked open. From her spot on the floor, she couldn't see who entered. She lay perfectly still on her stomach and waited for them to act first. Doggedly, the footsteps grew louder, until someone stood in a straddle over her inert body. He smelled of power and expensive aftershave.

In an instant, the intruder grabbed a handful of the knotted rag and jerked her head up from the floor.

She grunted from the coarse treatment, but bided her time to defend herself, only now realizing the man was untying her head bond in rough, jerking movements. The moment her mouth was freed she twisted her head to the side, and looked up. She squinted into the dark at the face close to hers, and easily recognized Magellan before she released a howling scream . . .

Angie bolted upright in the bed, her eyes wide and unseeing, and screamed uncontrollable wails, over and over again.

Matt crashed through the door with Buster at his heels,

fearing what he'd find. He saw Angie, and in a flash, threw back the netting to get to her. She sat unmoving, her face wet with tears and wrenched in a scream. She was seized by a dream. He dropped to the bed and grasped her upper arms.

"Angie, wake up." He shook her.

The scream in her throat died, but she closed her eyes and gentle moans replaced the earlier hysteria.

"Angie, it's Matt." He spoke gently. "Wake up. You're dreaming."

She opened her eyes and raised her hands in a fighting posture. Slowly, recognition began to surface. She threw her arms around Matt's neck and buried her face there.

"It's okay," he said, over and over again, and rocked her back and forth. "It was only a bad dream." Matt held her tight so that her sniffles were muffled against his body. He could only hope his comfort would keep the dangerous nightmare at bay.

He couldn't remember how long they sat there and exchanged simple comfort. He only knew that when she turned her face deeper into the crook of his neck, his pulse leapt with excitement. Suddenly, her breasts were heavy and warm as they crushed against his chest, and their heartbeats seemed to thud as one continuous drum-roll.

He knew, instinctively, that it was time to pull away. He felt her indecision, too. Comfort had become a reluctant embrace and seemed the most natural position in the world, and neither was letting go.

Angie raised her face to Matt's and, like a moth to a flame, his shiver of desire would not be denied. Hungrily, he covered her mouth with his.

LOVE

You can hide the fire, but what about the smoke?
—Anonymous

CHAPTER NINE

"Look at the time." Jillian glanced at her watch before she gave Reed a pointed stare. Dinner had long vanished from the table and the evening had been spent catching up on the past. "I really should be going." When she pushed away from the table and stood, the others did, too.

"We enjoyed seeing you again," Maddy said.

"I hope I didn't impose tonight," Jillian added with a smile. "I'll make sure I call next time."

"Drop in any time." Reed was sure she caught his sarcasm. He propped his arm across the neighboring chair. "Mom and Dad wouldn't have it any other way."

When his parents had insisted she stay for dinner, he had used that opportunity to study her. As smooth as the silk that brazenly caressed her chest, she had finagled herself back into their lives and his plans. A smart woman.

Reed dropped his napkin to the table as the women left the room.

"She's grown into quite the lady, don't you think?" Wesley raised his brows at his son.

"I believe you and Mom think so."

"Always suspicious, aren't you?" Wesley slapped his son across the back before they walked across the room. "She was your sister's best friend in college, a damn good settling influence on Angie."

"You know, I've tried, but I can't remember her visits."

Wesley turned to glance at Reed. "That's 'cause you were never home, and you missed the wedding. By then, you were spending a lot of time out of the country. She shared quite a few holiday breaks with us and, naturally, we became close."

They reached the den, as the subject of their discussion prepared to leave.

Maddy gave her another hug. "Stop in tomorrow if you're in the area."

"I promise," Jill said, and turned to give Mr. Palmer a goodbye hug, as well.

"You have a good evening, young lady," he said. "Let me walk you out to your car."

"I can do that, Dad." Reed escorted her through the foyer and out the front door.

When the door closed behind them, he pushed his hands into his pockets and openly studied her in the warm night. Her perfume gently merged with the aromatic sweet woodruff that grew in abundance near the walk.

"You can drop the chivalry act." She stepped away to the edge of the stone porch as she searched her purse for her keys. "No one's watching."

He ignored her barb. "Are you trying to ease your guilt by working with me to find Angie?"

The quiet night was finally broken by the sharp jingle from her keys. She fingered them a moment before she took an abrupt step toward Reed.

"I won't say this again." Her voice was low. "Angie is my friend and I respect your parents too much not to try and undo damage I may have caused, no matter how inadvertent. My guilt is a given. Nothing will ease that."

"I don't want you here, upsetting my parents—"

"You mean second-guessing your decisions," she finished. "Angie was right."

"About what?" Reed frowned.

She leaned toward him and exhaled in agitation. "I think the pedestal she's put you on is wobbly. She got the high-handed part right, though, including your suspicious nature."

Turning, she hurried down the wide paved steps to the driveway and her car.

Reed watched her, his interest peaked, before he followed. By the time he reached her, she had already slid into the driver's seat. Before she could slam the door, he insinuated himself between it and her.

"Did Angie ever give you the real story on Philip?"

She studied his face. "You're talking about his connections?"

He sighed as he returned her stare. "I won't beat around the bush. She was dealing with an explosive situation, and you either knew about it, or you didn't."

Jillian swallowed hard before she nodded. "She told me what she found. He was up to his neck in illegal activities, which she had been led to believe were in his past."

"That's why I don't want you stirring things up and informing my parents of every new detail you find." Reed spat out the words in a controlled voice. "They don't know much about that side of his business."

Her brows narrowed in anger. "Is that why you glared at me all evening? Afraid I would blurt out Philip's dirty secret so your parents would worry even more? Give me credit for having a brain."

"You already suggested Coast Guard involvement. I don't want that done until I have an idea of Angie's whereabouts. To protect her, I have to keep my efforts low profile."

"All right, Reed. I'll play things your way." She crossed her arms and looked contrite. "I'll follow your lead, if that's what you want. I'll even go along with whatever plan you have," she implored. "But, don't pat me on the head and send me home."

He looked at the plea in her brown eyes. In that moment, he did an about-face. "Be at my place in the morning, ready to go."

She jotted down the address he gave her, with an appreciative smile. "You won't be sorry."

He hoped not. He stepped away from the car as she pulled out onto the street.

Angie's body was a tight flower that slowly unfurled as quivers of want playfully rippled through her. Matt's firm mouth, moist against hers, demanded she respond. Parting her lips beneath his, she raised her head to better receive his possession and enjoy the luxury of his warm embrace. As she savored the kiss, Matt's head pulled up. The intimacy was broken.

He stared into her face, at her softly mounded lips, the sound of her breath, faint and even, the smell of rose-scented soap. He set her away from him.

"I'm sorry, Angie," he whispered. "I had no right to do that."

"I kissed you back." She said the words slowly as she raised her gaze to his.

His finger trailed down her cheek before he released her and rose from the bed. His swift stride took him across the room and through the door. It closed with a firm thud.

Matt stood in the dark living room on the other side of the door and rested a hand on his hip. A mass of tension, he drew in a deep breath to clear his mind while his body slowly relaxed.

He had steered clear of entanglements, women, since Paula's death. So, what was it about this woman? He groaned at the thought.

He had accepted her allure from the start. It had been as evident as the tattoo he'd found on her nicely rounded butt. One minute she was helpless; the next, tough as nails. She was also nosy, opinionated, and, considering her present plight, sympathetic.

He shook his head. He was on dangerous ground. But, he could handle his attraction as long as he got to call the shots. He'd just have to keep his distance, that's all. Staring into the ceiling, he sighed. He needed a long swim. He shot a glance toward Angie's room before he headed through the door to the beach.

Angie lay propped against the pillows in her dimly lit room when she heard the faint bang of the screen door. She touched her mouth. The weight of Matt's lips lingered. She had returned the kiss of a man she'd barely known twenty-four hours. Why? Did the simple fact that it felt right have anything to do with whether she should have given in to the urge in the first place?

One minute she had been asleep, the next she had been in his arms. She had dreamed again, and she had screamed. Why? She shifted on the bed, queasy with apprehension, and tried to recall what her subconscious wanted hidden. Images flashed across her mind's eye, as fleeting as they were indistinct. This time, one remained. She sat up in the bed and rewound the dream, attaching herself to the senses it evoked.

As they washed over her, she knew, instinctively, that she'd recalled a piece of the puzzle that fit into her past.

* * *

An hour later, Matt staggered from the frothy surf to the damp white sand made luminous by the moonlight. He bent to rest his hands against his knees, his heavy breathing a sure sign that he hadn't killed himself in a foolhardy attempt to clear Angie from his mind. A night of swimming against the tide and waves had been both dangerous and exhausting, and he'd welcomed both. He looked at the house, brightly lit from the floodlights attached at the eaves, and walked heavily toward it.

Buster met him at the door. The quiet seemed a portent of unfinished business with Angie. He tried to shrug off the feeling as briskly as he toweled the excess water from his body. Heavy with the thought of their earlier encounter, he went to her door. He rapped against it as he called her name. When she didn't answer, he nudged it open.

Her scent remained in the air and assailed his nostrils as he quickly moved across the floor to her side. She lay in innocent sleep, half-sitting against a pillow that was propped against the headboard. Her covers had been kicked aside and exposed the simple ankle bracelet.

Its mysterious key was a neon sign reminder that she was not available for a stolen kiss or touch. He wouldn't breach their trust again.

When he reached out to check her brow, he stopped his hand. Shaking his head clear of its charmed fog, he left her there, untouched and undisturbed.

CHAPTER TEN

The next morning, Angie awakened to the crisp smell of fresh air. As she savored the cool, pleasant breeze, a shrill noise came from outside. She turned her head to the open window, then, as her circumstance returned in a rush, abruptly sat up to look around the room.

It was still early. The door was open with Buster gone. She rubbed her hands over her face and let last evening's events wash over her. Matt's kiss, the frightening dream, and the vague revelations, all commingled into a paisley pattern. She had tried staying awake until Matt returned to the house. Instead, she had drifted to sleep.

She pulled her legs into her chest, her mood lifted by the first real possibility that her memory would return, when she saw the key and chain on her ankle. She touched the metal nameplate as though the motion would transport knowledge. *Who are you, Angie?* She squeezed her eyes tight for a revelation, but nothing broke through the barrier in her head; only the same, unnamed fear and suspicion she'd felt before: she should be doing something. What?

She gave up as she spied another of Matt's shirts that had been laid out for her use. Leaving the bed, she slipped the shirt over her nightshirt and ventured into the living room. He wasn't there. The noise from outside had become a series of screeches. Curious, she sought out the source.

The house was built in an airy ranch style, with light woods and brightly colored accents. It winged out around an interior garden and skylight. As she walked through the house, she passed two other bedrooms and faced a large double window set into the wall at the other end of the hall. She could already see Matt and Buster through it. He threw a large red disc that the dog chased. When another screech rent the air, she followed the sound from the window. Two large, colorful parrots were the culprits. They sat poised on a perch strung from the trees at the edge of the garden.

Her attention returned to Matt. With his back to her, he stood in a pool of clear, blue water that reached his ankles. He was naked. He pulled on a metal chain attached to the pole in front of him, and a spigot released water over his head and down his back. Intrigued by the sight, she blinked, and realized he used an outdoor shower that washed out to the sea.

Angie's eyes widened as they poured over Matt's body, from wide shoulders that flexed with every move, to his tapered waist and strong, muscular buttocks, down to his long, thick legs, all handsomely wrapped in earthy brown skin.

She turned from the window and leaned against the wall as a smile played on her face. Turnabout is fair play, she thought, and didn't feel the least bit of guilt that she spied on him. She returned her expectant stare to the window and watched him retrieve the disc from the dog. He raised from his stoop and turned in her direction before he reared back his arm and gave the toy a hard toss. Her face burned with delight as she witnessed the easy grace with which his evenly muscled body moved.

Matt's impromptu glance toward the window wrenched Angie from her ridiculous preoccupation. She slid from view, then chanced another peek. He had quit the shower and now swam with Buster into the surf. She released a breath she had forgotten she'd held and stepped away from the window. With a heady, satisfied smile on her face, she returned to her room to get dressed so she could join them outside.

"Jillian, you're early." Reed's perusal was fast as she stood in the carpeted hallway of his condo, vibrant and fresh in a cream-colored pantsuit. "Come on in."

"I wasn't sure how long it would take to find you, or where I would park." She tilted her head at him. "Is there a problem?"

"No," he answered, and threw his door wide open. "Actually, I'm ready, too." He motioned her into the living room. "Have a seat while I take care of a couple of things."

No sooner had the words escaped his lips, than a noise from the back of the residence drew their attention. A beautiful woman in a cloud of brunette curls, clad in a long terry robe, waltzed toward them. She drew a towel around her shoulders.

"Is she one of the things?" Jillian's low voice was riddled with sarcasm.

He acknowledged her jab with a tight smile. "This is Tessa. Tessa, Jillian."

"Hi." Tessa had reached them at the front door and flashed Jillian a wide smile below green eyes. She leaned over and tiptoed to give Reed a quick kiss on the jaw. "Thanks, Sweetheart. You were great about this morning." She gave his arm a light squeeze before she moved through the doorway.

Reed closed the door behind her and turned to face Jillian's critical squint.

"At least you're an equal opportunist," she offered with a raised brow.

The gauntlet had been thrown. "I invited you here, didn't I?" he said in good humor. He strode to his bedroom to retrieve his jacket, a smile building on his face. He did enjoy a battle of words with a worthy opponent.

He could have explained that Tessa was just a good friend in the building, and had innocently asked to use his shower when her floor lost water pressure that morning. He enjoyed the fact that her curiosity over Tessa would only rise with no information from him. In fact, he could guarantee she would bring up the subject of Tessa before the day was over. Women could be quite predictable about some things.

He shrugged into his jacket as he returned to the living room. "I'm ready."

Jillian stood near an étagère with her back to him, and held a framed photograph. It was of Angie.

This time, he called her name.

She turned, startled. "Oh, you're back." She replaced the picture. "And, please, call me Jill."

Her long-delayed suggestion made him smile. "All right, Jill." He opened the door. "Let's go find Angie."

Preparation with the items Matt had left in her room took Angie longer than expected. Her burns were healing, and she'd rubbed them with the salves he'd left on the dresser. After she donned her bathing suit, she remembered Matt's comments from last night about her dress, or lack thereof, so she buttoned one of his clean shirts over the suit before she joined him outside.

She found him at the stone garden table dressed, appropriately enough, in a T-shirt and shorts. He was eating a breakfast of sliced fruit and muffins. It was an altogether different scene from the one she had gazed on earlier, and she smiled at that secret knowledge.

"Good morning." He pushed the platter of fruit toward her as she sat on the bench opposite him. "How are you feeling today?"

"Stronger. Hungry, too. The mango smells good."

"Dig in," he suggested. "Silverware is optional." He smiled when she reached ready fingers to the plate and fished out a peeled wedge. "I thought you'd sleep late this morning."

"After you left me last night, I had no trouble getting back to sleep." She slid the juicy fruit between her lips and chewed the soft pulp.

Matt ran his hand across his thickening beard. "I know. I kept an eye on you just in case your nightmare returned."

"Why did you leave me?" She looked up and met his frown.

He cleared his throat. "About last night."

"You kissed me." She made light of his serious tone as she chewed the fruit. "I kissed you back."

"It's not that simple; and just because we were willing, doesn't make it right, either." He rested his elbows on the table. "You see, patients can experience overwhelming gratitude toward their doctors, and that's sort of what I am to you. It happens all the time." He gave Angie a hard stare. "What's important is that I know better and it won't happen again."

Her eyes narrowed. "My overwhelming gratitude?"

"Well, yes."

Inexplicably disappointed at his confession of guilt, she was also irked by his choice of penance. "So, in the future, you intend to save me from myself?"

"Again, you're oversimplifying—"

"I can make it even simpler," she snapped. "We kissed and you ran."

"It's a good thing I did. One of us needed to keep a clear head. You don't seem to exercise the best self-control."

She froze, too startled by his take on her to speak.

Matt frowned. "That came out all wrong. It's just that I've been around you a few days now, and already I know you're . . ." He searched for a word that wouldn't offend. ". . . Unrestrained." He smiled as her silence lengthened. "That's a good thing, though," he added. "Take me, for instance. I'm the opposite. I'm used to figuring out all the angles before I act. See? We're just different, and that's neither good nor bad."

"What was there to figure out last night?" As she prepared to goad him for being overly apologetic for the brief kiss, her attitude and mood relaxed again. "You obviously wanted to kiss me, and acted on it. I did the same."

A gust of wind tossed the towel to the ground. Matt sighed as he got up from the bench to retrieve it.

"The breeze is wonderful," Angie said.

"It's a little more windy than normal." He turned toward the ocean, where the sun reflected brightly off the distant turquoise water. "The sky is clear now, but we could be in for another afternoon storm."

Angie felt the hackles rise at her neck. "Storms? Are they bad?"

"Blowing rain, mostly, and they're in and out. Nothing serious. How about I show you around the island today? We can even fish for tonight's dinner."

She rubbed her arms and nodded her agreement, but the mention of the storm was disquieting, and had turned her thoughts elsewhere. She studied Matt as he reclaimed his seat at the table. His solitary trip here, his wife's death, and his reluctance to talk about himself, all added up to as many questions about his past as her lost memory held about hers.

* * *

When the young police officer left to copy the missing person's report, Reed let out a thunderous breath and sat back in the hard, straight chair at the small precinct in Miami. It had been exasperating explaining to a stranger why Angie would not go off willingly with Philip. It had been nice to have Jill as backup.

The gray, cluttered room was small, though filled with office furniture and similar paraphernalia. Phones rang continuously, probably because only a few were answered. Paper, stacks of it, covered every desk. Although only a few officers occupied the room, they were outnumbered by civilians who, upon being called, left a long bench to join an officer at a crowded desk.

"You were right," Jill said, and crossed her legs in an attempt to relax after their interview with the police. "They don't believe she's in danger. He's making a report because he's required to."

"He's doing it by the book and that's okay. I didn't expect much more. They still help us when they rule out the hospitals and morgues. We'll stay focused on what we can find, then, we'll present evidence that—"

"Reed? Reed Palmer?" The heavy voice's boom commanded Reed's and Jill's attention. They looked across the room for the owner, who made his way to them. He was a tall man with a serious face; he wore his authority, as well as his dark suit, with equal care.

Slowly, Reed stood and narrowed his brows at the smiling man who came to a stop in front of him. "Tony King." A broad smile now broke from Reed. "What are you doing here?"

"After that last assignment, I left to come back home. I'm a lieutenant now, in Special Operations."

Reed thrust his hand out to his friend. "It's been a long time."

Tony's smile became a grin as he gave Reed's hand a spirited shake. "Not long enough that I forgot you owe me another go on the obstacle course so I can win my money back."

"Aww, you're still sore about that? When you count inflation, my man, you'd better get ready to make back to back bets." They laughed and slapped each other's shoulder in friendly competition.

"So, what are you doing in my backyard?" Tony asked. "D.C. isn't busy enough for your services?" His gaze transferred lower. "And, who's the lovely lady?"

Jill had quietly observed the two men. "I'm Jillian Madison." She deferred to Reed to explain further.

"My sister, Angie, is missing." He then quickly explained the circumstances of their visit and the progress the young officer had made with them.

"Whoa," Tony said. "No wonder you're worried. I've been hearing some rumblings about Philip Manchester from friends on the Fed side. Why don't I check it out and get back with you?"

"That would be great," Jill said.

"Here's my card." Reed handed it to Tony.

"Meanwhile, I'll ask the officer on your case to give things a push by putting out an immediate APB on both of their cars."

Reed pressed his hands into his pockets. "Time is important, so whatever you can give me—fact or rumor—at this point, it can only help."

At that moment, the officer returned with the copied report. After thanks were given all around, Reed and Jill took their leave and headed for their next appointment.

When Reed and Jill's sojourn to Philip's legal counsel, Mackenzie McNamara, offered nothing, they had called it a morning.

"You weren't surprised by McNamara's reticence, were you?" Jill had asked in the car, testy after no good news.

"Nope. He doesn't know anything. Philip only used them to handle the legal points of the divorce. If Philip is involved in Angie's disappearance, he would have played it close to the vest. You know, the answer could lie in his own office."

That was their next stop—Philip's law partnership. Reed had been careful to make the visit during the lunch hour, and had laid out a plan of action to Jill.

"Why now?" she asked, as they made their way through the high-rise building. Under her arm, she carried a makeshift wrapped package, which Reed had prepared in the car for their purpose.

"Don't you know?" He winked at her. "It's the best time not to find someone."

She groaned at his attempted joke. "I hope you know what you're doing. If not, we could be in a lot of trouble." They walked through the glass doors of the law firm.

"You said you could help, so improvise. All we want to do is get past the front desk." He motioned toward the desk. "Head's up. There's the receptionist."

"Hello, may I help you?" She was young, pert, and sat under the firm's huge silver and black logo. She deferred her question and smile to Reed, ignoring Jill.

"Yes, you can." Jill aggressively offered her name as she leaned on the desk. "I have some papers that I must personally deliver to Philip Manchester's assistant, Deirdre Watson. He and I are working a case together, and I know he's out this week—he told me he'd be on vacation." She offered a nervous laugh to highlight this bit of inside information. "But, his instructions were to leave these documents only with her." She hefted the bound package in her hand.

When the receptionist turned an inquiring eye to Reed

that questioned his presence, Jill quickly added, "Oh, he's just my paralegal."

While the receptionist made the obligatory call to Deirdre's desk, Reed stepped aside with Jill and whispered, "You don't have to lay it on too thick. Just enough to get us through the door."

"I hope you have a back-up plan if the assistant comes out to get this bogus package," she whispered back.

"She won't." Reed winked. "I made sure beforehand."

"Oh, Miss Madison," the receptionist called out as she hung up her phone. "Deirdre just left for lunch. Do you want to wait for her?"

"I can leave it on her desk," Jill offered, and started for the door to the offices, Reed behind her.

"But Miss," the receptionist protested, you don't know—" Her phone's ring interrupted her words. At the same time, the door opened as two others came through to the reception area. Reed caught the door before it closed.

Jill didn't stop, nor did she turn around. "Oh, I've been here before. I'll just store them safely on her desk and be back before you know it."

Reed took the lead when they were out of sight. He headed for the corner office he knew to be Philip's. "All right, blend in with the rest of the office personnel. Write a nice, long note at Deirdre's desk and I'll see what I can find inside his office."

Jill exhaled heavily as adrenaline moved her alongside Reed. "How I let you talk me into this, I'll never know."

"Because you like adventure. Didn't Angie tell you that about me?"

Ten minutes later, the two of them beat a retreat through the glass-doored law office and stepped into an empty elevator.

Reed quickly pushed the lobby button as Jill slumped against the wall with a noisy sigh.

"I have never been so scared," she said. "What were you thinking when you took his day planner from his office? And, I don't even want to know about the lock you picked to get to it."

Reed was already quickly flipping through the leather bound volume. "You act like this is your first time breaking the law." He turned to the date Philip met with Angie.

"I take that to mean it's not yours?"

He shot her a glance. "Hey, don't get self-righteous on me. I'll return his property when he shows up. With Angie. And don't forget—you asked to work with me, not the other way around."

As they rode in silence, he looked up from his reading and saw that she'd settled a frown on him. "By the way, you're a pretty good actress. I couldn't have pulled this off without your help. Thanks."

The elevator doors opened to the lobby and they stepped out.

"I keep thinking someone's gonna lay a hand on my shoulder and arrest me," Jill said as she jogged to keep up with Reed. "Did you find anything in his book we can use?"

He smiled at her sudden interest in the planner and nodded. "We have an address. I believe it's time we paid a visit to Philip's right hand man, Daniel Otero." He didn't mention two other occurrences he'd found, the more interesting one being the name of a U.S. Attorney he'd crossed paths with before, J. Ryan Harrison.

CHAPTER ELEVEN

Matt intended to give Angie a good day on the island, free of stress. Other than the memory loss and headaches, she appeared healthy, which meant there was an excellent chance her memory could be coaxed to return under the right conditions. With Buster gamely alongside, they hiked toward the other end of the island.

He was surprised at how nimbly she'd traversed the slippery, above-ground roots of the mangrove trees, and was further impressed at her agile climb across a wide out-cropping of smooth boulders to reach the fishing site. They dropped their fishing lines in the calm, blue cove just below the boulders, where schools of fish darted through the shaded water. After he pulled their first catch from the water, it didn't surprise him when Angie balked at lessons on how to clean and dress it for the night's dinner.

The day continued to progress in a carefree manner as morning faded into afternoon far too quickly. While they enjoyed the familiarity and comfort their forced closeness required, neither broached the subject of their respective pasts.

Tired of fishing, they returned to the beach and ate from a packed lunch. Sated from food and sun, they both stretched out on soft mats. They were hidden from the sun's rays by low swaying palm trees, but the warm, fragrant breeze was stronger and added to their lassitude.

"Tell me what you think of the island now."

Angie smiled, and guessed correctly that he was proud of the place and wanted her to like it here. She did. So far, what she had seen was breathtaking, a paradise.

"It's beautiful," she said, with her eyes closed. "The colors are like the ones you find in a child's crayon box. Pure, bold, unadulterated." Her eyes drifted open and revealed Matt propped on an elbow, smiling down at her. His gaze warmed her inside. "What's funny?"

"I knew you'd like it here once you got a chance to see it up close. There's a waterfall near the sanctuary—"

"If it's near the cave, no thanks." She tried not to stare at his mouth.

This time, he grinned wide and revealed strong teeth as he nodded. "We can always avoid a repeat performance at the cave."

"Really?" She mimicked his excitement.

Matt recognized her impertinence and dropped to his back beside her, resting his hands behind his head. "I'm sorry you're stuck here. But, if you don't want to make the most of your time and see the place, then suit yourself."

"I was only kidding." Angie quickly struggled to sit up, but when she saw his face, she realized it barely held his grin inside. She punched him hard in the arm.

Matt's laugh came out in a howl, and he grabbed her hands before she inflicted more pain.

"I was trying to be on my best behavior today."

"Oh . . . You have to work at it?"

She tried punching him again, but her hands were firmly

in his grasp. With only a slight tug, he playfully pulled her off balance so that she landed softly on her back and under him. She laughed as Matt leaned over her. He smiled, his breath warm and fruity as it brushed her face.

The moment froze for Angie—much longer than the few seconds that actually passed. Her heart raced as her eyes fluttered closed to receive his kiss.

In the next moment, she was being pulled up by him. Surprise lit her wide eyes. He had wanted to kiss her—Angie was sure of it. But, he had stopped, just as he'd promised, and she felt a measure of disappointment. She sat back on her legs and brushed the sand from her arms.

"I'm playing too rough with you," he said, and rubbed the beard at his chin. "I forget you're still healing."

"Except for the occasional headache, I'm okay." Her stare had settled on his mouth. "Do you always wear a beard?"

He scratched at the hair on his face before he smiled. "No. Only when I come here. Why?"

"I imagine it itches." In a capricious move, she touched his bearded jaw. "It's soft, and rough."

Before her hand could travel any farther, Matt caught it in his own. "It takes a little getting used to." His gaze captured hers. "Sort of like unexpected company."

It was Angie's turn to smile at his thorny point. "And when it's time for you to leave, you'll get rid of it and return to a normal life, right?"

"You have this habit of twisting things so that you end up with the upper hand." He chuckled and released her. "I'll bet you're used to getting your way with passive aggression."

She snorted at his analysis. "That doesn't answer what'll happen to me when you leave and my memory hasn't returned. You'll dump me in the nearest hospital and say, good riddance."

Matt slowly shook his head. "I wouldn't abandon you.

WIN A CHANCE TO BE IN A BET ARABESQUE FILM!

Arabesque films

lack Entertainment elevision (BET) has entered he world of movie making! his fall, BET Arabesque ilms will be the first studio o "greenlight" ten African-American themed original nade-for-TV movies. With ilm adaptations from the Arabesque Book Collection, BET will be the only studio committed to exploring the lives of African-Americans in a variety of genres, including romantic dramas and suspense thrillers. Join the ranks of today's hottest movie stars, including Holly Robinson, Loretta Devine, Vanessa Bell Calloway, Richard T. Jones, Phil Morris, and Allison Dean, and make your cameo appearance in one of BET Arabesque's upcoming productions: *Incognito, Intimate Betrayal, Rendezvous, After All, Rhapsody, Midnight Blue, Playing With Fire, A Private Affair, Hidden Blessings,* or *Masquerade* (in the *Love Letters* anthology).

This fall, BET Arabesque Films will create 10 original African American themed, made-for-TV movies based on the Arabesque Romance book series.

The list includes some of the best-loved Arabesque romances, including Francis Ray's *Incognito*, Donna Hill's *Intimate Betray* Bridget Anderson's *Rendezvous*, Lynn Emery's *After All*, Felici Mason's *Rhapsody*, Monica Jackson's *Midnight Blue*, Dianne Mayhew's *Playing with Fire*, Donna Hill's *A Private Affair*, Jacquelin Thomas' *Hidden Blessings, and* Donna Hill's *Masquerade*.

And now BET is offering you the chance to win a cameo appearance in one of these upcoming productions! Just think, you can join some of today's hottest African-American movie stars—like Richard T. Jones, Loretta Devine, and Holly Robinson—in the creation of a movie written by, and for, African-American romantics like yourself! All you have to do is complete the attached entry form and mail it in. Just think, if you act now, you could be in one of these exciting new movies! Mail your entry today!

PRIZES

The **GRAND PRIZE WINNER** will receive:
- A trip for two to Los Angeles.
  Think about it—3 days and 2 nights in L.A., round-trip airfare, hotel accommodations.

- $500 spending money, and round-trip transportation to and from the airport and movie set...sounds pretty good, right?

- And the winner's clip will be featured on the Arabesque website!

- As if that's not enough, you'll also get a one-year membership in the Arabesque Book Club and a BET Arabesque Romance gift-pack.

5 RUNNERS-UP will receive:
- One-year memberships in the Arabesque Book Club and BET Arabesque Romance gift-packs.

WIN A CHANCE TO BE IN A
BET ARABESQUE FILM!

Yes! Enter me in the BET Arabesque Film Sweepstakes!

NAME _____

ADDRESS _____

CITY _____ STATE ____ ZIP _____

TELEPHONE _____ AGE _____

SIGNATURE _____

(MUST BE 21 OR OLDER TO ENTER)

www.arabesquebooks.com

In fact, when your memory returns, chances are you'll dump me. I'd like to think that, no matter what happens, we'll be friends."

"What about you?" She rested her hands on her lap. "You came here to work out your own problems."

"Since you showed up, it's given me something to do. I don't know if that's good or bad." He looked out to the shore. "Maybe I'll just stay here. It's peaceful, don't you think?"

"Hide out from the world? That's not you."

"You don't know me." He picked up a shell and threw it hard across the sand. It dropped into the distant surf. "Lately, I'm not even sure who I am."

"Then, we're simpatico." She smiled before she added, "It's the anniversary of your wife's death, and you're still dealing with it."

He jerked his head around at Angie, his brows narrowed.

"Well, you did say she died about a year ago," she offered. "Talking could help." When he said nothing, she added, "Maybe."

Buster had found his way back to their side and sank to the sand between them. Matt sighed as he scratched the dog's ears.

"The only thing that could have changed the course of my life was my own hand in shaping it. No one asked my opinion, so here I am. Talking won't undo what's done." He glanced at her and smiled. "I guess we've both been dealt a bad hand."

"We have free will to go our own way."

"Yeah, or so we think. You can't escape the fact that we live in the same space as the leeches that feed on that soft underbelly of ours called weakness."

"Why are you being cynical?"

His words were short. "What makes you think I'm not always this way?"

"All right." Angie petted the dog's wet coat, looking

away from Matt. "This anger is about your wife. You must have loved her very much."

He didn't respond, and she darted a glance at him. His brows had narrowed in thought. "Which is worse, Matt, the leech or the weakness?"

"The fault is equal."

"One can't survive without the other."

He scooped up another shell and sailed it across the sand. Buster tired of them and ran off to chase after it. Matt turned to her, his brow now soft with humor. "When your memory returns, I won't be surprised if it turns out that you're a shrink . . . or a private investigator." He smiled. "Maybe both."

"I'm serious. You should talk about whatever it is you've got locked inside. Didn't you say everything happens for a reason? Maybe I was put on your island to listen to you, act as your muse." She raised her eyes to him before she continued. "Even help you get through this bad time."

She waited for him to react badly to her comments. After all, she had mentioned his wife again. Leaning toward him, the gusty, warm wind billowed her shirt.

The fact that she had mentioned Paula was not uppermost in Matt's mind—not at the moment. Earlier, he had wanted to kiss her again. It had been hard to turn his thoughts from what she innocently offered.

Even the wind now worked against him. The strong breeze separated her shirt and exposed her cleavage to his stare. Her nipples were hard and defined, and pressed against the Lycra suit. He swallowed hard and raised his eyes, only to meet confusion in hers.

"What's wrong?" she asked.

He swallowed again. "I like listening to you." It wasn't a lie. Her voice had fascinated him from the start. "Coming from a small woman, your voice is . . . throaty."

Once again, she snorted at his observation, and raised up off her legs. "I've heard that most of my life."

"You have, huh?" Matt's brows arched in a question. "Are you remembering more?"

Her hand flew to her mouth. "I don't know." She seemed equally incredulous at the ease in which the words had slipped their bounds, and frowned. "It just came out."

"It'll happen more often, and before you know it, your full memory will be back." He touched the short, slick hair near her temple where the cut from her accident was healing. "Your body will knit, and so will your mind. Give it time." His hand dropped to her chin and he gently lifted her solemn face. "Something else is on your mind. I can tell. Out with it."

"The nightmare from last night?" At his nod, she said, "I remembered a part of it."

His hand dropped. "You were screaming when I found you sitting up in bed."

"In the dream, it was a dark and closed space. I was scared and could hardly breathe. I thought I'd suffocate."

"That's a good start," Matt said, pleased with her revelations. "Think back, focus on your senses. Did you see a face, hear a name, touch or smell anything?"

She closed her eyes and tried to revisit the dream. "I just sense the darkness and familiar things." Her eyes popped open again. "I know the place. It wasn't unpleasant, but familiar. I can't remember why, though."

"Why didn't you tell me about this?"

"I don't know. It was so vague I didn't think it was important." She dropped her shoulders.

"Hey, don't let this disappoint you." He offered her a smile. "More will come next time, and the dreams will get easier to remember."

"What do you think it means?"

"I don't know, Angie. If we're to believe your dreams are your subconscious memories coming out, then it sounds like something extraordinary happened in your ordinary and familiar world. It was enough to shake you up pretty badly before you got here."

"Suppose I brought that danger here, to you and Buster?" Her eyes had turned sad. "Sometimes, I get this feeling—"

"Hey . . . don't worry yourself like that. How could you harm us? You were probably in a boating mishap that frightened you. Whoever accompanied you on that boat is still looking for you."

Buster sidled up to Angie and now shook his coat free of sand and seawater. Their hands flew up to avoid the stinging spray.

"Buster's taken to you pretty quickly." Matt shooed the dog away as he pounced to his feet. "I believe a storm could blow through before long." He looked back at Angie. She hadn't moved from where she sat on her heels.

"Come and join me for a swim," he offered.

She hesitated before she stumbled over her answer. "I don't know . . . not today. Maybe I'll try tomorrow."

He watched her a moment. "I don't blame your being scared about going back out there so soon."

"I'm not scared," she bristled.

"Sure you are. You had a rough time on the water. You almost drowned."

When she didn't answer, he stooped down beside her and tried to allay the uncertainty she wore on her face. "I'm a strong swimmer and I won't let anything happen to you." He stood and held his hand out to her. "We can take it a bit at a time."

She sighed loudly before she pushed her shirt from her shoulders. Matt stripped to his trunks.

"Okay, but promise you'll stay at my side." She reached out and clutched his hand.

"Deal," he said. They walked down to the surf while Buster pranced around them.

* * *

It was midafternoon when Reed drove past the entrance to Gateshead Park and onto the neat streets of the quiet, suburban Coral Gables neighborhood.

He stopped the car in front of a neat, though ordinary, house. It was one of a number of homes set within a square patch of green, manicured lawn.

"He lives here?" Jill peered at the house from the car window. "Seems a little middle class for him, don't you think?"

"You stay put," Reed directed as he got out of the car. "I'll be right back."

He walked up to the door and rang the bell. The door opened to reveal a man of average height and build, with black hair that grazed his shoulders. The man's tanned, olive complexion crinkled around the eyes when he squinted at Reed.

"What are you doing here?" he asked, visibly suspicious.

Reed's shove sent Daniel Otero stumbling backward into the house. "Looking for your boss." He followed him inside, then slammed the door. "Where is he?"

Daniel shrugged as he cautiously eyed Reed. "How should I know? I'm on vacation." He walked into the adjoining room and dropped into an armchair.

"Yeah, sure." Reed walked around the neatly decorated room, taking notice of its contents. "You two don't take separate vacations. Isn't that bad for Philip's health? Where he goes, you go, like a ball and chain."

"He wanted to be alone this week."

"Why?"

Daniel's furtive glance washed over Reed. "You're here, so you know why."

"Humor me."

Daniel spoke low. "He wanted some time alone with your sister on the *Angelica*."

"That seems kind of strange. They're getting divorced."

"You know how women are when it comes to Philip," he leered. "She probably changed her mind."

"You bastard." With lightning speed, Reed grabbed Daniel's collar in his fists, then wrenched him from the chair. He drew Daniel close enough to inhale the pungent combination of aftershave and fear. "Where did he take her?"

Daniel struggled, his windpipe jammed under Reed's fist. "I don't know," he gasped. "He didn't tell me."

Reed swung him into the wall. "Tell me something I want to hear, and tell me fast."

Pinned as he was, Daniel clawed at Reed's hands. "I swear I don't know where they went."

The door slammed.

"Reed, what are you doing?"

Jill's shrill cry drew his attention. He threw an angry glance at her, but continued to hold Daniel. "Damnit, I told you to stay in the car."

"You can't do this," she argued, as her eyes darted helplessly between the men. "Stop it."

"Keep out of this," Reed warned.

"Wait," Daniel finally managed to shout. "Maybe I do remember something."

Reed eased his hands from the man's throat. "All right, let's hear it." He pushed him away.

"Like I said, I don't know his plans, but I was supposed to get a call over the weekend for instructions." He rubbed his neck as he cast a suspicious eye at Jill. "Who's she?"

Reed's look told her not to answer. "What kind of instructions?"

"That's just it. I never got them. I've been sitting tight for the last few days and he never called. I've been worried over it myself."

"Why?" He circled over to the window and took a cautious look out before he returned to stand next to Jill.

"Philip hasn't upset anyone, has he? Is something going on?"

"I swear, Reed, I don't know."

"What was Philip doing before Thursday?" When he saw Daniel's hesitation, he added, "Angie is missing. The last time she was seen, she left to meet your boss. Is she in trouble?" He advanced on Daniel.

"No," Daniel shouted. "I mean, I don't know. He had a lot of meetings last week, and we changed our usual protocol. So, I never got a chance to see who he met with. All I know is he was gonna spend time with your sister and he'd let me know over the weekend when he wanted me back at work."

"Don't you think it strange that he changed how he was doing things? Did he meet with Magellan?"

Jill looked at Reed. "Nicolas Magellan?"

"Hey," Daniel interjected. "I never said I saw him talking with anybody."

"Yeah, sure." Reed grabbed Jill's arm and strode to the front door. "We'll be in touch, Daniel." He quickly left the house.

"What's this about Nicolas Magellan? And, what were you doing beating up that man?" Jill asked her questions as she endured Reed's fast escort to the car. "I mean, there you are roughing up the guy, talking about this notorious drug lord, and I'm an officer of the Court."

He gave her a long sigh before opening her car door. "That's why I told you to stay in the car. Daniel is Philip's right hand in everything, from navigating the *Angelica* to pressing suits for special engagements." She slid into the seat and he closed her door.

"So, what do we do now?" She asked the question as he got behind the wheel. "Wait until Philip calls Daniel?"

"I don't believe for a minute he's been sitting around waiting for a call that didn't come. Did you notice the inside of the house?"

"Besides being immaculate, what about it?"

"Angie told me Daniel is a chain smoker, and lived with them when he was on duty. I could smell smoke on him, but none in the room, and no cigarette butts or filled ashtrays were around. I don't think he's been at the house long—he hasn't even had time to check his phone. The answering machine had twelve messages waiting. He's there for appearances only."

"That's pretty good observing. I'm impressed."

"Don't be." He started the car and pulled out into the street. "Someone's pulling Daniel's chain, and I'd like to think it's Philip. If not, who?"

He turned the car into Gateshead Park. A white Chevrolet Lumina faced them and was parked on the grassy shoulders. They slowly passed the car, occupied by a business-man whose head tilted against the back of the seat. Reed stared into the rearview mirror to see his license plate. It was government issued.

"So, why are we riding through the park?" Jill asked.

"It's a shortcut back to the highway and my place for your car."

"What do we do tomorrow?"

He glanced her way. "I'll go through Philip's planner and wait for the reports from the police department. Hopefully, we'll have more leads to follow by then. You have a business to run, don't you?"

"I'm going in to handle some things in the morning, but I'll be ready to help you by midmorning."

"All right. I'll pick you up at your office around ten." He watched her settle in her seat. She was obviously satisfied with his answer, a long way from how their day had started. Maybe having her around wouldn't be a chore after all.

"You never asked me about my houseguest this morning."

Jill had a puzzled look on her face. "What guest?"

"You remember Tessa, my neighbor. She was at my place using the shower this morning. Hers was broken."

"So, why tell me?"

A smile tugged at Reed's face.

While Reed sped down the highway, the phone rang in Daniel Otero's house. He reached out a sweaty hand to grab it up.

"Does he know anything?" The deep voice on the other end of the line was insistent.

"He showed up, like you said, and he was real pissed about his sister." Daniel spoke eagerly. "I don't think he knows where she is."

"You're sure about that?"

"He damn near choked me to death." When he was met by silence from the other end, he answered more responsibly. "Yeah, I'm sure. Now what?"

"We'll let you know. Stay put until we pick you up. Mr. Magellan appreciates your cooperation and, by the way, so did Philip." The connection ended.

Daniel hung up the phone and, out of habit, looked over his shoulder into the dim room. He swiped his hand across his damp face as he fingered the empty cigarette package with the other. He needed a smoke, but they'd told him not to leave the house. He headed for the bar in the dark corner to pour another drink.

Matt pulled Angie into the protection of a group of small palms at the edge of the beach. Buster followed as his barks collided with the thunder's rumbling echoes. A short time before, Angie had found confidence in the ocean water and had repeatedly swum into Matt's waiting arms. Too soon, though, his prediction of rain had come true and, as the sun-burst sky darkened, they had sought protection from the cloudburst. Now, the three of them crouched tightly together and waited for the steadily increasing onslaught to reach its apex and subside.

"At least we know you can swim," Matt declared over the din of the weather. Alerted by her vigilance, he tried keeping her thoughts off the storm.

"Do they last long?" She shivered as her arms folded across her chest.

"Usually no more than ten minutes." Her short hair stuck out in spots, and he thought she resembled some sea creature. Another thunderclap cracked the air and she jerked around. Buster relaxed on his haunches just behind them.

"Before I make these trips, I always get a long-range forecast to make sure there's no surprise weather, like a hurricane," he joked, but she didn't relax and continued to hold her body stiffly. "These storms blow through fast. You'll get used to them soon enough."

A bolt of lightning flashed before them. As a whimper escaped her throat, she buried her face in his chest. The succession of bold thunder crashes behind the bright flash had reduced her to a shuddering mass. Matt cupped his hand to the back of her head and held her against him.

He whispered at her ear. "It's all right. I didn't know you were afraid of storms."

Unable to speak, Angie nodded repeatedly against his chest, but didn't move from the circle of his arms. The jagged flashes seemed to have opened a corner of her mind. She remembered a boat, a lost oar, and the fear that came from capsizing in a dark ocean with no one to hear her screams. Another crash of thunder, and Angie whimpered again. Her fingers curved into his skin and she held onto him for dear life.

Matt dropped his chin to the top of her head. The storm had crested and the wind sprayed rain into their small shelter. He held her tight, their bodies warm and pliant, and murmured a solace in her ear. She raised her face up to his. Drawn to her moist, parted lips, he was led into a fantasy of his own creation, one that had been building the entire day. Alarms sounded, but he ignored them when she closed her eyes. He kissed her.

It was not gentle and curious, like the night before, but hard and dangerous, like the weather that swooped about them. His mouth slanted across her lips. He wanted more, all of her. His tongue's assault into her warm mouth granted the wish but promised to send him to the edge.

Angie welcomed his lusty possession. The fear and dread brought on by the storm was replaced by luscious waves of want. She stroked his face, and never felt more alive than when his rough beard rubbed into her skin and his tongue explored her. His mouth released hers and slid downward.

His lips trailed along her rain-slicked neck, to her shoulders, and still further to the tops of her breasts. He placed reverent kisses on her exposed flesh.

A crack of thunder drew them back into reality and the cramped space they shared with Buster. Angie's eyes were sharp with terror and she lurched with each flash and roar from the weather. Matt reached for her.

"I don't want to argue about the kiss right now." She rushed the words. "Can we deal with it later, after the storm?"

He drew her back into his arms, a wry smile on his lips, and kept his thoughts directed to her safety.

That night, Angie picked at the half-eaten filet of grilled fish on her dinner plate. "The pictures just popped into my head during that awful storm, like a slide show that I could actually feel."

Matt sat across from her at the table. "Tell me again what you saw."

"First a boat on the dark ocean, then rain, hard rain

like today. It was so hard, the boat flipped over." She pulled her feet up in the chair and curved her arms around her knees.

"Was it a dinghy like the one you were on?"

"It was small."

"Have you considered the possibility that you're seeing the danger you were in prior to washing up here?"

"The person in that boat was afraid," she whispered.

"Afraid of the storm?"

"More. Of being rescued. But, by the wrong people."

CHAPTER TWELVE

Angie sat up in the bed and rubbed her eyes. Matt's suggestion after dinner that she retire early had been a good one. She felt better, rested.

Evidence of a clear day could be seen through the window. As before, Buster was gone and she could hear the birds from the sanctuary. Matt would be outside. Consumed with the idea that he played with Buster in the garden pool again, she slipped from the bed and headed for the window in the hallway.

Stealthily, she approached the window, and stood to the side. There was no sign of Matt or Buster. She leaned toward the window for a better view. Finally, she moved to the front of it and boldly scanned the yard and beach area.

"Angie? What are you looking for?"

Startled, she whirled around and faced Matt, who had come up behind her. He was already dressed for the day in shorts and a shirt. As the heat of embarrassment swept her face, she tugged on the hem of her short nightshirt.

"Oh . . . I, um, thought you'd be outside." She looked around him. "Where's Buster?"

Matt smiled as his gaze swept over her. "Outside." He joined her at the window and peered out. "There he is, sunning on the patio." He rubbed his beard before he turned to her again. "So, you were looking for me from this window?"

She offered an awkward smile. "I should change. I've been in bed too long this morning, anyway." She backed away before she turned and hastily fled his presence. She could only hope he didn't have a clue of her secret pleasure.

Reed stared at the name in Philip's planner. J. Ryan Harrison, called J.R. by everyone, was the Assistant U. S. Attorney who had made a name for himself by working to upend the incoming drug trade that filtered through the Miami ports. One well-known drug broker in particular had eluded his grasp: Nicolas Magellan.

He picked up his watch, a gift from Angie, and remembered how desperate she'd been to leave Philip after she'd innocently uncovered incriminating evidence of his business dealings in the illicit drug trade. At one time, Nicolas Magellan had been Philip's client.

Reed had warned her what to expect upon her exodus from what everyone had considered wedded bliss. His words hadn't shaken her determination to be free of Philip's velvet trap. He flipped to two other entries in the planner, which had drawn his curiosity. The word "halo" had been penciled in and circled on two separate occasions during the week prior to Philip's meeting with Angie.

The phone's ring tugged at Reed's attention. He glanced at his watch. Not yet nine, he had plenty of time left to meet Jill at her office. He picked up the phone and spoke a terse greeting into the receiver.

"Reed, it's Tony King."

He immediately straightened with anticipation. "You have something?"

"A lucky break. The APB produced Angie's car last night."

"Where?"

"It was reported abandoned by an attendant in an obscure public parking lot off the causeway. We had it transported to a lockup last night."

Reed was already up and grabbed for a pad and paper. "Which police lot?"

He jotted down the information that Tony provided, thanked his friend, then hung up the phone.

Jill could wait awhile longer. He reached for his jacket and keys, and headed out the door.

Soft waves washed across Angie's feet as she walked in the surf with Buster. The heavy heat, tempered by the ocean breezes, allowed her to relax. For now, she was at peace with herself, and raised her head to squint into the sun.

At that moment a surge of vertigo swept over her. Everything became white before the flash of pictures started, one after the other, then ended at breakneck speed. This time, the memory images were intense and unmistakable: A man's hands encircled her ankle as he attached a key. It was silver. He spoke to her. "Find help, find halo." Halo? Dizzy and confused, she whirled from the visions and tripped over Buster before she tumbled to the sand.

Matt could see Angie from the living room. When she dropped to the surf, he feared something was wrong, and raced to the beach, shouting as he ran.

"Angie, are you all right?"

She had begun to pull herself up from the sand when

he arrived. He helped her up even as she tried to wave him off.

"I'm okay now, really." She didn't look at him.

"Now? What happened before?" He gently nudged her face around to his.

"I got a little dizzy and fell on Buster. He didn't like that too much. He moved and I hit the ground."

He tilted her chin so he could see her eyes, which avoided his. "That's all?"

She narrowed her brows at his insistence, but nodded anyway.

"You are stubborn. I'll bet you were a regular terror with your family."

Angie swatted away his hand. "In that case, my return should be a real comfort to them." She walked away from him, her water-soaked beach skirt clinging to her hips.

Within a few seconds, he had caught up with her. "I'm the one who's supposed to be tight-lipped. You aren't keeping anything from me, are you?"

She glanced his way and caught him studying her. "Why do you look at me like that?"

He blinked hard. "Like what?"

"Like you have to ask a question twice to get all of the answer." When she thought she saw an expression of relief flit across his bearded face, her brows narrowed again.

"Oh, that." He laughed. "Now who's being cynical?" He reached out and caught her hand in his. "I was going to show you the waterfalls today. Now is as good a time as any. What do you think?"

Angie smiled a half-hearted agreement at his suggestion.

"I guarantee the island will win you over and make you smile," he teased.

She didn't think so. Her concerns about her past lurked at the back of her memory and replaced her earlier joy. He was trying hard to make her stay on the island palatable; but, he didn't know that there was something increasingly frightening about the pictures in her head. Who was the man that instructed her to get help and find halo? And, more consequential, who was he to her?

"It's in good condition, no outside damage." The bespectacled lot supervisor escorted Reed down an aisle of cars and stopped at a green, late model Millenia squeezed between two other vehicles.

Reed bent to peer through the tinted side glass. It was Angie's car, all right. Her blown-glass butterfly, which she considered a symbol of her newfound freedom and used as her business logo, was attached to the dashboard. He noticed powder all over the place. Tony had made sure they did a thorough job. He turned to the small man who rocked on his heels nearby. His shirt proclaimed his name as Lou.

"Have the police finished going through it?"

"A crime scene team was here early this morning, did the dusting. Didn't find anything obvious inside." He frowned at Reed. "Said they'd be back to check for more physical evidence, and to keep it locked up in this special section."

"Special section?"

"Yeah." Lou turned and pointed to the cars that occupied the corner where they stood. "Special attention from multiple jurisdictions."

Reed noticed that he wasn't the only interested observer in the section. A dark-suited man had stooped to observe a car a couple of rows over. "Don't worry," he cautioned Lou. "I won't ask you to break your vows to the team."

He returned his attention to the dark suit and the car he inspected, a silver Mercedes SLK roadster. As both acknowledgement and surprise clicked in his head, he moved to the other aisle.

"Do you need me for anything else?"

"No, Lou. Thanks for the report," he responded absently. "I can find my way out." He walked steadily toward the other aisle until he stood over the man at the Mercedes.

The man looked up, and upon seeing Reed, rose to his full height.

"Well, well, well." Reed crossed his arms as he took in J.R.'s wary features. "What brings a man of your caliber down to an impound lot? I thought you had people to do the grunge work."

J.R. pushed his hands into his pockets before he answered. "Vested interest in the results, that's all." He narrowed his brows. "I could ask you the same question. I didn't think you handled low-level investigations anymore."

"Maybe we can help each other."

"What makes you think you have something I need?"

Reed rubbed his chin and started to circle the car. "You're investigating Magellan again."

"If you were in town, you'd know that's off. It was all over the news." J.R.'s gaze followed Reed, who rounded the car. "Not enough evidence to get a strong indictment."

"Is that why you're here, checking out Philip's car?" He watched J.R.'s eyes narrow in search of a plausible explanation.

"Let's talk like two old friends, okay?" Reed stopped on the other side of the car. "I think you've reopened your case and I suspect you're using Philip, my mangy former brother-in-law, to do it. Now, he's missing, isn't he?"

"Where'd you get that from?" He looked around as though to insure they were alone before he joined Reed. "Have you been talking to him?"

"No, but I want to find him, too." He turned and faced J.R. toe to toe. "You help me and I can help you."

"Sorry, but you've got it all wrong." He hesitated a moment before he continued. "My interest in Philip is strictly that his name surfaced in my previous investigation on Magellan.''

"That's your story and you'll stick to it. For now." Reed gave J.R.'s stern face a tight-lipped smile, then strode off to the exit.

Damn. Reed walked hard to work off his excess energy. Both of the cars had been abandoned, which meant Angie and Philip had disappeared together after all. J.R. would learn that soon enough and on his own.

In the meantime, Reed had to find out more about J.R.'s deal with Philip. It was his only leverage to get J.R.'s help in finding Angie. He suspected that wherever Philip and Magellan surfaced, Angie would be close by. Experience also told him that Angie would be third on the Fed's list of persons to protect.

The forest was warm and sultry, much like the day Angie had ventured into it alone. This time though, with Matt at her side, she took the time to enjoy the lush beauty that surrounded them on the trail. Delicate orchid buds sprung from woody trees. Fragrant, flowering shrubs abounded in parts of the thick underbrush. They'd come across ducks, marsh hens, and more of the screeching, brightly-hued parrots. The abundance of plant and animal life in the habitat amazed her and lightened her mood considerably.

"See." Matt pointed to another of the white square signs posted on a tree, as he adjusted the bag on his shoulder. "The trail is well marked. The sanctuary is safe as long as you know where you're going or you stay to the path."

"Look—another iguana." The lizard was at least two feet long and moved slothlike just ahead at the base of a tree. Angie slowed as they neared the creature.

"It's harmless." He stood behind her and rested his hands on her shoulders. "Do you want to feed it?"

"No!" She jerked her head around and saw his laugh. "Any more surprises?"

He clasped her hand again and led her from the path, and around the lizard. "How are your feet holding up?"

They both looked down at the rubber thongs from storage he had almost cut in half to accommodate her feet. "So far, so good," she said.

As they neared their destination, Matt stopped and turned his head to a sound.

"What's that?" she asked, as she also turned. "Sounds like a grunt or something."

Matt let out a soft whistle and Buster appeared at their side. "It's a wild boar."

Angie gulped. "That's bad, isn't it?"

"Not if it's a baby. They're one of the not-so-nice inhabitants that live deep in the interior. They seldom stray beyond their nests."

"Is that why you don't let Buster stray far at night?"

He nodded. "A wild boar is just a mean pig. They make a great roast if you can catch one." He pointed to the belt at his waist. It had a series of tools hooked into three leather loops, including a wicked-looking knife.

Angie wrinkled her nose at the idea. "No thanks. I'll stick with the native fish and fruit diet."

He laughed. "I was hoping you'd say that. Let's get out of here."

Soon, Angie could hear moving water. Light trickling had turned to loud splashes. "How can there be a waterfall in the middle of an island?"

"Actually, it's a waterway, a finger flowing from the surrounding ocean." He pushed past low palms and moved aside for Angie to come through. "We're here."

Her eyes grew wide as she stepped into the clearing. "Oh, Matt. It's beautiful." A wall of water cascaded down from a small mountain of stone, over tiered rocks, and crashed into a crystal clear pool of pale blue water.

"I like to come here and think. I figured you'd like it, too." His voice rose above the din of splashing water.

Angie had already started to unsnap her skirt. "Is it safe to get in?"

Matt had walked to the other side and dropped the bag. He tied Buster onto a long restraining leash near a tree. "Go on. I'll join you."

Angie stepped to the edge and waded in. She laughed, despite the unsettling memories that forced themselves into her conscious mind. From behind her, Matt's hands grasped her waist on either side. She placed her hands on top of his.

"Don't be scared. It's only deep toward the spill off on the other side. There's also an inland ocean hole, called blue holes, not far from here."

She looked over her shoulder at him. "What's that?"

They moved deeper into the water. "They're these steep, porous limestone walls in the ground that the ocean water flows up through. They make great freshwater swimming holes. Marine life flows through them, too."

"So why are they called blue holes?"

"Because they're fathomless, and the water is deep cobalt and ultramarine blue." He whispered at her ear. "You have to see them to believe the incredible color."

"No wonder you love this place."

Matt gave her a hard shove, which landed her in the depths of the pool, before he swam away on his back.

Angie shrieked first, then laughed and sputtered when she bobbed to the surface. Matt stroked by as she wiped the water from her face. His blue stretch Speedos left little to the imagination.

Warmed by that pleasant thought, another flashed through her head: a faceless man, also in Speedos, with a large cross that lay on his chest.

She lost her smile as she tried to hold onto the fading

vision. Was he the same man who had held her ankle in the other memory? Confusion swirled in her head.

"Angie, are you all right?"

She treaded the water as Matt swam to her. He caught her into his arm while he kept them afloat with the other.

She threw her arms around his neck. "Hold me, Matt. Just hold me." He did as she asked.

Reed opened the door to Jill's law office and met her secretary for the first time.

"Well," the young woman behind the desk proclaimed. "You must be Reed Palmer." She glanced at the clock. "And, if it's four o'clock, that also must mean you're late."

Reed liked her sense of humor, and hoped her boss shared it. He nodded toward her private door. "She hasn't left, has she?"

"Brenda!" Jill's voice sailed in from behind the closed door. "Send him in here."

"In case you didn't hear that, I'm Brenda Thompson." She stretched out her hand for his.

"I don't suppose she's in a good mood?" He shook her offered hand.

"Enter at your own risk." She motioned to the door and smiled in commiseration.

He pushed Jill's door open. She sat behind the desk with her feet on its corner. Clad in a pants suit and tank top, sans the jacket, she had a bound legal brief in her lap that she appeared to be reading. She didn't look up as she spoke.

"If you wanted to blow off my help last night, all you had to do was say it. There were other avenues I could have pursued to find—"

"I got a call from Tony this morning. They found Angie's car."

Jill's mouth hung open a moment as she raised her head

and looked at him for the first time. She swung her feet to the floor and tossed the brief on her desk.

"Sit down." She motioned Reed to a chair as she circled to the front of the desk and pulled herself up on its corner. "And, tell me everything."

He recounted the call, his subsequent trip to the impound, and his run-in with J.R. inspecting Philip's car.

He crossed his ankle atop his knee. "If we can learn J.R.'s connection to Philip, maybe I can figure out where he may have gone with Angie."

"Why do you think the U.S. Attorney's office is involved?"

Reed told her about the occurrences he found in Philip's planner. "J.R.'s name was in the book. Philip's name surfaced once before in J.R.'s investigations, but Philip would never cooperate—not against a client like Magellan, who had an arm longer than any enforcement agency."

"Maybe Angie was right. When she asked for the divorce, Philip promised things would change."

Reed rubbed his chin in deep thought. "You know, you may be onto something. I found the word *halo* in his planner. It showed up twice during the week before he disappeared, and it was pencilled in again for the day after he met Angie." He raised his gaze to Jill's. "We both know what Angie found that led to her divorce . . . evidence that Magellan had Philip paying off crooked officials."

She nodded and crossed her arms over her chest. "He couldn't explain it away and didn't even try. You think he finally decided that Angie was more important to him than Magellan?" She turned to her phone on the desk and picked up the receiver.

"What are you doing?"

"Calling this guy I know over on the Fed side. He gets an ear of rumors every so often." She cupped her hand over the mouthpiece. "It'll probably cost me, though."

"I hope it's not too steep."

"Just a date," she said, smiling, and spoke into the phone.

Reed sat back in the chair and watched her in action, accepting that she was a continual surprise. As his eyes slid over her lithe figure in front of him, he decided the surprise was definitely on him.

CHAPTER THIRTEEN

"I didn't see a face, Matt. There was only the impression of one." Angie sat on the grass, away from the pool's edge, with her arms wrapped around her drawn-up legs. She met his eyes with a subtle challenge. "I've told you everything I can remember."

"You act like you're afraid of your own memories," he accused, as he leaned closer into her, the water still glistening on his skin. "You're frightening them away."

"Aren't you afraid of yours? I don't see you all fired up to talk about your past, and I don't want to talk about the memories right now."

He let out a long, audible sigh. "This isn't about me. You can't be scared of what you see. Let it come out on its own."

She looked away from him, and knew he was right. She was afraid of the images she'd been getting. Something sinister lurked along the periphery of every memory that had reared its head. Even worse, she didn't want to acknowledge the possibility that the danger she and Matt suspected she'd survived may not be over. She shivered at the thought.

Birds chirped overhead against the cloudless blue sky and heralded the perfect afternoon. The beautiful, almost surreal clearing they sat in seemed an odd place to talk of fears and evil intentions.

"Are you even listening to me?"

She turned back to Matt. "You're right." He had kneeled in front of her, his knees apart to brace his weight. His virile appeal was caustic, and she deliberately shut out the effect.

"Let me know when something's going on in your head. Just now, in the water, you could have drowned. When you fell in the surf with Buster, you had a memory flash then, didn't you?"

She nodded. "I didn't want to say anything about it. It's just that . . ."

"All you have to do is tell me." His voice lowered an octave. "I thought you trusted me."

"I do." In fact, she took comfort in his very presence. Angie rested her head against her knees as he stroked her wet hair. "I saw someone attach the silver key around my ankle, and tell me to get help. There was no face, and I don't know where I was, but I sensed urgency."

His hand stilled a moment before it continued to stroke her hair. "Don't you see, Angie? This is a good thing. Your body is getting healthier and knows you're ready to handle the truth."

"Something is wrong with the memory flashes, though. They aren't of my family life, pleasant events, or childhood memories. They're dangerous things, and I get a distinct impression that the danger isn't over." She raised her head to him. "See, you don't understand."

"Yes, I do. Maybe too well." He drew his hand back and rested it on his thigh. "I'm not a psych doctor, but when your past is unknown and can't provide a compass in your present, the future direction can be scary. You don't know what happened to you out there on the water, and you're manifesting fear into your visions because they're unknown. Stop worrying about what'll pop in your head, and just let it appear."

"It's not that easy." Even as she shouted her frustration at him, his demeanor remained the same, and she became contrite. "I'm sorry. I shouldn't be angry with you."

He placed his hands on her shoulders. "Play a game with me, Angie, a word association game."

She was immediately suspicious and dropped her hands from her legs. "What will that do?" She leaned back against the tree. Matt moved with her.

"It might trigger something in your consciousness, below the surface. Follow along and give me your one-word thought, the first thing that comes to your mind."

She cocked a brow at him and tried to mask her discomfort. "You're going to play around with my head using that one psychology course you took in medical school, what, seven or eight years ago?" As he kneeled there, his hands on his hips, like a well-sculpted bronze, she realized he was serious.

"Okay," she agreed. "Bring it on. You, doctor, me, patient."

"Name," he started.

"Angie, I guess." She pointed at him. "Matt. And Buster. See, I can do it. And we haven't triggered anything, either."

"Boy."

"Girl."

"Man."

She smiled. "Woman, me and you. Here."

He also grinned at her reference. "Come on, be serious, and use one word. "Butterfly."

"Freedom." She thought about it. "And independence."

"Sun."

"Moon. Comfort."

"Day."

"Night." She shifted her legs as the déjà vu of prior visions washed over her.

"Dark."

She hesitated this time. "Danger." Her gaze caught Matt's as another word came at her.

"Lightning," he thundered.

"Fear. I . . . I don't want to do this anymore." She tried to get up, but Matt pressed her back.

"Key."

"Halo." Panicked at her odd answer, she shook her head and tried to move.

"Black."

Her eyes grew wide. "Man."

"White."

She gulped in air. "Another man. Stop, Matt," she whispered. "I don't want to do this." Unnerved by the revelations, she strained against his hands."

"Visualize, Angie. Do they mean something?"

"I don't know," she cried. Tears had welled in her eyes. "They're on a boat with me, and that's all I see . . . nothing else."

Matt pulled her hard against him, her small frame buried by his. "None of the pieces make a whole lot of sense, and why would the key make you think of halo?"

"Has anything about me made sense? Not my washing ashore with no memory, the ankle chain I wear, nor the memories that creep into my head when God knows I don't want them there."

"Come on, dry your eyes. I brought you to my special place so we could enjoy ourselves." With his free hand, he rubbed her tears away.

She withdrew from his hold and raised her face to his. "This is your special place?"

He nodded. "That means you can't tell anyone else

about it." The ridiculous comment broke the tension and they both grinned wide. He joined her beside the tree and sat pressed to the smooth bark.

"I suppose it's my turn to play a game with you." Angie looked up at him.

"Fair enough," he agreed. He drew his legs up to rest his arms.

"I want to play twenty questions, though, not association."

"Fire away, I think."

She let her head loll on his arm. "Tell me about your work back home in Atlanta."

"I have a practice with three other doctors, a professional corporation."

"And your family?"

"That would be my mom. Her name is Jewel. She, by the way, is a registered nurse, and acts as director to a community clinic I started a few years ago."

She could hear the pride in his words. "You're a doctor and you're philanthropic. What about your father?"

He shifted his arm to draw Angie next to him. "Never knew him. My mother raised me alone after he was killed playing the good Samaritan one night."

"I'm sorry, Matt."

"Don't be. I was only three years old at the time. I've been hoisted up as the poster boy for 'kids that make good despite the odds' more times than I can remember."

"Watch it. You're turning cynical again. So, that leaves your wife, Paula." She felt his arm around her shoulder stiffen.

"What about her?"

"Why are you so closed about her death? I know it's your right not to talk about something as painful as that, but you just taught me how that can help. I'd like to understand why she died."

She listened to his deep sigh as he shifted again, which

signaled his withdrawal, both emotionally and physically. She held his arm, though, and temporarily stayed his physical separation.

"Paula didn't have to die. There's irony in the situation, don't you think? I'm not the consummate healer you want to think I am."

Angie gleaned understanding from his words. "You blame yourself for your wife's death, don't you?"

"The doctor you keep thanking for saving you has clay feet after all. Satisfied?"

Angie didn't respond to his puzzling remark, and knew from experience that he'd closed the door to discussion. She nodded and changed the subject. "Do you enjoy other things besides your practice and clinic?"

"I wouldn't call it a joy to see sick people. The enjoyment comes from helping them overcome health problems . . ." He paused a moment. "When you can."

"Let me put it this way, then. What do you do for sheer pleasure?"

He squeezed her against him. "Don't you know? I come to this island and rescue damsels in distress."

She smiled up at him. "Do you believe in fate? I think you do. I never knew your wife. But, our lives are intertwined."

"What are you talking—"

"No, listen," she interrupted. "I can't explain fate, but you said it yourself, I would have drowned, unconscious in the surf. The island would have been vacant had you decided not to come here to mourn your wife's death."

She turned in his arms to face him, and found herself dangerously close to his mouth.

"I am frightened by the visions, Matt," she whispered. "But, it's because they threaten the freedom I'm enjoying."

He smiled. "I guess that's why you have a butterfly on your butt." He turned and accommodated her across his lap.

"I like waking up, knowing I'll be with you and Buster."

"I like that, too." Matt's voice was thick and unsteady.

She warmed at his words. "I don't want to find out I have a past that'll make me cynical or angry . . ."

His breath, heavy and audible on her cheek, brought on a knot of passion that rose in her throat as she finished. ". . . Or doesn't include you."

When she found understanding in his dark eyes, she let him pull her to his chest, where she buried her face and could almost taste the salt and musk of his smell.

He tilted her chin up and kissed her hard. It was a heady sensation for Angie, and she let it take possession.

As his mouth slanted across hers, again and again, he caressed her buttocks before he cupped the soft mounds and pulled her across him until she straddled his lap.

His lips left hers to brush her shoulders, where his mouth coaxed the straps away. Angie held onto him as he explored the pulsing hollow at the base of her throat and moved further down.

The swim top had slipped downward, and Matt's eyes and mouth feasted on the display. He whispered against her satiny skin, "Angie, I'm not made of stone."

The hard bulge she pressed against said the contrary, but as her blood pounded in her brain and the pleasure radiated outward, she could only marvel at his strength and restrained ardor.

He raised his head and found her mouth again, and this time his tongue devoured her senses. At her groan of contentment, he whispered, "Tell me to stop." He nibbled her lip. "Soon, you'll remember who you are and we'll regret this."

She caressed his neck. "Then, I don't want to remember."

He dragged his mouth from hers to look in her face. "Don't say that."

"I mean it." Angie's breaths were harsh and uneven under the heat of his gaze.

"I promised I wouldn't do this." His broad shoulders

heaved in a sigh as he brushed her short hair back. "I can't keep breaking that vow."

"When you're with me, I'm not afraid. I . . . I take comfort from you."

"That'll change once we leave and find your family. They'll be there for you." He cupped her face. "And, when we find them, I'll be the outsider."

"No." She straightened against him. "You're part of who I am now."

"This isn't right. I can't keep touching you, knowing you . . . intimately without being affected."

Angie didn't want to hear him declare her off limits and stroked his chest.

He grabbed her hand. "You provoke me on purpose, I think."

"It serves my point. If we want each other, then it's all right."

Matt's face became grim as he pulled the straps of her suit back onto her shoulders. He lifted her from his lap and set her away from him. Rising fluidly from the ground, he stomped off on powerful legs toward the water.

"Where are you going?" she called out.

"For a swim," he retorted over his shoulder, before he dove into the water.

Angie stubbornly crossed her arms, bereft that he'd left her. "You and those Speedos are going to send me for a dunking soon, too."

Late that night, Angie sat on the floor on the far side of her bed and stroked Buster's coat. With her other hand, and by the light of the nearby oil lamp, she jotted down all the memories and visions she had seen, including the ones she had not shared with Matt: the name Magellan, the reference to halo in connection with the silver key, and the man who wore the Speedos and gold cross. She looked at the list. None of them made a connection in her mind.

Crash!

The sound of breaking glass startled her and the dog. As Buster rose and trotted to the door, she realized the sound came from somewhere in the main part of the house. She tossed the pad and paper to the bed and hurried to the door after Buster.

Looking out, she didn't see Matt, and rushed down the hall to his bedroom. The door was closed.

"Matt?" She rapped on the door twice before she turned the knob. Buster unceremoniously rammed his way through, causing the door to spring open wide and hit the wall.

Matt stood at the window. Wearing only a pair of fleece gym shorts, he turned at the interruption. As Angie slowly broached his doorway, he quite openly studied her. Her nightshirt caressed her body in all the right places. The knowledge that she was accessible only angered him more.

The smell of liquor was rife. An open bottle of rum sat on the desk, which was covered with stacks of papers, all surrounding an opened briefcase. The large bed was rumpled, and had not been turned back for sleep.

Angie's glance followed Buster to the other wall, where the dog sniffed at amber liquid and broken glass that mingled where the floor met the wall.

"Buster, come back," she called, but kept a watchful eye on Matt. "You'll cut yourself." As the dog made his way back to her, she gave Matt her full gaze. "Are you all right?"

"Do I look all right?" His words were gruff and unfriendly as he came toward her. "You, on the other hand, look mighty damn fine, as usual." He brazenly took in her dishabille, then returned his gaze to her eyes, where they registered the shock he wanted.

"What's wrong with you?"

"Everything, since you rode in on your wave." He turned

and gave her his back. "Get out of here and leave me alone."

"But—"

He spun back around. "Don't you get it, lady? I want to be left alone."

"No, you don't." She crossed her arms in defiance. "For some reason, you want to feel sorry for yourself, and I won't let you. What are you going to do, drink yourself into oblivion to forget?"

He offered her an ugly laugh. "Don't flatter yourself. I'm not trying to forget you." He stepped closer. "I don't have to." In an instant, he reached out his hand and brazenly fondled her breast.

She gasped, and jumped away from his hand. "What are you doing?"

"Just goes to show," he leered. "I'm not your damn knight in shining armor."

"I know. Tonight, you've become a drunken bastard. Come on, Buster."

When she cleared the door, he slammed it shut, hoping to close off the active participant in his pain.

He found himself at the desk, faced with the newspaper articles that had set off his guilt. He ran his finger over the coroner's report, as though to enforce his decision to steer clear of her. He had no right to intrude into Angie's life any more than she into his, without knowledge of their respective pasts. They couldn't act on what they both wanted.

Frustrated with his thoughts, he picked up the rum bottle and sailed it against the wall, where it fell to join the other broken glass.

CHAPTER FOURTEEN

The sun had peeked in on Angie as she slowly awakened. No dreams had invaded her sleep, but the clarity of daylight revealed Matt's behavior as the stuff of nightmares. She lay in the bed, shrouded in the covers, and relived last night's scene. He'd been drunk, but was that a good enough excuse for the way he had acted? It was just as well that their frustration in handling their attraction was out in the open.

She spied the pad of paper on top of the cover that contained her jotted-down memories thus far. Weary of allowing her misgivings a voice, she sat up and looked at the entries she had made, one by one.

They all puzzled her. Frustrated, she tossed the pad aside and left the bed.

As she neared the bedroom door, she saw a sheet of paper taped to it. It was a note, with Matt's name scrawled across the bottom. She let out a breath of anticipation before she pulled it from the door. It read that he had gone for a run with Buster and would be back soon. She smiled at his feeble attempt to make peace. Balling the paper in her fist, she tossed it in the wastebasket and proceeded into the living room.

With a pulse-pounding certainty, she knew she was falling in love with him. How could that have happened in so short a time? He was a good man, with good intentions, and something intense flared within her when he was around—that was how.

He was aware of her, too. His touches and kisses didn't lie. But, he'd reminded her last night of who he kept in his thoughts. It was his wife, a woman he obviously still loved. He needed to find peace from the guilt that surrounded her death. What had happened that had shattered him so completely?

The sea breeze blowing in from the open windows was exhilarating on her skin as she walked to the front door. She could see the bright ocean through the screen door, even smell the sprays that floated over the sand. She loved it here, the freedom, the beauty . . . a flicker of apprehension coursed through her. There was also the danger and unease that accompanied her memories.

She turned from the door. The only way to escape the dread was to remember. As she paced the room, her eyes fed on the walls and tables and stopped when they reached the uppermost shelf of the bookcase.

The briefcase from Matt's room sat there. It was the same one he'd closed down on the papers about his wife's death a few days before. She stared a full minute before her impetuosity got the better of her. She dragged a chair from the kitchen and used it to reach the briefcase. When it was safely in her hands, she took it to the table.

"He can share his pain," she said out loud. "Maybe I can help."

Luck was with her. When she depressed the levers, the clasp on each combination lock sprang open.

The briefcase was packed with carefully stacked sheets

of newsprint and official-looking reports. The coroner's report she had glimpsed days ago was on top. Giving it a cursory study, she read again that Paula Sinclair had died of heart failure. She set it aside to look at the newspaper articles. Some were clippings, others were full folded pages.

The first headline caused her to drop into the nearby chair: "Prominent Doctor Questioned In Wife's Death."

She devoured the short story. The doctor had found his wife unconscious and attempted to resuscitate her. She died later at the hospital. Originally declared heart failure, police now questioned the validity of that diagnosis as more evidence was uncovered. The article seemed to tease the reader into considering whether the doctor was guilty of culpability in a cover-up of drug abuse or out-and-out murder.

What? Angie reeled from the paper's accusation. A picture of Matt's wife accompanied the article. She studied the grainy black and white photo of a tall, beautiful woman dressed in a ball gown.

Two more articles were variations on the one she had read, all printed within two weeks of each other. However, the next big headline trumpeted new troubles: "State Medical Board Now Investigating Ethics Violations by Dr. Matthew Sinclair." Her eyes raced over the words. The medical board's investigation would overlap the one currently being run by the police and include serious charges of medical ethics. It went on to list his lengthy community activities and charities. Witnesses were to include Dr. Sinclair's embittered mother-in-law. In all of the articles, Matt had been steadfast in his "no comment" to reporters' questions.

She thumbed to another article, and was stopped by a blatant, two-part headline, " '. . . He Murdered My Daughter.' Gripping Testimony from a Grieving Mother." Angie's hand flew to her mouth. It can't be.

Buster's bark drew her attention to the screen door. She

swallowed hard as a surge of panic twisted in her stomach.
Matt was back.

"The news is good this time." Jillian referred to the
prior day's lack of progress as she came from around her
desk to meet Reed.

"Let's have it, then," he said, and closed the door
behind him. He wore a wide smile at her show of exuber-
ance.

Propped against her desk, she crossed her arms. "Someone in the U.S. Attorney's office is definitely trying to swing
a deal with Philip. But, get this, Philip instigated it."

"Philip?" Reed's brain raced ahead in search of plausible reasons.

She nodded sagely. "My source doesn't know who the
go-between is because the entire arrangement is coded."

Reed knew that meant no names were used. Everything—meetings, phone calls—was exchanged via codes.
And, no official record would be kept to reveal the details
that led to the deal.

"Obviously, J.R.'s not ready to give up on his indictment."

"You're right. He wants Magellan."

Reed mused aloud. "So, what could they offer Philip
that he wanted badly enough to sell out his former client?"

"Hmmm . . . respectability again? A way out?"

Reed's head snapped to attention. "Bingo. He wanted
Angie, and that's the only way he figured he was going to
get her back." He turned to the door. "Come on, let's get
moving."

Jill hopped from the desk and grabbed her purse and
jacket from the chair. "Where are we going?"

"To the park."

"What?" she asked, perplexed.

"To make our own deal with the U.S. Attorney's office."

* * *

Angie heard the screen door slam as she rushed to sit at the edge of her bed. Out of breath in her haste to replace the briefcase on the shelf before she was caught, she now forced herself to breathe evenly. She turned an alert eye to the door and waited for Matt to appear.

When she saw the awesome shadow he formed in the doorway, her heart skipped a beat. Was it fear mixed with something else? Surely he couldn't be a murderer. Not her gentle Matt. He rapped at the opened door.

"Angie . . . can I come in?"

"Yes." Her voice was low and wary.

"Did you get my note?" He was shirtless as he came across the room, dressed in sandals and the same fleece shorts from last night. He wiped his face with the towel that draped his shoulders. When it dropped away, she could see a frown build across his face even as his stare caught her. "Are you all right?"

Angie shrank away, further onto the bed, and nodded repeatedly. "Sure."

When he reached her side, his eyes settled on her. "I don't blame you for giving me the cold shoulder." He rubbed the back of his neck sheepishly. "The way I remember it, I acted really badly last night."

She cleared her throat and avoided his stare. "You'd been drinking."

Matt shook his head and proceeded to sit next to her on the bed. "That's no excuse. And, for the record, I never drink like that."

When Matt reached for her hand, Angie was too startled by his action to object. Speechless, she watched as he stroked it.

"What you said made sense," he said. "Maybe I do feel sorry for myself. Bear with me though." He smiled. "I'm not used to opening up. To anyone. It's always been hard, and it's worse with you since you seem to be the object of a great deal of my, well, emotional turmoil."

Angie raised her eyes to his. Although she saw a tenderness in his expression, she stiffened at the warring resolves that had settled within her. She had to take a look at those papers again and find out more about his wife's death and the result of the charges leveled at him.

Matt's eyes wandered beyond Angie and to the pad that lay on the bed. "What's that? Are you writing your island memoirs?" he teased.

She snatched her hand from his and reached to gather up the pad to her chest. "They're personal observations, that's all." She offered him a half smile. "I'd rather keep them to myself."

"I'll respect your privacy, then." He stood to leave. "Why don't you get dressed and we can eat outside in the garden?"

When he left her room, Angie didn't move from the bed, miserable that she hadn't respected his privacy—but, in fact, she waited for the opportunity to invade it again. She tried to force her confused emotions into some semblance of order as her brain screamed her dilemma: What if you're falling in love with a murderer?

Reed and Jill sat in his car on a grassy lane in Gateshead Park. Up ahead was the same, nondescript white Lumina that had been there before.

"With Philip missing, J.R. figured, like I did, that Daniel would know where he'd disappeared to," Reed said, and drummed his fingers along the door handle.

"So, he set up this stakeout on Daniel?"

He nodded as he sat up at attention. "Looks like my message got passed on to J.R. Someone's shown up."

Another white car, this one larger, had swung into the

park and made a wide U-turn to pull alongside the small white one ahead of them.

Within a few moments, the Lumina pulled out of the park just as the driver's door opened on the big car. J.R. Harrison got out and brushed his dark gray hair away from his face. He wore a none-too-pleased expression as he straightened his tie.

"Well, well, well, if it isn't the Assistant U.S. Attorney himself, all dressed for a GQ shot. I must have said the right thing in that note." Reed climbed from the car as Jill did the same on her side. "I know it won't do any good to tell you to stay put."

"You're learning," she said, and joined him to meet the Assistant.

J.R. immediately started in on Reed. "You, again. What do you mean by interfering in my operation and sending a message that I'd better get here? What in hell do you want from me?"

"If I made your stakeout, don't you think Magellan knows you're watching Daniel, too?"

J.R. sighed as he tilted his head at Jill. "Who is she?"

"An interested party, like me. You had Philip in your pocket, but the man knows both you and Magellan want him. All I need to know is where you think Philip is holed up."

"He isn't your problem, Reed." He turned and feigned an interest in the surrounding woods.

"He is when he involved my sister." He paused a moment. "How do you think I know about Halo?"

J.R. jerked around to Reed and stared a split second too long to contain his bluff. "You don't know a damned thing."

"But, you're scared that I do. I could blow your operation to the local press, and maybe I will."

In an exasperated voice, J.R. asked, "What's this about your sister being involved?"

"She disappeared with Philip on the eve of their divorce, the day before he was to meet his contact." He watched the almost imperceptible rise of J.R.'s brow.

The Assistant gave an impatient shrug. "I'm sorry."

"Like hell you are." Reed's voice was cold and exact. "You don't give a damn about anybody but your source and your target. Angie is a distant third on your list." He took a step toward J.R. "What's your justification for putting her in danger?"

"I want Magellan in jail for the rest of his life." His complexion turned florid with anger as he ground the words out between his teeth. "He feeds drugs to children. That's my justification."

The men were at a stalemate as neither said a word. Then, J.R. motioned with his head that they should walk up the path.

Reed indicated to Jill to stay put before he joined him.

"We both want something out of this, but don't go bandying information through the air. The wrong people could hear it."

"If I have to rattle cages," Reed argued, "I will. Someone or something made Philip take off, and my sister wasn't a willing participant."

J.R. stopped and nodded sagely. "You'd do that, wouldn't you?" He continued on, his head bent in thought. "What's your noise?"

"It's simple enough. You've reopened your operation, meant to target and bring Magellan down. When Philip came to you, he became your ace. And, of course, there are those meetings of his with Halo." He glanced at J.R., who'd crossed his arms. "If Philip is still alive, the TV stations will go crazy with that info and blow your deal."

"All right. I'll cut you in since your sister is involved, but only on a need-to-know basis. And, because I owe you one."

"Deal." He stopped in midstride and turned to J.R. "By the way, I take it you're Halo?"

J.R.'s face became enigmatic. "In some ways. First, though, you and I'll go back to the car and find out what you really know that can help me."

"You don't trust me anymore?"

J.R. smiled for the first time. "No. But I know a bluff when I hear one, and it sounds like you don't know Jack."

CHAPTER FIFTEEN

Angie dumped the shells she'd gathered from the beach and sand dunes into the hammock. Strung between two palms near the house, it sagged under their weight. The spot set back on the beach also afforded Angie a clear view of the gardens and Matt. That was where her attention returned, time and again.

He was busy cleaning snorkeling equipment. She agonized as she waited for an opportunity to open his briefcase again. He wouldn't tell her the truth about his past, so she'd have to find out herself.

Her fingers locked around a conch shell. Its distinctive shape, all of a sudden uneasily familiar, turned her head. As her unfocused stare transferred to the shell, her hand became someone else's, someone who picked the conch and other shells from a sandy beach—not this beach, but one filled with people laughing and playing in the water. She could hear them now. Angie turned, drunkenly, and tried to follow the sounds. They were gone. She blinked, then refocused her gaze. The people were gone too.

The shell slid from her grasp as she sagged against the palm, disturbed by another vision.

She raised her head and saw that Matt still sat in the garden, unaware of her distress. Shaken, she rubbed her eyes and walked to the beach. She was the woman in the memory, and she had done this before. It unnerved her, these memories that she'd begun to decipher. But, what frightened her was the malaise that remained from each one. She was supposed to remember something else. Would it be too late when she finally did?

Matt looked up and saw Angie walk across the sand to the shore, followed, as usual, by Buster. His eyes latched onto her lissome figure in the oversized shirt until she was out of sight.

He shook his head. One night of drinking hadn't purged her from his system. He'd tested the waters, and that they wanted each other was beside the point. There was too much baggage between them. Didn't last night's fiasco prove he wasn't ready to shed Paula's shadow?

A loud yelp rent the air, followed by his name. Matt threw aside the sports gear and quickly left the garden. As he crossed the sand, he saw Angie, doubled over on the beach. He took off at a gallop.

Reed maneuvered the car out of the park and entered the traffic. He turned to Jill seated next to him. "That didn't take too long."

"Easy for you." Her hair bobbed as she tilted her head away. "You didn't have to wait like a third wheel."

He smiled at her petulance. "Believe me, J.R.'s not happy sharing anything with me, either."

"So, what did he say?"

"Philip was supposed to turn important evidence over to the Feds. Apparently, DEA is in on it, too. All of them were salivating, bending over backward to give Philip what he wanted.''

''A way out?''

Reed nodded. ''Immunity and secret testimony was part of the deal. They knew about the divorce, but they swear he never mentioned Angie being involved. They figured Philip was tired of the innuendoes about his soft ties to traffickers, and wanted a clean break. Either that or Philip wanted to make a first strike before Magellan made his.''

''What did Philip have to deliver? It must have been pretty big.''

''If J.R. knows, he didn't say.'' He darted a glance to Jill. ''The problem is, Philip disappeared before they could get it. With the DEA directly involved, I figure it's either trafficking records or something else big enough to roll heads.''

''That would explain why Magellan would be after Philip, too.'' She shifted in her seat to face him. ''Do you think Philip took off on his own with Angie?''

Reed nodded again. ''I prefer that scenario to the alternative.''

They rode for a while, in individual thought, before Reed's voice broke the silence.

''When we started out a few days ago, I blamed you for Angie's disappearance.'' He glanced in her direction.

''Nothing I hadn't already done to myself.''

He smiled. ''Well, it's okay if you beat yourself up, but I shouldn't have been the one to do it. My dad was right, you know, when he says Angie is strong-willed. If she hadn't wanted to meet Philip, you could have talked 'til you were blue in the face and she'd have stayed put.''

''I'm sorry that we couldn't have met under better circumstances.''

''We all have to live with the hand Fate deals us. Which reminds me, I have to go by my parents' house and update them on what's going on." He made a turn off the highway. "We're almost at your office building."

"What's on for us tomorrow? Shouldn't we question Daniel again to get a bead on Magellan?"

He adjusted the rearview mirror. "I'm going out with J.R. to search for the *Angelica*."

Jill sat at attention. "What? When do we leave?"

"After I filled in the details about Angie's plans to meet Philip on the boat, he wanted to arrange a Coast Guard escort out to sea." He turned to Jill and frowned when he saw her own stubborn one. "You're not going, and that's that."

"The hell I'm not. You purposely kept this from me, didn't you?"

"No, it's—"

"All this talk about forgiving me and crap was to keep me off the track you're following with J.R." She crossed her arms. "You must think I'm stupid."

Reed pulled into her building's parking lot. "I never said anything like—"

"Oh, yes, you do. You may not say it in words, but you see a woman and right away her ability to compete on your level is reduced mightily. I've worked hard to find sources for help. I've helped you find information for this investigation, and you have no right to keep me from going out and—"

Reed braked hard before he shifted the car in park and released his seat belt, all in one motion. He turned to grasp the shoulders of a startled Jill.

"Shut up," he said, and covered her mouth with his. When her arms came up across his back, he relaxed and slowed the urgent kiss on her warm lips.

Too soon, he raised his mouth from hers, and gazed into her eyes. He straightened in his seat as Jill, quiet now, found her purse. She opened the door to get out.

"I guess that's that," Reed said.

Her subdued smile was grim as she slammed the car door.

Reed watched her walk across the asphalt to enter the building then disappear. He let out a deep breath, rebuckled his seat belt, and turned the car in the direction of his parent's house.

Angie watched as Matt entered her bedroom with a glass of water and a painkiller. The man-o'-war's bite had not been severe, but Matt didn't want to chance an unknown reaction or infection, and made her elevate the foot on a pillow while she rested in bed.

She took the offered glass and capsule, and as she downed the medication, guiltily let the thought slip through about her safety. Is he dangerous? She watched as he watched her.

"Are you in pain?" He sat next to her on the bed.

His stare pulled Angie back into the present, and she tried to close out the doubts she had begun to feel. "No. You said it would be all right, didn't you?"

He replied without inflection. "You looked like something was wrong." He crossed his arms, as if he didn't know what else to do with them. "So, what are you going to do with all those shells you've collected?"

She handed the glass to him and raised herself up. "I don't know." Reaching for her ankle, she touched the key and chain. "I liked how they looked, so I picked them up."

"Maybe they're another clue to your past."

Angie lay back against the pillow as she remembered the vision. "I'd like to rest for a while."

"Sure." Matt stood and, again, stared at her as he rubbed at his beard.

Uncomfortable under his scrutiny, Angie sat up again. "What?"

"I don't know. You tell me. What's going on that's got you as tight as a clam. I don't think you've been this quiet since you arrived. Are you still angry about what I said last night?"

"No." Angie's voice was noncommittal. "I . . . I'm getting a little tinge of pain from the sting, that's all. After I rest for a while, I'll be okay."

He backed away, his dark eyes telling her he was not quite convinced by her answer. "I'll check on you later."

"No, you don't have to," she protested. "You can go snorkeling or run like you usually do. I'll be okay."

Smiling, he nodded and left her.

The minute he cleared the room, Angie slid from the bed and retrieved her notepad from the dresser drawer. If her luck held out, it would be just a matter of time until he left the house and she could peek into his briefcase. She reclaimed her spot on the bed and proceeded to write out the latest memories she'd experienced.

Time passed as she became engrossed in the task. And soon, the medication took effect. Without realizing the extent of her stupor, she nodded off to sleep. The pad slipped from her fingers and fell to her chest.

Reed sat on the coffee table in front of his mother and held both her hands in his. "I promise you, when I get back, I'll either have Angie with me or know where she is so I can get her."

From the light of the table lamp, Maddy Palmer's eyes were red-rimmed and bright. Upon hearing Reed's latest news, she had finally given in to the lingering doubt that her daughter would walk through the doors, laughing that she'd just returned from an impromptu trip.

"We never believed Philip was a saint, but Angie didn't tell us these details."

Reed's glance took in his father, who stood nearby with

his hands deep in his pockets. "Her guilt was overwhelming for putting you both through that whole marriage. She didn't want you to worry even more, or cause you grief. She made me swear not to tell you what she suspected was going on after they married." He shook his head. "Her disappearance changes things and all bets are off."

"That's okay. Your mom and I have decided we're going to find her a nice young doctor when she gets back."

They all smiled, needing the levity his comments brought out.

Maddy raised her hand to Reed's heavy brow. "What about you? You can't want this publicity." She turned to her husband. "Wesley, maybe you should go."

"That's right, son. What about the limelight these political types like to bask in? Will you be all right?"

"I can take care of myself. Right now, J.R. wants it to stay low key, too. It's just a short jaunt into the waters with the Coast Guard." He leaned toward his mother. "Let me tell you, I feel pretty good about where all this is leading. We're going to find Angie and she'll be okay."

The doorbell's ring drew their attention. Reed squeezed his mother's fingers before he sprang up from the table. "Dad, stay with Mom. I'll get it."

A short stride later, Reed opened the door. When he recognized the visitor, he leaned against the jamb and let his eyes wash over her soft face.

"Why are you here?"

Jill pushed her hands into the pockets of her fleece jacket that covered her matching fleece pants. "To tell you that I'm going with you tomorrow." Her words were haughty and forced.

"I thought we settled this in the car?"

"That's your opinion. I said no such thing."

His smile baited her. "You're right. You didn't say much of anything when you got out of the car."

"Listen, I've been kissed before, and better." They both sized the other up for battle.

"Reed, aren't you going to invite Jill in?" His father had come up behind him.

"Sure, I was just getting to it." He stepped away from the door and allowed Jill to enter and greet his father.

As she crossed the threshold to enter the den and join his mother, Reed grabbed her hand. "First, though, we're going out to the greenhouse." At his mother's questioning look, he added, "To see your roses."

Without a word, and a clench to his jaw, Reed pulled a willing Jill through the house. He exited the kitchen to the patio. A short walk across the backyard grass near the lake sat a gray metal structure screened on all sides. It was twilight, and the houses on the other side of the large, man-made lake sparkled like holiday tinsel.

"I forget how beautiful it is living out here," Jill observed as Reed pulled her into the greenhouse, before he turned her loose. "Well, where are the roses?"

He flicked on the light. "Don't be smart. I didn't want to upset my parents by arguing with you in their presence."

"We don't have to argue. I'm going with you." Her voice was matter-of-fact as she strolled down the narrow aisle between two tables heavily laden with potted flowers.

"It'll be rough out there, and it's no place for a woman." He hunched his shoulders and tried to get a bead on her mood. "Who knows what we'll find on the boat."

"Nothing I haven't dealt with before." She came around the table and gave Reed a hostile glare. "It's interesting that you thought that little kiss in the car would just throw little old me off, and I'd forget all about what I wanted."

Liking the challenge she offered, his reply was sarcastic. "Obviously, it didn't work. This time."

"Don't patronize me. I'm going to see this through to the end."

"Jill, I need you here. If the search with the Guard

doesn't pan out, I'm going to have to check other ports. It'll be rough, and no place for a woman.''

"Will you shut up about this woman stuff. I can do anything you can,'' she shouted.

"No you can't,'' he shouted back. "All kidding aside, this is dangerous work with dangerous people. You're too gentle and . . . and nice for this.'' He looked at her and saw the defiance in her eyes and posture. He didn't want her hurt. "The truth is, I don't want you in jeopardy. Later on, you'll understand that I'm looking out for you. There are limitations you can't get around.''

"Don't be so sure,'' she countered icily. She drew back her right arm and, with her entire body, threw her fist into his jaw.

Surprised, he staggered backward, but kept his balance.

"How's that for gentle?'' Her playful words were anything but that as she shook out her fist.

Reed worked his jaw open and closed as he tenderly fingered the area. "Pretty good,'' he mumbled, and blinked at Jill with grudging respect. He then tempered his anger with amusement. "Meet us at the marina tomorrow morning at ten.''

Matt had come to Angie's room to check on her. She continued to sleep as he studied the newest welts across her foot, only slightly less red and angry than before. As she fidgeted in her sleep, he wondered if she dreamt of her past. He touched her brow. Cool to his touch, she stirred under his hand. Damn, she was beautiful, like some dusky angel. An undeniable magnetism had grown between them, and he tamped down the longing that had started to build.

As he backed away, he saw that her writing pad was wedged between her arm and side. He pulled it out, intending only to straighten the crushed pages and put it away.

When he saw her notes, listed as events, the first was read with an innocent eye. It was a description of one of her dreams, a detailed memory he wasn't familiar with. Confused, he read the next, and the next. After that, he was trapped in the knowledge that she had lied to him. These were memories, not memoirs, and most he didn't know about.

He looked from her angelic, sleeping form to the pad of paper. Had her memory returned and was she playing him for a fool?

CHAPTER·SIXTEEN

Matt could only stare at the tablet that detailed Angie's memories. He ran his hand across his head in exasperation. What else hadn't she told him? Did she know more than she'd let on about her arrival on the island?

A moan came from the bed, and he turned to her, a sleeping siren cloaked in innocence who'd come to test his resolve about his past. She appeared agitated, and her head moved restlessly on the pillow.

He took another glance at the page before he tossed it to the bed, then bent over her. She smelled of the fragrant soap he'd given her. As she squirmed in sleep, her chest heaved with each deep breath. He quietly spoke her name. "Angie . . . Angie . . ."

Her miserable stare swept across the dim cabin to the steps that led to the ship's deck, where he knelt as he leaned against the wall and called to her. She was also huddled on the floor, between the bed and chair, her legs tucked beneath her.

"I'm mad about it, too," he said. "But, we don't have time for that."

Her eyes burned from unshed tears held back by sharp anger. "How could I let you do this to me? Why did you do this to yourself?"

"I swear it wasn't supposed to play out this way." He looked over at the steps. "We don't have long before he gets here." He shifted closer to her. "I have to give you something."

"What?" She wiped her face with her beach skirt as he moved closer to her. He fumbled with the gold cross around his neck and, once again, it occurred to her that the jewelry was both ostentatious and not his style. When his hand moved away, she saw that the cross was actually a locket, and he took something from the inside.

He made a careful, backward glance toward the doorway before he turned to her again. "It's a key," he whispered. "An important key."

Angie looked at the thin, silver key. "What are you going to do with it?" She also whispered.

"Give me your ankle."

Before she could digest his words and decide if she'd comply, he had already reached for her leg and drew it from beneath her. "What are you doing?"

"Buying us time to keep you safe." He fumbled with the gold chain on her ankle. "I'm putting the key on your chain." With her help, he unclasped the chain and slipped the key onto it. After they refastened the jewelry, he turned the key so that it lay to the inside of her ankle.

She looked from her ankle to his face. "Is this what he wants?"

"Yes—"

"Then, for God's sake, give it to him," she interrupted with a harsh cry. "It's not worth your life."

He put his hands on her shoulders. "Yes, it is," he said solemnly. "But, not yours. That's why I'm giving it to you." He swallowed hard. "You don't know these men, Angie. They're ruthless. You should be safe because they don't want you." Fear poured from eyes that stared into hers. "If something happens to me, I want you to contact the U.S. Attorney's office in Miami and speak to an operative, code named 'Halo.' Talk to no one else, understand?"

She nodded rapidly, and the dislodged tears jogged down her face from the motion. "I'm scared. For both of us."

A noise came from the deck above them. "I know. I didn't set out to be a hero, and I'm scared, too. They want me, though, and I won't let anything happen to you." He smiled. "If I did, Reed would find me, even if it meant a trip to hell." He wiped away her tears. "We have to split up. I think they're back."

He moved away and returned to his spot near the steps. "Remember," he whispered out. "Give it to Halo."

Angie looked down at the key and touched it. "I won't forget."

As heavy footsteps descended the short set of steps, she became quiet, filled with the fear that comes from the unknown . . .

Angie heard her name flow through the fog of events that unwound in her head. Afraid of what came next, she didn't answer. As the voice continued to urge her, she opened her eyes to Matt's bearded face. His dark stare burned into her.

She gasped and let out a scream, colliding into him as she strained to sit up.

"Angie." He spoke sternly and wrapped his arms around hers. "Wake up. You're having a dream." Under the influence of his repeated words, her struggles lessened.

Disoriented, recognition slowly descended upon her. The alarming dream, coupled with her newfound knowledge of Matt, clashed to create a wall of doubt. Hastily, she drew away from his arms, her breathing still hard.

Matt frowned and let her escape his arms. "Are you all right? Do you know where you are?"

She nodded as she licked her lips nervously. She burst at the seams from the knowledge she'd gleaned from parts of the dream. She couldn't share it with Matt—not until she knew the truth that was contained in his briefcase. She raised her head to him.

Matt's frown became deeper, but when he moved closer, she also retreated. "You had another dream, didn't you?"

Angie hugged her arms to her chest. "Yes . . . no . . .

well, nothing I can remember." She averted her gaze. "I'll be all right."

He shifted on the bed to better draw her gaze. "I don't think so."

She rubbed her eyes. "Did I sleep long? What time is it?"

"Late, near sunset, but don't change the subject. Something scared you. I saw that look in your eyes when you woke up. Is there something you want to tell me?"

"No."

"You're sure?" he pressured.

"Yes," she blurted, aggravated at his insistence. "Maybe you just don't want to believe me, no matter what I say." She'd answered much too quickly, and stole a glance at him to see if he read anything in her response. "Just leave me alone for a while." She stretched out her leg with the stung foot and propped it on the cushion. When he didn't move, but sat there with his eyes narrowed, she added pleasantly, "Please?"

He spread his hands regretfully, and with an impersonal shrug, said, "Sure. If that's what you want." Rising from the bed, he looked at her intently. "I'll be outside, and will probably take a swim. If you need me, let me know." He turned and strode through the door.

The moment he left, Angie let out a breath and forced herself to settle down. Pieces of her dream floated back to her, and beckoned her to remember more from the fragments. She looked around for her writing tablet and saw it, along with the pencil, partially covered by the sheet. She grabbed them up and wrote down her impressions.

She'd been angry and fearful in the dream as the man with her had instructed her to give something to halo. She didn't know what that meant. Was he the same man who, in another vision, had wrapped his hands around her ankle? The gaudy cross around the man's neck. It had opened to reveal a silver key, the one that was on her ankle. Give the key to halo? Is that what he'd meant? What about the man who had put it there—was he a friend, or more . . . her husband?

The screen door clanged shut and her head shot up from her writing. Matt had left the house. He had warned her not to force her memories, that they'd return on their own. Would they? She laid the pad and pencil down and turned to peek from her window. He walked across the yard toward the beach. She watched him in a private moment of longing—his yard-wide shoulders were like a molded Atlas, and she mentally caressed him. But, her desire for him was couched by disappointment, and guilt—her own. Matt knew something was wrong. She could tell it in his eyes, and it saddened her that she now repaid his earlier kindness with suspicions and an invasion of his privacy.

When he disappeared out of view, Angie got out of the bed. She'd have to gird herself with resolve to do what had to be done. It was time she found out who she was losing her heart to: a man who not only had her respect, but could melt her with his touch—or a murderer.

Matt was puzzled as he walked to the beach. What was with her keeping her memories a secret? He should have confronted her with the tablet, but forcing the truth out of her, and so soon after another nightmare, wouldn't have done either of them any good.

When he reached the water, he turned and looked back at the house. She was there, and that's where he wanted to be. He couldn't help it, but he was falling in love with every aggravating and unknown part of her. He rested his hands on his hips and shook his head at the admittance. It was time to try and put away his past, maybe even come clean about his entire ordeal. Tell her about it. For the first time, the thought wasn't totally distasteful. Maybe it was possible to start over with a clean slate. His hands dropped as he considered his painful choices.

From her chair, Angie reached her arms up and grasped the briefcase from its spot on the top of the shelf. She carefully avoided toppling the sculpture. Favoring her sore foot, she slowly lowered the briefcase to the safety of her arms, then hopped down to place it on the kitchen table.

The clasps were just as she'd found them that morning—closed but unlocked. She opened the case and once again revealed the newspaper articles stuffed inside with the reports. The papers were in the same order, with the newsprint folded at the bottom. She sorted through them to get to the ones that were unread.

A noise came from behind her. Angie whirled about, guilt licking at her face. When she saw Buster saunter into the room, relief flooded through her.

"Buster," she whispered, "You've got to stop doing that to me." With one more cautious glance thrown to the window, she returned her attention to the briefcase and its contents.

She skimmed her fingers through the top third of the papers, and carefully laid them aside. The remaining newspapers quickly produced a headline that caught her interest: "Police Probe Tightens Around Local Honored Doctor." The one below it was equally caustic: "Doctor and Dead Wife Hid Rocky Past."

Her eyes perused the first article at breakneck speed as she hungrily grabbed at the words. It read that the doctor's version of events didn't add up when matched with evidence found at the scene, and his doctor's bag was being analyzed for evidence.

"No, no," she whispered. Immersed in the contents of the article, she felt as if her breath were cut off. "Oh, Matt," she wailed out loud. "Would you have killed your wife? Is that why you're here, hiding from the authorities?'' Distressed by the article's content, she backed away from the table, and bumped into an unyielding wall. She spun around to Matt's face.

Shock flew through her as they both froze in a stunned tableau.

BETRAYAL

There is no reason to repeat bad history.
—Eleanor Holmes Norton, 1970

CHAPTER SEVENTEEN

Matt's astonished gaze impaled Angie as the newspaper clipping fluttered from her frozen fingers.

She darted a nervous glance to the floor before she returned her stricken stare to his face. "I didn't hear you come in."

"I think you were too damn busy." He pushed past her to the table and the briefcase. He knocked it closed before he faced her again. "What in hell are you doing?"

The anger in his stony black eyes was devastating, and she slowly backed away into the living room. "I'm sorry," she managed to speak in a broken whisper. When he next slammed his fist to the table, she jumped with a gasp.

"Save it, Angie," he growled, and began his advance on her.

"I thought I could help you get over your past." She responded quickly over her racing heart. "And, I figured the answers were in your briefcase."

"You found what you were looking for?" His tone hardened.

Angie's voice was lost as their tenuous trust unraveled before her eyes. Disappointment melded with dismay at his growing anger.

He dropped a hand to his hip. "Are you scared that I'll get rid of you the way I did my wife? You think with just the two of us here, no one will ever know?"

Forced to listen to his sarcasm, her own voice returned. "Stop telling me what I think. The story's in the paper," she stammered, and looked toward the stack she'd left on the table. "It's all there, that the police investigated you for your wife's death."

His frown grew as she tried to explain.

"And that others, mainly her mother, accused you of her . . . ," she paused, then whispered the unspeakable word, ". . . murder."

As he continued toward her, Angie's panic increased. "Did you do what they said?"

"Now, you're asking me?" He let out a hollow, ugly laugh. "I thought your mind was made up. Didn't I just hear you say I was hiding out here from the authorities?"

Angie's backward steps had reached the living room. "Matt, what am I supposed to believe?" she reasoned. "You wouldn't tell me anything. I had no choice but to try and find out for myself," she said, with easy defiance.

"You had a choice, all right," he bellowed. "You could have trusted me and let my past stay private until I chose to bring it up."

"I wanted nothing more than to trust you, and I've done that." She tried to see past his anger. Why did he comment as if the answers to her questions were obvious? "What I did may have been wrong, and I didn't read all of the articles. Tell me what happened."

"You read just enough to pronounce me guilty in your eyes."

"No, never." Her voice had risen to equal his. "I won't ever believe that's true." She had backed into the sofa, and now Matt towered over her, boldly intimidating. "All I know is your past is tearing you up inside, and it's keeping us apart."

"But, it was mine to share," he insisted harshly. His mouth tightened as he looked at her. "And, what about you? How much of your memory has come back?"

Angie gave him a blank stare.

"You've also been keeping your past from me. The difference is I gave you the space to deal with yours."

He must have seen her tablet on the bed. Surprised at his discovery, she looked away. "I don't know what to say."

"That's a first," he growled. "You want to know what keeps us apart?" He pointed his finger at his chest, then hers. "We're our own worst enemies. You try to hide your demons, yet you think you know all about mine."

"No, I don't, Matt. Tell me the newspaper is wrong, that there's an explanation." Her heart ached each moment he remained silent. "Please."

Abruptly, he turned from her. She opened her eyes and saw him grab up the briefcase from the table, return to her side, and toss it to the sofa, where the contents spilled out.

He walked to the window where he looked out on the darkening horizon. "One day last year, I returned home and found Paula, my wife, on the floor of our bedroom, unconscious and in respiratory arrest. I tried everything to get her to breathe while I waited for the ambulance. She was pronounced dead at the hospital, of cardio-pulmonary arrest." He pulled in a deep breath.

"You must have thought it was happening all over again when you found me."

He nodded. "It was either a sick joke or my chance at redemption. I decided on the latter and swore I wouldn't lose you." Leaning against the window, he continued. "Right after the coroner's report was issued, the police questioned me, looking for evidence to charge me with murder. The medical board's inquiry on my . . . ethics, or lack thereof, came next."

"Oh, Matt, why would they—"

"Because they suspected a young and reasonably healthy woman's heart failure could have been simulated, and the possible drugs to induce that could be traced back to me."

Angie's spirits sank lower, and she dropped onto the sofa.

"I tried to save her, and I couldn't—didn't." His voice dropped an octave.

"But didn't you explain it? Didn't you tell them you didn't do it?"

"They were right. The culprit was a fatal dose of epinephrine, taken while she was on antidepressant medication. She took an ampoule from my medical bag."

Her eyes widened with knowledge. "She injected herself—"

"They never knew that she did . . ." Matt turned from the window, and she could see the raw hurt that glittered there. ". . . Because I never showed anyone the suicide note she left."

Angie stared, wordlessly, shocked at his admission.

"Weeks before it happened, all the signs were there, but I ignored them, and I only blame myself." He nodded at the newspaper articles. "You want to know what my city thought, what my friends and enemies alike thought, then read about it. But your wants gave you no right to snoop into my life." His voice had been firm, final. Like an angry wind, he strode through screen door and left her there.

Without warning, Matt's parting words provoked a wave of déjà vu, and raised the fog in her head. A series of flashing pictures, in another place, swirled in her consciousness . . . a combination safe being opened . . . by her own hands . . . to reveal a neat stack of paper. . . bearer bonds . . . a safe door slammed shut . . . a person entering the room . . . angry words exchanged . . .

Her eyes stretched wide, as though to hold the fading visions in place, and she dropped her head to the back of the sofa. Was she fated to relive her entire past as a score of moving pictures while on the island? When Buster sidled up to the sofa and nudged her hand, she was grateful for the dog's continued devotion to her, and scratched his ears.

Repentant at the grief Matt had recalled, and her part in it, she turned to the newspaper articles spread over the sofa. The more she learned about the past, the more her future resembled a vague haze fraught with shadows and mystery.

Frustrated by a sense of helplessness, salty tears worked their way down her face. She read, then replaced, each article in the briefcase, Matt's pain becoming her own.

Matt gently swayed in the hammock in the sultry night, glad that he'd nixed a shirt. He counted the stars in the clear night sky. It had become a lazy habit of his, while on the island, when he wanted to clear his mind and grab a corner of peace. Only, it didn't work this time. None of his old tricks had worked during this trip. Angie was the difference.

What did she think of him now? It was a given that she couldn't think too much less than he did of himself. He sighed and adjusted his frame in the hammock so that his hand rested under his head.

His other arm hung over the side when Buster came up to the hammock. "Hey, fella." Surprised, he raised his head to greet the tethered dog, before he saw Angie standing just beyond.

He dropped his head back to the hammock as a chill black silence surrounded them.

"Matt, forgive me." She dropped to the sand next to the hammock. "I regret that I damaged our trust . . . my doubts and interference, our argument tonight, the memories I kept from you.''

He didn't acknowledge her apology, nor did he turn to her. "Did you know that when a month has two full moons, the second is known as a blue moon?" He stared into the clear, moonlit sky as he explained the lunar anomaly.

She followed his gaze. "Is that what you're looking for?"

"Not tonight, but one will occur our last night here." He finally turned so he could see her face, washed pale by the settling dusk. "It's an unusual event, and it doesn't happen often. On the rare occasion when it does, legend has it that it offers redemptive powers to those that look upon it and truly want some measure of healing."

"For their souls?"

His sigh was deep and lifted his chest as he closed his eyes. "I turned a deaf ear to Paula, and she died as a result."

Angie was losing him to the horrors in his past. She had to do something. She rose from the sand and sat on the hammock so that she faced him.

"Look at me, Matt. It's over, and it wasn't your fault. It was no one's fault. You were cleared of wrongdoing because there was never evidence to bring charges. And, I don't think public opinion was ever against you." She touched his brow in a comforting gesture. "The only person that keeps you prisoner is yourself."

His eyes flashed open as he caught her hand in his. "You read the entire coroner's report?"

Angie nodded.

"Then, you know."

"I'm so sorry . . . ," she blinked back the tears as she considered the enormity of his loss, ". . . that you lost your unborn baby, too."

"It was kind of ironic, wouldn't you say? A few years after we married, she became obsessed with having a baby. Our baby. After what must have been a hundred tests on both of us, the results were the same. She had a genetic infirmity that made it difficult to conceive."

As she listened to his broken voice, Angie felt completely helpless at offering a platitude that would lessen the sting of his ordeal.

"I didn't pay her depression much attention at first, until she developed a dependence on prescription drugs. That's when we started seeing a marriage counselor, and she bounced in and out of drug therapy programs."

"Did you consider adoption?"

"That was my immediate choice, but her drug counseling was a matter of record and made it difficult; but, she wouldn't think of it as an alternative, anyway. By then, our marriage was this secret life where I hid her addictions to protect her from scandal. In the months before her death, her depression grew worse."

"You tried to get her help."

"She was a different woman, outgoing and funny, between her bouts, as we called them. Only after I'd threaten her with exposure to her family would she agree to therapy. I used the threat so regularly, it became a pattern, and we grew apart. This last time, she only stayed in rehab three of the six weeks and released herself."

He squeezed Angie's hand, as though for support. "When she came home from the clinic, I told her that was it, and I would divorce her. I was the one who had always protected her, so it must have been a shock she wasn't ready to handle to find I had abandoned her again. She ended everything two weeks later."

"She was only seven weeks pregnant, so she never knew?"

"No. She didn't mention it in her final note to me."

"Why did you keep quiet about the suicide note? It would have saved you from the hell of being investigated in her murder."

"I couldn't, and she knew it. I'd spent our entire marriage protecting her from herself. And with her family so proudly Catholic, it was something I did for her in death that I couldn't in life—save her from humiliation and the glare of pity from others." He turned to Angie. "More important, knowing that she took her own life wasn't going to bring her back."

"But, suppose the authorities had decided that you did have something to do with her death? What would you have done?"

"Thankfully, I never had to consider that. I think of her death as an accident because that's what it was. She loved attention, and always figured I'd save her from herself, as usual." He lifted his legs and dropped them to the ground, so that he sat next to Angie in the hammock.

"It's over with, you know, and you can let your guilt free," she said. "Don't you think she'd want you to get on with your life?"

"Do you know what she said in that note?" He darted a glance at Angie. "She said my sense of honor was skewed, and since I'd never end our misery, she was doing it for me." He sighed deeply again. "She wanted me to think of her on the days I'm most happy and know it was the one thing she did right for me."

"Matt, that's sick."

"It doesn't matter. She was right, and I won't ever be free knowing that if I'd saved her one more time, I'd have saved my unborn baby."

Angie dropped her head against his shoulder and held him tight around the waist. Slowly, he reciprocated, and they swayed on the hammock in the soft evening breeze.

After a while, Angie spoke in a whisper. "Sometimes, the comfort of another is all that's necessary to start the healing."

Matt pulled his head back to look at her face. "Do you want to stay out here with me awhile longer?"

She smiled. The sadness in his piercing eyes was palpable. The strange surge of affection she felt was just as frightening. "I'd like that. Anyway, it's my turn to open up and be honest about all the dreams and memories I've been having."

"Come on," he said, and pulled her with him so that they dropped onto the hammock as one. With his arm acting as a pillow for her head, he stretched his long legs out so as to balance them in the swing before he drew her close and rested his hand around her waist.

Contentedly, Angie rolled into the warm lines of his body, the shadows gone from her heart as she listened to the crashing waves. It had been a day of revelations; and, if he could share his dark and certain past, surely she could trust him with pieces of her unknown one.

The room service cart, laden with covered silver trays, rolled into the penthouse suite located at the top of the four-star hotel in the Grand Caymans. The young black waiter, uniformed in white, had performed this duty countless times before, having passed the rigorous inspection required to enter this level of security. He now made himself as insignificant as possible when he entered the living room, and proceeded to set up the meals from the cart. He kept a watchful eye on the powerful, swarthy man whose aura filled the room, Nicolas Magellan.

"No one keeps me out of the States," Magellan intoned from behind the desk. "No one. Not even an almighty U.S. Attorney. I go, I live where I choose."

He stroked a sleek and aloof Persian cat as it lounged at the corner of the desk in the well-appointed suite. The diamond necklace that adorned the animal's neck glittered like a hundred prisms, and didn't seem at all odd in the luxurious surroundings.

Magellan's words were directed at the three other men in the room. One stood relaxed near the window. The other two men held an obeisant posture directly in front of the desk. And while all appeared to be successful, their appearance made the nature of their business subject to interpretation. A clatter of silverware drew their attention to the service cart.

"Fool, leave the food, leave the food." Magellan waved his hand in a gesture of dismissal as he barked the order at the stunned young waiter. "Wait until the grandchildren arrive. I'll call you back."

The young waiter bowed his understanding and quickly recovered the chafing dishes. As he slowly backed from the room, he watched the cat stretch lazily from its corner position on the desk and saunter to the opposite side. The vacated spot revealed a Smith & Wesson 9mm neat, with a steel-gray frame. Nice piece.

When the door closed after the waiter, Nicolas Magellan looked hard at the two men who had stood stonily in front of his desk.

"Ricardo over there doesn't believe I should return to Miami." He nodded toward Ricardo, both his trusted lieutenant and bodyguard, who stood at the window with an expression that was both dour and alert.

"It's a chance you don't have to take, Sir. Why rub your appearance in the Fed's faces and piss them off?" He returned his attention to the window.

Nicolas smiled, and leaned back in his chair. "And, if you two do your jobs, I won't have a problem."

The two men finally shuffled a movement, but only to dart a glance at the other.

"So tell me good news." Magellan sat forward. "Did you find her?"

The shorter man spoke with obvious deference and respect. "Sir, everyone's reported back. She's disappeared, for sure. No one's seen her."

He slammed his hand to the desk. "What do you mean? We already know she disappeared." He mocked the man with a smile. "Hell, she disappeared off the damn boat. I want to know if you found her and if she has what we want. Or, did she drown?"

"Yeah." The taller man agreed with his own smile that showed little deference. "She's probably swimming with the fishes by now."

The smile that had played along Magellan's features slowly turned into a dissatisfied frown. "Get that smirk off your stupid face, Manuel. The only reason I don't kill you is that you're my cousin's son." He sighed. "If she's with the 'fishes' as you suggest, I want some proof. The boat, her clothes, the damn key. Something."

Both men again straightened under his scrutiny, and the shorter man asked, "What do you want us to do next, Sir?"

"I want that damn key Philip passed to her. If she's already dead, then show me her bones if you have to." When Magellan punctuated his bellow with another slam of his fist to the desk, the cat scampered down and fled across the room.

"I want to know she's not a threat anymore. We can't let her pass on that key." He snapped his fingers as he tried to remember something, and called to Ricardo. "The two men you put on the boat job. What were their names?"

Ricardo turned to his boss. "Elgado and Murphy. They work as a team."

"Quite efficient, too. Find them," he ordered. "They know what she looks like. Sweep the local islands around the anchor spot." He nodded to the two men still frozen in front of his desk. "One of you join them. I want a report in three days. Is that clear?"

The two men nodded their understanding and turned to

follow Ricardo from the room. As they cleared the doorway, another guard stepped inside.

"Mr. Magellan, Father Adolphes is here. For the weekly alms to the poor," he explained unnecessarily.

Magellan looked at his watch and sighed as he opened a side drawer and dropped the gun into it. "Show the good Father in."

CHAPTER EIGHTEEN

Angie awakened to a crisp morning breeze and the sounds of rough waves. She also came to the slow realization that she was cradled on top of Matt, comfortably nestled on his chest, between his arms and legs. They'd talked for what seemed like hours last night before falling asleep in the hammock.

She raised up slightly and looked into his sleeping face. In repose, his features were relaxed and soft. She stroked his bearded jaw and stored the memory. As he began to stir, something else did, too. He had grown rock hard beneath her. The encounter was a sensual jolt, and explosive currents raced through her. She tried to rise from his groin without disturbing his sleep, but it didn't work. His arms tightened gruffly to hold her in place, and there she lay ensconced, snug against his morning erection. Then, when his hips forcefully rotated into hers, heat rushed to her wide-eyed face. He must be dreaming.

This time she used his chest for support and raised herself up to break free of his arms. However, the hammock wouldn't cooperate and began to tilt. She held onto Matt for the inevitable. Her uneven weight rolled her, first to his side, then over the edge to the sand.

"Oh, no," she grunted, as Matt tumbled over after her.

He was now fully awake and avoided falling on her when he looped his arm around her waist and rolled with her on the sand. They came to a stop much like they had been in the hammock. She was again on top of him. With no hesitation this time, she scrambled from his lap, even as he quickly moved to help her get up, and nimbly leapt from the ground.

"Angie, I . . ."

"I think the evening did both of us a lot of good," she said, attempting to ease their embarrassment.

His lazy smile became knowing. "You're right. I feel . . . better. Much better this morning."

Her pulses raced from his gaze. She brushed the sand from her arm and looked past him to the patient dog tethered at the tree. "Why don't you let Buster take his morning run while I go inside? After last night, who knows where the day might take us."

Her delight grew as she watched him digest her cryptic words. She turned away slowly and walked off.

Matt steeled his teeth as he watched her cross the sand, her hips swaying to some lusty beat. It was amazing what she did to him. Her urging him to talk of the past had worked, but it also opened a floodgate of checked emotions directed at her.

He had dreamed of them together this morning, a dream so real that . . . he flexed his jaw to relieve the tension that gnawed through his loins. His visions of her supplanted clear thought, and were getting increasingly erotic. He knew what he wanted—but, at what cost in the future?

Buster's bark drew him from his self-imposed reverie. He sighed and got up from the sand, but before he com-

plied with Buster's wish, he looked off in the direction
Angie had taken. Where would the day take them?

The Coast Guard cutter, *Prosperity*, had taken off from
the marina at the appointed time, and without a hitch.

Reed had been quiet, his eyes remote, when Jill met up
with him for boarding. The seriousness of this journey was
not lost on her, either. It was obvious that J.R. had been
warned that she'd accompany them—he didn't bat an eye
when she was helped aboard and issued a life jacket. J.R.
had reached into a large black gear bag stowed on the
deck and pulled out a crushed navy windbreaker that bore
the Agency's initials and imprint. He'd instructed her to
don it once their patrol had found its target.

Now, as the cutter skimmed the water in pursuit of its
mission, Reed stood away from her and conversed with a
DEA agent who already wore an official slicker with his
agency's initials. They leaned against the rail as though
contemplating the blank horizon, not knowing what
awaited them when they got there.

Jill was soon joined aft by J.R. She looked away from
Reed when J.R. took the seat next to her on the bench.

"Don't be concerned about him. He gets this way when
there's business to tend to."

"How do you know Reed?"

"I take it he hasn't discussed our past stellar relationship?"

She shook her head. "Why would he?"

"I thought you two were—"

"No." She quickly disavowed him of the notion. "I'm . . ."
Upon second thought, she amended her intended answer
slightly. ". . . A close family friend."

"I see." He motioned toward Reed again. "When he
told me you were joining us, I couldn't figure out why he'd
agreed."

She smiled at his unintended condescension. "He gets overprotective on occasion. Men can be forgiven for that. All it took was a gentle reminder to pull him back into reality." She narrowed her brows and smiled. "Maybe not so gentle."

He smiled with her. "There's a reason for that."

Jill tilted her head at him. "You two worked together before?"

He nodded. "A joint investigation that changed our lives. The details are no secret.

"So, what happened?"

"Some years back, we developed a problem with a case. His fiancée, also an Agent at the time, was caught in the cross fire." He paused a moment. "She was killed."

Her voice rose in surprise. "I didn't know."

He nodded. "Reed called her death a sacrifice and never forgave me for my part in the operation."

"Was he right? Did the Agency sacrifice her?"

J.R. sighed and shifted on the bench. "Who knows. This justice business is complicated, and people can get hurt for the larger good."

She managed a shrug and spoke offhandedly. "No wonder he doesn't trust you with Angie's life."

"Now you know why he takes his sister's involvement so personally. I imagine yours, too. He said you insisted on coming, but I know he doesn't want you anywhere near this operation."

She thought about what J.R. was saying, and about the time she'd asked her question to Reed, which had been pointedly ignored. "Does he still work for the Agency?"

"He's a former operative out of Washington. I believe he left covert operations behind after his fiancée's death."

"What does he do now?"

"I can hazard a guess, but I think he prefers it that way."

A young crew member came up to them. "You're wanted on the bridge, sir."

When J.R. left with the crewman, Jill saw that Reed still conversed with the agent at the rail. Having no desire to join them, she leaned back on the bench and closed her eyes. The Dramamine she had taken earlier had done its job.

"What was J.R. talking about?" Reed had taken the seat next to her.

When she opened her eyes, they blinked, then quizzically narrowed on him.

"Nothing important. A crewman came to get him." She reached out and touched his arm. "Are you okay with this patrol and what it'll turn up?"

"That doesn't matter. It's something that has to be done." He sat forward and rested his hands against his knees. "I was talking to the DEA Agent. His name is Lee Gordon. They believe Magellan had begun to diversify into new arenas. Designer drugs. He'll check out the boat in detail. After all, smuggling was Magellan's favorite way to get around customs."

"They suspect the *Angelica* was used that way?"

He peered at her. "You look a little green around the gills. Shocked or scared?"

"Neither," she answered quickly. "Not after what Angie told me about Philip. Plus, these guys have guns and the boat moves pretty fast."

"It's a cutter," Reed said. "Built for speed and armed to deal with smugglers. If we come across unfriendly types, I guarantee they'll run first."

"Reed!"

His head snapped around at J.R.'s voice.

"We've got a sighting on the *Angelica*."

He was up and skipped over the riggings that covered the deck, Jill right behind him.

* * *

The day did, indeed, turn out to be filled with promise for Angie and Matt. From their breakfast in the garden that morning to their swim in the waterfall at lunch, they had enjoyed the other's company, and on one level, resembled carefree lovers. On another level, the love was painfully unrequited, held in check by the fear that the past might damage the delicate tightrope they walked in paradise. Nothing had been mentioned of Matt's briefcase and its contents, or the nagging memories that danced around Angie's psyche. Neither had yet accepted the idea that their pasts could reside comfortably in their shaky present.

Matt reclined in the tidal pool, where the water graduated with the incoming tide and reached from one to a few feet deep before the cemented bottom slanted down to join with the ocean. Farther down on the beach, Angie tossed a toy bone that Buster chased.

Her shirt was dappled with water and rode up on her hips, exposing the bright green bikini bottom. They'd never resolved the clothing problem. He smiled thoughtfully as he drank his fill of her, and it still wasn't enough. A delicious tremor built deep within him, its eruption controlled with a hair trigger.

Like a voyeur, he continued to watch her, a shameless act that under ordinary circumstances, he might have condemned. But, the circumstances he found himself in were anything but ordinary, and she was an extraordinary woman. How did you explain falling in love with a complete stranger in such a short time, one whose past memory could return at any moment to wreak emotional havoc? When her memory returned, would she still believe his soul was salvageable?

He felt good, and it was feeding his guilt. He turned his gaze from Angie and looked out to the sea. The horizon was clear—just billowy white clouds against an azure sky.

"Buster's tired of chasing the bone. Where's his other toy, the disc you throw for him?"

Matt looked up from his sobering thoughts as Angie stood over him.

"What are you talking about?"

Her hands rested saucily on her hips. "I saw you throwing a disc one morning—" She abruptly stopped, her brown eyes wide from discovery.

He'd seen her at the window before he swam off that morning, and knew she'd watched him. Openly amused, he didn't ease her discomfort. It would serve her right.

"You did? I only throw that thing for Buster when I'm in the shower out here."

"Well," she answered petulantly, and sank into the water near him, "I just happened to be near the window when you were . . . cavorting."

"Cavorting? I was in the shower." His mood had lightened once again and he laughed at her description. "I should have known better than to think I'd have privacy with you around." His gaze was unrelenting. "I don't think I wear anything when I shower."

She smiled and arched a brow. "I didn't say it wasn't a pleasant morning."

He skimmed the water with his hands so that it splashed over her. "Like today?"

She screeched at the soaking her shirt took, and returned his action in kind. Matt warmed to the play, and pretty soon, they were laughing as they frolicked in the pool, dodging the other's tags. He picked her up as she let out a whoop of protest and, wading deeper into the tidal pool, soaked her thoroughly in the seawater.

"Look at you." Matt laughed as he waded away from her. "Now you're soaking wet." He turned and sat on the edge of the pool.

Angie struggled to stand, then slowly plodded through

the water toward him, her breaths heavy from their play. "You took advantage of me. You're bigger."

Matt's grin evaporated in the rush of heat that stroked his loins. Her shirt was pasted to her skin and exposed her dark, hard nipples. The seawater dripped down her lush, tanned thighs. "You're ... ," he swallowed hard, ". . . Better looking." He couldn't seem to divert his gaze.

She watched him rise from his seat, the hunger clear in his eyes, and didn't look away from it. "We've been dancing around this all day." She reveled in his open admiration that fell upon her as soft as a caress. Sensing his vulnerability with his past, she wanted to offer comfort and support. In return, she wanted the same from him. She reached for the first button on her shirt.

He didn't move as he watched her. Then, with an imperceptible shift of her shoulders, the shirt slid backward from her body, exposing her round, tanned breasts. After quickly tossing the shirt to the pool's edge, she lifted her arms and slowly covered her breasts.

His eyes raked over her. "You covered yourself like that when we first met," he said huskily.

She nodded.

"That seems like a long time ago. I'd like to think we know each other a lot better now."

A hot ache began to build inside her. "We do," she said, and dropped her arms.

He reached out and pulled her roughly to him, then bent to kiss her hard. Standing on her toes, Angie put her arms around his neck and met his punishing kiss with her own hunger, swept away in the passion.

Turning in their locked embrace, Matt lowered her to the shallow pool where his kiss turned to nibbles that grazed her earlobe, then moved to her neck and shoulders. The pit of Angie's stomach was in a wild swirl as his rough beard scraped her face and shocked her with desire.

"It's taken every bit of my strength to keep my hands

off you these last days," he whispered in her ear. "You have no idea what you do to me."

She curved her hands around his neck and pressed her open mouth to his. "Matt, I think I love you."

His tongue explored her lip's soft fullness before he moved his head downward and found her sensitive, swollen nipples. Angie gasped at the caress, rocked by her own eager response to the touch of his lips. Her head lolled back on the pool's edge as his tongue tantalized the dark buds.

His hand made a path across her stomach and ventured to the bikini bottom she wore, where he eased his fingers under the Lycra and roamed intimately and leisurely. Angie's eyes closed as he found pleasure points that elicited her groan of pleasure. When he had eased the bikini down her hips, she lifted her head and saw the dark, smoky passion that sparked in his eyes.

"I want you, Angie, and it's like nothing else I've ever needed."

"I like hearing you say that," she whispered, and trailed a hand to his muscular thigh. She closed her eyes and raised her face for his kiss, but when it didn't come, she opened her eyes. Matt's face had turned grim. "What's wrong?" she asked.

He slowly shook his head. "No matter how much we want to make love, we can't do it. Not until we know who you are."

His words knocked the wind from her. "Why is my past so important now?" She let her fingers massage the taut muscles along his thighs before she slipped her fingers into the hem of his trunks. "What's important is that we want each other."

He caught her hand up in his. "We can't think about only what we want. You don't have a memory, Angie, and it wouldn't be right for you. I'm sorry."

"Sorry?" She looked away from him and felt her face

grow hot. "I'm naked as a jaybird and . . . and humiliated."
She raised her arms over her breasts.

He drew her into his arms. Turning, he eased her from
the pool. "God help me, we have no right. Try to understand that until we know who you are, you're not mine to
have."

She stiffened away from him, her shame giving way to
anger at this turn of events, and grabbed up her shirt. "You
don't want anyone else. Why can't you find the courage to
admit it?"

"I stopped because of you."

"No, you didn't," she shouted. "You're preserving your
sainted dead wife's memory. Can't you see it? Everything
else is an excuse." She gave him her back as she pulled
on the wet, sand-caked shirt.

Matt lowered his head as he tried to reason with her.
"Why are you bringing Paula up? This has nothing to do
with her and everything to do with you not remembering
your past."

Angie whirled around at him as she angrily buttoned
the shirt. "How do you do it, huh? Just close off your
feelings?"

"Don't you think I want you, too? I haven't been able
to get you out of my head since I first found you."

"Then, explain to me what happened just now."

"I don't want to wake up one day and find I've fallen
in love with a woman who remembers that she belongs to
someone else," he shouted.

Momentarily taken aback by his words, she could only
stare at him.

"And you," he continued. "You don't have any idea
how all this will play out, yet you blissfully want to rush
right into a relationship with no thought about who gets
hurt by your selfish decision."

Affronted by his attack, she defended herself. "Maybe

I'm not stuck in the past and am willing to take a chance on love.''

"Or maybe you're too damn impulsive and haven't given it a thought like you've done since the first day you landed here." His face twisted with anger.

"You bastard." Without a thought, Angie swung her hand back and slapped Matt with all her might. The effect on his jaw was not as great as the surprise on his face that he had angered her enough to slap him.

Held-back tears burned Angie's eyes. She shook her numbed fingers and turned to run for the house, humiliated enough for one day.

"Angie," Matt called to her, "I'm sorry, I didn't mean that."

When she didn't stop, Matt let out a deep breath. "Damn." And then, he remembered what she'd said. She loved him. "Damn."

The deck hummed with activity after the discovery was made aboard the yacht. Reed separated himself from J.R. and strode hurriedly through the crew members that worked the scene to find his way to Jill. He jumped down from the *Angelica* to the deck of the *Prosperity*, his eyes seeking her out.

She sprang from her seat there, guarded by two crewmen, and ran to him with her arms outstretched. "What did you find?" she cried.

He let her plow into his chest before he wrapped her in a tight embrace. "She's not on the boat, thank God," he whispered in her hair. "She's not there."

Jill slumped against him in relief, then raised her head. "But, after all of you went aboard, they called back that they'd found a body."

He nodded. "Philip's. He's dead." At her gasp, he pulled her back to him.

"Oh, Lord, Reed, what happened? If Angie's not here, where is she? Where's Angie?"

"We don't know." He released her and they stepped apart. "I have to get back over there. I didn't want you wondering about Angie."

"How did he die?"

"They're not sure. He's been on the boat for at least a few days. There's a lot of soft tissue damage to his face, so he was beaten before he died."

Jill turned kind eyes to his mouth, which was tight and grim. "This must be hell for you."

"I don't know what I'm feeling—relief, anger, fear for Angie's safety." He observed Jill and tried to appraise her commitment to finding Angie. "Because she is still alive. You believe that, don't you?"

She nodded. "Angie is resourceful. She's surviving whatever situation she's in." Her hand dropped to his arm. "I can't stand sitting over here waiting for information. I want to board the *Angelica* with you. Please?"

He turned with her. "The entire boat is a crime scene, so be careful."

The crewmen lifted her up from the *Prosperity,* then handed her over the side to Reed, who waited on the *Angelica.*

As he set her safely on the yacht's deck, J.R. and Lee came up from the cabin steps. Each wore a mask and gloves and carried items in their arms.

Reed frowned at the white cloth draped across J.R.'s arm. "What did you find down there?"

J.R. slid the mask from his mouth. "Are these familiar to you?"

Jill stepped forward and carefully displayed a piece of the draped material from his arm. It was a long wrap skirt. "This is Angie's."

"And that's her purse and shoes," Reed said, indicating the items Lee took from a brown bag.

Lee also removed his mask. "The victim wore a pair of swim trunks."

"So, Angie probably changed on the boat, too," Reed mused aloud.

"But, she wouldn't have left her purse, unless it was against her will or she was in a hurry," Jill added, and turned to look around the deck.

"This isn't your everyday piracy robbery." J.R.'s words were hesitant.

Lee agreed. "Did you get a load of that gold chain around his neck?" He handed J.R. the bag.

"Didn't look much like Philip's style," Reed answered. "Robbery wasn't a motive, not when they left a chain easily worth a few grand."

"We think he died of a forced drug overdose." J.R. rolled the clothing and pushed them into the brown bag with the shoes and purse. "The drug, we're not sure."

"It follows the pattern of a hit. He was taught a lesson," Lee said. "Whoever did it didn't try to hide that fact. The hypodermic was left next to the body." He left them.

"Magellan." Reed slammed his fist into the palm of his hand as his thoughts flew to Angie's safety. "Damn. He's got her."

"If he does," J.R. said, "it's for leverage or information."

"Yeah," Reed agreed. "If he wanted her dead, she'd have been on the boat."

"This murder is Miami's problem." J.R. handed the brown bag to Reed. "They've been notified and are on their way to handle the scene. I'll stay and meet them. In a few hours, though, it'll be all over the news."

"Jill and I will leave on the cutter with Angie's things."

"We don't want Angie's name connected to this too soon. We can buy a few days, provided you're not around when they get here."

Reed nodded his understanding. "Miami PD won't be

happy finding two civilians in the midst of their crime scene."

"You got it. Until I locate the evidence Philip had for me, I can at least throw Magellan off." He turned on the deck. "Where's Jill?"

The men turned and saw Jill bent precariously over the side of the boat.

"Jill," Reed called out, "What are you doing?"

"Look at this," she called back to them.

When they joined her, she pointed over the side of the boat. "Shouldn't the safety boat be lashed here?" Two leather string ties flapped harmlessly in the wind. The imprint of a canoe-sized boat was left against the bleached white boat side.

"She's right," a nearby Coast Guard crewman said. "Depending on the boat design, they can be latched to the sides or on the deck."

"Well, I'll be damned. It's missing, all right," J.R. said.

"Someone got away from here on that boat." Reed's voice was eager, and a hopeful smile began to form on his face as he turned to Jill. "Maybe it was Angie."

They all turned their attention to the circular stretch of horizon and water that surrounded them.

Jill said what they all thought. "But, where is she now?"

"I'm leaving tonight," Reed said, and pushed off the railing. "To find her."

"Where?" J.R. asked.

"You continue putting the pressure on Daniel Otero and work Miami," he replied, as he looked from J.R. to Jill. "I've got this feeling that she's out here, hiding from the danger. And, if I have to search every land mass between the Bahamas and Miami, I'm going to find her."

When he tilted his gaze to Jill, he saw the commitment strong in her eyes, and modified his words as he reached out for her. "We both are."

* * *

Angie burst through the screen door and let it bang shut behind her. She dropped onto the sofa, oblivious to the sand she left in her wake, and curled up in the corner.

Her tears flowed openly now and helped to wash away her humiliation. She'd practically thrown herself at him, and he'd turned her down. After last night, she was sure Matt was ready to move on. Those damn newspaper stories. She let her gaze clamp onto the briefcase, which had been returned to its place on the bookcase. What kind of person carries around that kind of baggage that can, literally, cripple growth? Not a person that wanted to move on. Matt had not yet realized he was his own worst enemy.

She sat up and wiped her eyes as an idea began to form in her head. Clenching her jaw to stop the sob in her throat, she let it take flight and soar.

Once again, she stood on a chair and removed the briefcase. Setting it down, she flexed the clasps, and they popped open to reveal the articles. She gathered matches from the kitchen and the metal wastebasket from under the desk. And before she lost her resolve, emptied the contents of the briefcase into the wastebasket.

When she struck the match, she shivered as though a winter breeze embraced her, and spoke her pain out loud. "Matt, you'll never be free as long as these reminders are around."

She dropped the lit match into the metal can and watched as the small, growing flame bounded up from the bottom to eat away at the edges of Matt's guilt.

Mesmerized, she watched the flames slowly multiply and dance about. As her gaze flitted across the curling newsprint, she saw a name. Magellan. She jerked upright. The name from her dream? In a surge of panic, she scooped the sheet of paper from the can and dropped it to the floor, before following it there to read.

The fire had singed the headline about Matt's hearing on one side, but she flipped the charred paper over and saw a smaller, but bold, headline near the bottom: "Magellan Indictment Quashed."

CHAPTER NINETEEN

The headline stuck out in bold relief, and the implication made Angie gasp. Only a few lines of the Associated Press story had escaped the fire:

Nicolas Magellan, the frequent Miami resident considered by many to be a notorious South American drug lord, has once again beaten the odds and avoided an indictment by the U.S. Attorney's Office and the Drug Enforcement Administration. Magellan's name had also been included in a pending FBI file on a well-known South Florida judge suspected of taking bribes . . .

That was it. The rest of the story had charred and crumbled in her fingers. Her mind raced through her prior visions. Did she have a connection to a criminal in the drug world? Her head shook in denial as she threw the damning article back into the can with the other paper. Hugging her arms to her chest, she backed away from the burning pyre. It was just a name, a weird coincidence. The name had meant nothing to Matt when she'd shared her nightmares with him. So, why did she feel a chill to her bone, a foreboding that made her skin crawl?

As surely as if her thoughts had beckoned him forward, Matt came through the door like a towering oak, big and forceful. The flames and smoke from the wastebasket drew his attention.

"What have you done?" He crossed the room in the time it took Angie to draw a frantic breath, and knew all she'd done in one glance.

He grabbed up a towel to beat out the flames, but he was too late. All that remained in the can were the charred pieces of newsprint.

Angie's wide eyes darted to his broad back, then sparked for the upcoming combat.

Matt threw the towel across the room and turned on her. "This is it, Angie. The last damn straw." His eyes filled with contempt as he angrily gestured with his hand. "You get mad at me and then you come in here and do this? Who do you think you are?"

"I don't know," she shot back at him. "You're the one that has the screwed up past that he can't forget. I guess I'm lucky."

"How could you do this?" He looked at the mess in the wastebasket. "What gives you the right to destroy my personal things?"

"I care about you, damn it." She was breathless with rage. "I'd do it again if I thought it would help."

"You can't even help yourself," he yelled back. "How in hell do you expect to help me?"

"Get off your guilt trip. All you do is make excuses for your wife. You almost went to jail for it. You're under the impression that you married some paragon of virtue."

"I won't talk about this with you, not anymore."

"You put her on a pedestal, and it did something to you

when she fell off. But, you have to face the truth. She left you. She didn't die accidentally. She did it on purpose."

"Shut up, Angie."

"No, I won't tiptoe around the subject. I'm alive, and a real woman with real feelings. What about you?"

She spun from him to leave, but he grabbed her arm and stopped her, his gaze hard on her face.

"What am I supposed to do, Angie?"

"Move on." She spoke quietly. "Life has a way of continuing with or without your permission."

"I know," he sighed, and dropped to the sofa. "That's why I came here. To heal."

"With a suitcase of clippings to remind you of the pain? My God, Matt, did you love her so much that you won't let anyone get near your heart again?"

He turned his head to her. "Love her? Angie, by the time we reached the end I think I . . . I hated her."

Angie's anger was blunted by his anguished admission.

"Because of that, I owed her and our baby some level of respect and peace when they died."

"And it's why you hold onto your guilt."

"I learned humility. I didn't divorce her because it meant the great doctor had failed on some level. So, I stayed and kept up a public pretense, hating her for what she'd become, and my part in it, as well."

She sat down next to him and took his hand. "That's why I burned those papers, Matt. Don't you see? You only kept them as a bitter reminder."

He nodded, choked by emotion that wouldn't let him speak.

"I know you, Dr. Matthew Sinclair." Her voice wavered with emotion as she stroked his hand in her lap. "You're a good man who'll get through this, but you've been holding everything inside too long."

"I don't want us hurt. The papers I kept reminded me of all the mistakes I'd ever made." He turned on the sofa to face her. "When I first saw you, you were not only beautiful, but you had this love of life in you. Even though your situation was pretty bad, you didn't want pity for yourself. I tried to control my feelings because it was easy to fall for you, Angie. I didn't realize how hard it would be to stay away."

"If you want to lay blame somewhere, then I'm also at fault," Angie said. "We've spent almost every waking moment together this past week, and all I think of is seeing you again."

Matt pulled her into his arms and groaned as he fell against the sofa with her on his chest. "You're amazing, you know that?"

She nuzzled against his neck. "I was thinking the same about you."

"We don't know what we'll face when we leave here." At her silence, he continued as he caressed her back. "I want you as a man wants a woman, Angie. Do you know how hard it's been to deny that?"

Angie raised her face to his and met his lips in a soft kiss, then ended it. "That's how I feel, and how can that be wrong? I won't ever believe that I'll feel differently about you when my memory returns."

She raised her hand to his jaw, stroked his beard that grew there, and brushed her lips across his.

"I want you to touch me, I want your hands on my body, Matt." She stroked her hand down his chest to his navel, where the circular motion she made had her own insides quickening. "I want to be yours." She shifted on the sofa so that she could see his face, then bent to kiss him again. Matt held her head with his hand and pressed her to him. She felt the pulse leap in his chest at her touch there.

She abruptly pulled away. "But, you'll have to come to me this time." She smiled at his strained features before she stood from the sofa. "I'll be in my bedroom."

* * *

The white jacket was quickly discarded before the young black man stepped off the main hallway, in the staff service area, and into a quiet alcove. He reached inside his pocket and pulled out a cell phone. Quickly extending the antenna, his fingers lit over the buttons before he placed it to his ear. Within a few moments, he spoke.

"Your report is ready and on the way. Your target continues his visit here with his family."

The voice from the other end acknowledged the information. "Good. Halo wants the surveillance continued, as usual. Were you able to secure a device after the morning bug sweep? There's a possibility that he has information on the whereabouts of an American woman informant. Be on the lookout for anything that might lead us to her. This is a priority."

The young man looked into the hall, in both directions, from the alcove before he continued. "We were successful with a mobile device this time and avoided detection. We know for a fact that he's also looking for a woman. It could be the same one."

"That's good news for Halo," the voice on the line intoned.

"Oh, one odd thing. His visitors list was busier than usual today, and they came in pairs, no extra security, so obviously internal business. One pair was Joaquin Elgado and Larry Murphy."

"The search and destroy mercenaries." The voice on the phone was matter-of-fact.

"You got it. They came late in the day, so we couldn't get a taping." The young man leaned casually against the wall as another employee walked by. After a moment's pause, he said, "The meeting was short and they left. No tail was assigned since we didn't know the level of importance."

"He doesn't know where she is, either, and he's hired them to find her," the voice suggested. "It's to our benefit to get to her first. Keep in touch with any news."

"I will." The young man scrambled the line before he lowered the antenna. Looking left, then right, he replaced the phone in his pocket before he stepped from the alcove. He slipped his arms into the white jacket and, whistling a popular tune, buttoned it as he walked down the hallway.

Matt had just lit the last of the candles when Angie came to her door. Her face glowed with surprise at his handiwork to her bedroom while she had been in the bathroom. The heady scent in the air came from a vase of fragrant bougainvillea he had placed near the bed. Their bright, loose buds cascaded down the side of the dresser.

"My goodness, Matt. When did you have time to do all this?"

"While you enjoyed that long, leisurely bath." His eyes clung to hers, analyzing her reaction to his seduction, as he walked up to her at the door. "You're a stunning woman, Angie." His voice was thick and unsteady with anticipation. "I noticed it from the beginning."

"And you're a romantic. I like that." Angie's throaty voice had also become unsteady.

She was like a wood nymph, her short hair wet and slicked back on her head, rubber thongs on her feet, and a clean shirt worn as a robe. She was beautiful and complicated and mysterious, and he loved every bit of her.

He stopped in front of her and bent to kiss her lips. She didn't back away but leaned into him as a pleasurable moan escaped her mouth. Together, they slowly stoked a growing fire.

"I've come to you," he said, and nibbled at her ear. "I want you." He reached for the buttons on her shirt, and straightening to gaze into her eyes, started to undo them.

"Do you know what you're doing?" she whispered.

"I know my way around."

She smiled. "No, not that." She brushed his arm before she turned her face up to his. "Are you sure?"

He touched her lips with his fingers and traced their fullness. "I want to love you, explore you, and see where it takes us. Now."

A warm glow flowed through Angie at his words. He lifted her up and carried her to the bed, where he sat her on the edge. When he joined her there, he resumed unbuttoning her shirt. A delightful shiver of wanting ran through her as his hands grazed her bare breasts beneath the shirt. When the shirt fell open, his stare was bold as he frankly assessed her naked body beneath it.

"You're beautiful." The husky words were smothered against her mouth as he hungrily recaptured her in a kiss. His arms encircled inside her shirt, one hand in the small of her back.

Pleasure radiated from Angie; she parted her lips and gave herself freely to the passion of his kiss. While his hands explored the lush curves of her waist and hips, her own craved to caress his bare flesh. She slipped her hands under his shirt and stroked the heavy muscles there.

Angie's touch jolted Matt upright. He separated himself from her and quickly pulled the shirt over his head. She stood with him and looped her fingers in the waistband of his swim shorts.

"Let me," she suggested, and tugged them down, below his waist. At his groan of satisfaction, her stare was drawn to his strong, brown body, and the heavy erection she had released. Spurred by the power of her own passion, she wanted him to find her just as desirable. He quickly stepped from the trunks, and in the same movement, slipped her open shirt from her shoulders, where it fell to the floor.

He was even more stunningly virile than Angie remembered. His strength and size engulfed her as they stood face to face at the bed. Aroused, her body arched toward him.

Matt swept her up, and she wrapped her legs about his waist, her arms about his neck. His lips teased a taut, dusky nipple, the touch light and painfully teasing. As he gently eased her down onto the bed, her limbs trembled with desire. Stretched out beside her, one hand slid across her taut stomach to the swell of her hips, while his mouth traced a sensuous path to ecstasy from her lips to her neck. His slow exploration took his kisses down her body—to her breasts and stomach, then down to her thighs. She squirmed with a heady invitation as he paused to kiss her, whispering his love for each part of her body he'd awakened with his intimate touch.

Raising up, he took her hands and encouraged them to explore. She was in an emotional upheaval as the thrill of his rough male skin pierced her senses. When his fingers reached down and felt her dampness, she groaned in pleasure. Her ardor matched Matt's, and she voiced that need to him, which only roused his own steadily growing one.

"Do you want me, Angie? Are you ready for me?"

"Yes." Her whisper was desperate. "Now, Matt."

He lowered his body over hers, and together, they found the tempo that bound them as one. The pleasure was pure, explosive, and sure as he pushed himself into her, again and again.

Finally, Angie cried out for release, as Matt gasped out loud in sweet agony. They both rode the wave back to sanity and collapsed together, exhausted, though sensually stimulated.

Matt pulled her into the crook of his arm before he bent to kiss her deeply. Angie saw the desire still bright in his eyes and gloried in the intimacy they'd shared.

"No regrets?" he asked.

Angie shook her head. "None. You are everything I wanted and expected."

"Then, why are you crying?"

She had thought the candlelit room hid the tears that came from her own private exasperation.

"Please, tell me what's wrong," he urged.

"Right now, everything is just perfect." She sat up next to him. "I'm falling in love with you, and I don't want anything to change between us."

"It won't, because I love you, too. I know this is only the beginning, and we'll explore these feelings a lot more when we get back to the States. The first thing we'll do is get an investigation going to find out who you are."

When more tears escaped her eyes, he quickly added, "I know a pretty good P.I. in Atlanta who can do the job. And, we'll get you the best medical attention that—"

Angie laughed at his enthusiasm as she placed her hand on his chest. "Hold on a minute. Just hold me. I want to feel safe in your arms." No sooner had the words left her mouth than she felt a shiver of apprehension flit through her body.

He squeezed her tight and placed a kiss on her shoulder. "You're cold. Are you okay?"

When a flash of lightning fell across the dim room, their attention was drawn to the window, where it had begun to rain.

"A storm is coming through," Matt said.

They snuggled down into the covers, spoon fashion, and Angie let Matt calm her fear of the storms with whispered words of comfort. Through his words, she gathered strength, and kept the burgeoning memories, which seemed to flourish with the storms, at bay.

Later in the night, as Matt slept with a hand holding her close, Angie awakened to the peal of thunder. Startled by the flashes of lightning that filled the room, she raised her head from Matt's arm to stare at the window. The rain came down hard outside.

The storm seemed to awaken some dormant entity that

wanted to burst from her, and she was frightened by the possibility that it could present itself in all its horrific glory at any time.

She wanted to make love with Matt again, now, before it was too late. Her eyes widened. Why did she feel that? They had the rest of their lives—or did they? Lightning flashed again as her desperate thoughts took root. Somehow, she knew tonight was perfect, just as she'd said earlier, and things would never be this way again. Matt had wanted to be cautious about their relationship. He'd warned her that there is no future without resolution of the past. He'd resolved his. What about hers?

She turned to him and pushed his shoulder so that he rolled to his back. As she straddled him, she felt when he instantly awakened, and bent to kiss his lips. "Make love to me."

He mastered her with his strength as he caught her to him and with one turn, she was now on her back.

"Sweetheart, there's nothing like riding through a storm together," he said, and raised himself to his knees. "I'll show you how."

Spurts of desire had begun to spiral through her. She closed her eyes and let the real world spin out of control.

Matt turned in the bed and reached a hand out for Angie. When all that found its way into his grasp was a handful of the sheets, he opened his eyes to daybreak that had begun to filter in through the jalousie windows. He sat up and looked around. Where was she? He smiled as he remembered their lovemaking throughout the storm-filled night, and wondered if she was okay.

Angie was not okay. Her aimless and desolate walk had started just as dawn broke, and had led her away from the house to the beach, close to the spot where she had come ashore over a week before. With her arms curled tightly about her waist, she had cried a silent wail that had left her eyes both sore and burning. The only remnants from last night's storm were the palm fronds scattered on the beach—and her rapidly returning memory. Angie treaded heavily across the sand and around the gray trunks of the towering palms as she wiped away more tears.

"Why, God, why?" She shouted the anguished plea for the world to hear. "Why give me back my memory now?" She had to return to Matt and tell him everything. When her choked sobs finally broke through, she left them alone, unchecked this time. She would tell him that she was Angelica Manchester. And, Philip Manchester was her husband.

CHAPTER TWENTY

Philip! The realization that it might now be too late to save him threatened her sanity. The memories from the boat came back to Angie in big chunks of fear. She doubled over and sagged under the weight of the knowledge that she was supposed to have gone for help. How many days had passed since their boat had been boarded by Nicolas Magellan's men? And, what had happened to Philip?

Memories careened through her head like out-of-control train cars and interlocked to form a solved puzzle—the yacht, the dangerous men that came aboard, the terror, and the warning to find help before she was set out on the water.

Her head jerked around as her mind flitted to other memories. Reed, her parents . . . my God, what must they think happened to her? Choking on another sob that squeezed at her heart, she continued down the shore. Angie alternately doused guilt on her own person and then lamented the Fates that allowed Matt to find her, only to set up an impasse to curb their happiness. Recognizing the boulders that jutted from the water ahead, she realized how far she had traveled from the house.

Suddenly, a school of flying fish, resembling a flock of birds, jumped out of the water and crossed her vision. They darted against the blue-tinted morning sky before slicing the ocean again. As she watched them disappear, she thought she heard the faint sound of an outboard motor coming from the dark, rocky outcroppings that dotted the shore. When it became louder, her head followed the drone-like noise.

A sleek motorboat slid into full view. Angie stopped, her hand frozen where she'd brushed away a tear. Was someone coming to the island? Surely it wasn't Matt's captain returning to pick him up. He wasn't expected until tomorrow afternoon.

Then, she saw him, the slim black man who stood with his hand resting on the bow, with a gun slung across his back. The hackles rose on Angie's neck as the air became electrified around her. His cocksure figure, sporting a gold earring, was unmistakable. Two other men, both white, were with him. She also recognized the pale one. She had thought of the two men as night and day because of their extreme coloring. Philip had called them ruthless thugs. Apprehensive, she wondered why they were here. Within a split second, she felt the color drain from her face as she answered her own query.

Fear leapt up and clutched Angie's heart—its fingers so tightly embedded she didn't dare breathe. She backed away, out of view, and fled to hide in the line of trees and brush. With a hand to her hammering chest, she saw that the boat was about to pull onto the beach. The men had not yet seen her. They were busy preparing to come ashore. She had to act, do something. Warn Matt. Her mind raced for a plan even as her feet danced across the sand in her retreat around the trees back to the house. What had she brought to his beautiful, peaceful island?

* * *

The small charter twin-prop plane gave off a cacophony of pops, creaks, and groans on its low flight to the Berry Islands. Reed had squeezed into his narrow seat next to Jill, taking it all in stride. The noisy drone was a monotonous diversion for him as he thought about Angie. His plan was to start a search in a square area that stretched from the Miami coast, across to Andros Island, and then up to the Berry and Bimini Islands.

Jill, neither comfortable nor trusting, warily watched the pilot. He had announced his name as, simply, Wally, and had a penchant for singing lyrical island ditties. Jill suspected she was only meant to understood the tamer parts. The racier portions were sung in an island dialect she couldn't quite grasp fast enough.

She leaned forward and read, from the pilot's control panel, a tattered bold warning: "Acrobatic Maneuvers Expressly Not Allowed, Including Spins And Rotations."

When she leaned back in her chair, Reed watched her expression turn sickly again and he smiled indulgently. Her stress at riding across bumpy air currents and open water had not eluded him, even though she'd tried to keep it concealed. He reached for her hand.

"We'll touch down soon."

"We'd have arrived faster if we'd just swum in from Miami, don't you think? Our chances of actually making it in one piece would've been much better, too."

He laughed at her take on their event-filled transportation arrangements from Miami. This was her first open complaint. After a flight into Andros Island, and then more channel hops from a speedboat and two other charter planes, they were now almost at their next destination, the northern end of the Berry Islands. Once there, they'd catch a mail boat that would escort them to small, colorfully named cays not even on the maps. The last twenty-four hours had been nothing short of an air/sea/land triathlon.

"Yeah, but we would've missed the local color and culture." His expression turned serious. "I talked with J.R. last night about our plans."

"You told me." She looked at him, puzzled, and sat up. "Has he changed his mind? Did he find out something else about Angie? You said last night that it's a fact that Magellan doesn't have Angie because he's searching for her, too."

He nodded. "He's also tying up loose ends that could find their way to J.R." He paused a moment. "Daniel Otero is dead."

"Dead?" she whispered.

"The stakeout closed in to pick him up for more questioning after we discovered Philip's body yesterday. They found him in the house. No sign of forced entry. Whoever did it was in and out."

"Oh, my goodness. We've got to find Angie before he does." She looked up at Reed. "Did J.R. say what it was that Philip expected to gain from this deal he made?"

"Philip was going to provide to his contact, Halo, extensive distribution records of Magellan's new designer drug."

"So, what went wrong? How did Magellan find out?"

"J.R. and Philip worked out a system to pass information anonymously. Somehow, though, the word got back to Magellan. We think the snitch was Daniel."

"But, Daniel was a good friend and longtime employee of Philip's," Jill mused with a frown.

"J.R. learned that Daniel worked for Magellan a long time ago, before he started with Philip. Maybe Philip forgot about that and let his guard down. Maybe he never knew."

"So, Daniel was Magellan's built-in security system. And in the end, he shut the system down." She shifted in her chair. "All of this cross, and double-cross. It's all too . . ."

"Bizarre? I agree." He picked up her hand and absently

stroked it. "You know, you deserve a nice vacation after we find Angie. I promise you'll get one, too. First, though, where did you hide all of the Dramamine you've been taking? And, why didn't you tell me you suffer from motion sickness?"

She looked up at him, surprised that he knew. "Because I had to help."

"These boat and plane rides must be hell for you."

"Only when I'm continually moving, like yesterday and today." She smiled. "As long as there's a dose in my system, the nausea stays at bay. I'll be fine." She darted a glance to her lap, where his hand still lay on hers, and looked up again. Her thick ponytail danced with the movement. "I want to be here, not only for me, but you . . . and Angie."

"I see why you two are close. Like her, you'd go the distance for a friend. You know, I didn't realize how much your being here has meant to my sanity."

"About that vacation," she said in a humorous tone. "All I've seen are airstrips with signs announcing that 'loose cattle will be shot.' I'll accept your offer, but only if you promise to deliver ecstatic views of green mountains and blue beaches." Her smile grew as she added, "With handsome men serving me rum punch in a courtyard perfumed with fragrant frangipani and jasmine. And, no more than one boat or plane ride a day."

She succeeded at drawing a smile from Reed. His eyes roamed her face briefly before he leaned over and let his lips brush hers as he spoke. "I'll make sure I'm the one serving our drinks." He was eager for her lips to be under his. As he pressed against her mouth, his did not become softer.

Angie had run back to the house at top speed. When it was finally in sight, Buster met her with enthusiastic barks, mistaking her urgency for play.

"Matt, Matt." She yelled for him as she stamped through the soft sand on her way to the house. Buster continued barking until Matt stepped from around the back of the house. When he appeared, a cry of relief broke from her lips, and she ran to him.

"What's with all the noise, you two?" he called out.

As he got closer, he saw fear, stark and vivid, bright in her eyes. "Angie, what's wrong?" He grasped her shoulders and looked hard into her face.

"Oh, Matt, we've got to do something. I just saw the men, they were down by the boulders. They're coming ashore and they're going to come here." She twisted from his hold, then pulled his arm toward the house with her. "Come on, we don't have any time. We've got to hide from them."

Matt's gaze was filled with incredulity as he resisted her pull. What in hell was wrong with her? "Angie, you're not making sense. What men? Where have you been?" One strong yank on her arm reeled her back to him. "What are you talking about?" He stared at her face, tear-stained and puffy. She'd been crying. Something was very wrong.

"The two men from my nightmares," she said. "They're here."

His frown was deep and troubled. "Someone from your past?"

"I don't know their names, damn it, and stop asking all these questions. We don't have time." She looked down the beach before she tried to pull him to the house again. "We've got to prepare. Now, before they get here."

"You know why they're here, don't you? Your memory's back." He rushed the words out. "When did this happen?"

"I'll explain everything later, I promise, but we have to act now." She tried to hold onto her fragile control as she explained.

"There are three of them, but I only recognize two, and I saw a gun. I know they're looking for me, but maybe they'll go away and not hurt you and Buster if they don't know I'm here. So, you must go and meet them. Don't let them come to the house. Tell them you've been here all alone and that you haven't seen anyone that resembles me. Please." She pulled him again from the open beach.

It finally dawned on Matt that her rantings were serious. He turned to look in the direction she had run from and saw nothing. He turned her loose and rested his hands on his hips. "I'll go see who it is that's frightening you, and—"

"Remember, don't tell them you've seen me," she interrupted.

"I want an explanation when I get back, you hear me?"

Angie nodded rapidly. "Okay, just go and meet them. Don't let them come to the house."

"Get inside, and stay there until I return. Then, we'll talk." His gaze pierced hers. "Is that clear?"

She nodded, and without a thought, pulled his head down to hers and kissed him. "I love you, Matt," she murmured to him. "Always remember that. And, I'm sorry." Her voice was trembling. "I'm so sorry."

For a moment, Matt stared into her eyes, his confusion evident. Then, he pointed to the house. "Go," he demanded gruffly. "Buster, come with me."

Angie ran to the house, looking over her shoulder in a panic as Matt strode off in the opposite direction. She'd have to tell him everything soon. But first, those men had to be tricked to leave the island. The thought of her short-term future tore at her insides.

No more than an hour had passed before the door to the bedroom closet that housed Angie's curled figure was thrown open. Startled, she blinked into the daylight and saw Matt. Buster pushed his way in and licked her face. She was drained and exhausted from all that had happened, but scrambled from her crouch to put her arms around the dog's neck.

"When you two were gone so long, I became worried," she said in relief. "Thank God, you're all right."

Matt reached his arm inside the closet and pulled her out. "I want to know everything, Angie. Who in hell are those men and why are they looking for you?"

She flinched at his tone as she stumbled from the closet. He didn't release her until they entered the living room.

Angie's gaze darted to the windows. "Have they gone?"

"Yes." His words were curt and short as he stood waiting for her explanation.

"Are you sure?" she insisted. "What did they say?"

His eyes had darkened dangerously when she turned to him. "They were looking for a woman that fit your description who'd fallen from a cruise ship in the vicinity. They were part of the search team dispatched to find you. They wouldn't give me your name because your next of kin hadn't been notified."

"They're lying."

"I figured that part out already."

She left him to look out the window. "Did you see them leave?"

He tread a line that led him to her at the window and whisked her around so he could see her face. "Is your memory back, Angie?" His voice wore an edge, and when she didn't answer, he raised it. "Damn it, is it back?"

She could tell he held his breath for her answer, and she tried to keep the tremble from her voice. "Yes," she shouted. "Every bit of it."

"How long?"

She looked away. "I had already told you that it had gotten stronger over the last two days—"

"Answer me," he demanded, and squeezed her shoulders.

She swallowed the despair in her throat. "This morning,

memories just appeared. Suddenly, with no effort, I could recall things, and they made sense." She raised her eyes to his.

"Last night, when you woke me, and we made love again, did you know then?"

"I . . . the storm brought on some memories, but they still weren't clear. I didn't know what was happening."

"How clear did they have to be for you to tell me? Or, have you played me for a fool from the beginning?"

"No, that's not true." Faced with his anger, she stumbled for an answer. "I wanted to tell you that something was different. Oh, God, I wanted to, but what I was remembering was scary, and confusing, so I went for a walk on the beach to clear my head. That's when I saw the men on the boat."

Matt's eyes narrowed. "Are you running from someone? They looked like hired thugs."

Angie rubbed at her temple, the pressure of tears building. "They are. You need to hear everything."

They both moved to the sofa where he sat down, his eyes keen on her every move. She perched on the edge of the coffee table in front of him and, raising her head up, met that hard stare as it pierced her like a knife.

"My name is Angelica Manchester, Angie for short. I live in Fort Lauderdale, Florida, where I design jewelry, from nature." She drew a deep breath, no longer able to hold his stare, and looked away. "I have a mother and father, and a brother I'm very close to. His name is Reed. They all live in Miami."

She swallowed hard and raised her head once again. "I had been on a private yacht a couple of days before you found me." She stumbled over her words. "During the evening, we . . . we were boarded by the two men you saw, and held against our will. But . . . I . . . I managed to escape with Philip's help."

Angie saw the twitch that marked his jaw as he heard the name, and she became increasingly miserable under his scrutiny.

"Philip Manchester. He's my husband."

CHAPTER TWENTY-ONE

"Your husband?"

It was an effort as Angie watched Matt close his eyes tight and rub the bridge of his nose.

"He was my husband at the time—"

"These men were hired by him?" he interrupted.

"No." She crossed her ankle over her knee and touched the chain and key. "They're after this." She lifted up the silver key.

His glance traveled from her ankle to her face, and then back again.

She sniffed as she wiped tears from her cheek. "I need to explain all this—"

"Tell me everything, Angie, from the beginning." His whisper was deep. "And, spare no detail. I think you owe me that." He avoided meeting her eyes as he rose from the sofa.

Angie's first thought was that he couldn't stand to look at her, and it broke her heart. She watched his broad, proud carriage as he strode past her and took his turn looking from the window.

"Philip and I were separated, Matt, our divorce almost final, when he contacted me almost two weeks ago." She watched Matt's head jerk to attention as she went on to explain how she happened to be on the boat when it was boarded by the men who worked for Philip's former client, Nicolas Magellan.

This time, Matt turned from the window. "I've heard of him." He pushed his hands into his pockets. "Did you know your husband did business with these guys?"

Angie felt shame at all the wrong decisions she'd made during that time. "I didn't know a lot of it, and I regretted that I hadn't asked enough questions almost immediately." Her glance found him. "He told me it was in the past, but I stumbled onto a safe stacked with millions of dollars in bearer bonds, marked for payoffs, and he didn't try explaining it away. It was the last straw and I left him."

"What happened when they boarded your boat?"

"They held us until Mr. Magellan arrived. Needless to say, I was mad as hell at Philip, then scared to death at what they'd do to us. One of the men got ugly with me. Then, he and Philip started to fight, and a gun went off. Luckily, no one was killed, but they put us below deck after that."

Angie rose from the coffee table to pace the room. "While we were below, Philip explained to me what was going on. He showed me a key that unlocks a safe-deposit box." She looked down at it. "He had kept the thing hidden inside a cross around his neck, so he decided to put it on my ankle chain for safekeeping before Magellan arrived on the boat.

"It seems he'd made a deal with the U.S. Attorney's Office to turn over evidence in their case against Magellan. And somehow, his deal got back to Magellan." She pressed a hand to her temple, her anxiety rising as she told the story. "If something were to happen to him, he told me where to take the key."

Matt's frown deepened at the incredible story, but he remained silent.

The fear and terror of that night had returned to Angie, and tears rolled down her cheeks.

"When Magellan arrived, and they came down for Philip, the men gagged and tied my arms before they left me in the dark." She sniffed quietly for a moment. "After what seemed like an eternity—when I heard noises and bumps from the deck that I didn't want to think about— Magellan came down with one of the men. They threatened me, slapped me around, wanting info about contacts and what Philip knew. But, Philip had been careful not to tell me anything, and I had not been around him for almost a year. They didn't even know about the key's existence at the time. Finally, they realized I couldn't help them and they left me alone."

She stopped her pace when, suddenly, Matt appeared in front of her. He reached out his hand to wipe her tears. "Is that when you got off the boat?"

She remembered the fear and darted her eyes away from his.

"Yes," she whispered. "They literally threw Philip down the stairs soon after that and, when I saw him, all battered and beaten," Angie's voice became strangled with grief, ". . . I knew our lives were over . . ."

A noise from the stairs turned Angie's attention in the dim light. The bandanna that had been tied around her mouth now dangled around her neck, loosened earlier by the black man who had accompanied Magellan. The noise was a body, sliding down the few stairs to the bottom. It was Philip. The door closed, but thin streams of light from the door slats flowed down to them. When she peered through the obscurity, the crumpled body moved.

"Ohhhh . . ." It was Philip groaning.

"Philip, are you all right?" Angie's ears perked for his response.

"Yeah," he whispered. She heard him shuffle toward her "What about you? Did they hurt you when they came down?"

"I'm all right." Relieved that he was still alive, she began to cry silently. "We've got to get off this boat, Philip. My God, what did they do to you?"

Indeed, Philip had crawled across the floor to her and she could see that he'd been beaten. Badly. One cheek of his beautiful face had been lacerated and blood oozed from the tear. Both of his eyes were already swelling in a face pocked with blood spots.

"You should see the other guy," he joked, but his own attempt to laugh only brought a tortured grunt from his lips.

"You must be in a lot of pain. Can you untie my hands?" She twisted around so he could work at her bonds.

"We only have a little time before they come back for me," he whispered. "I'm only here because Magellan got a call. He's getting information on the deal I made, I know it, so we have to act now. This could be our only chance."

Angie shook her hands loose to restore their circulation and looked around the dark room. "How far offshore are we? Maybe I could swim to another boat for help."

"No, no, they'd pick you off like a sitting duck, and what if there are no other boats around? I've got a plan."

As quickly as he could, he moved to the other side of the bed to a porthole. After he struggled with the latch, Angie realized what he was trying to do and helped him wrench the hole open with as little noise as possible. When it was open, he looked out and above and saw what he wanted: the dinghy latched to the side just above their heads. He pulled his head back into the room.

"Listen, Angelica. You're small enough to squeeze through this hole. I'll hold you while you reach up and unlash the lanyards that'll release the dinghy, got it?"

"But, how will I launch it without their knowing what I'm doing?"

"You're going to lower it for a short drop, then you're going through the hole and you'll swim for it."

"No. I can't. What if I can't reach it before the waves carry it out?"

"You're a strong swimmer. You have to. You have no choice."

Angie looked away and knew he was right. *"You'll be behind me, won't you?"*

"No. I'm going to go back up on deck and buy you some extra time. I'll keep them busy before they realize you're missing."

Panic closed in on her. *"Philip, no."*

"Yes. Staying on the boat is sure death. Magellan may be a businessman, but he's got two ruthless thugs to do his dirty work. If you ever get the advantage against either of them, use it. You have a chance in the water. There are patches of land and rocks all over the place. Chances are good you'll find one."

"You can't stay here."

"I have to. My deal to win you back didn't quite work out the way I figured. Now, come on. No more time for discussions."

He lifted her up so that she could stretch through the porthole. First her head, then her shoulders and hips, wriggled and cleared the small space. She reached up and pulled at the lanyard ties, one at a time. When the two uppermost ones were loose, the dinghy dropped backward onto Angie. While Philip held her legs inside, her quaking arms supported the falling dinghy, then it rolled over her head and quietly hit the water, bow end first.

She held her breath, expecting the men on deck to come to the side to find out what the splash had been. Instead, she heard Philip's voice from below her.

"It's up to you now. Paddle away from here as fast as you can. When you get to safety, find help and send them back. But first and foremost, take care of yourself. Don't forget what I told you about Halo."

Before she could complain or argue about the plan, he pushed her the rest of the way out of the porthole. With only a couple of seconds to assume a dive position, she did, and cut through the water, avoiding a loud splash.

She shot a few yards underwater before she pedaled to a stop and stroked to the surface. Pulling in air in great gulps, she *twisted in the water as she looked for the dinghy. It was only a few yards to her right, and she took off after it. As she thrashed the water with long strokes, every swimming horror story she'd ever heard came to mind. They only provided her with the needed impetus to get to the bobbing dinghy . . .*

Angie was now curled into the corner of the sofa. Tears continued down her cheeks as she'd told the story to Matt. His pacing had carried him across the room numerous times.

"When I reached the dinghy, I paddled away as fast as I could. A storm came through later that night, though, and turned me around. I was scared to death from the lightning and thunder, not to mention the rain. And, I'd lost my bearings. I didn't know where I was."

Matt wanted to rage at the ordeal she'd gone through, and his fists opened and closed with each step. He was torn, though, by his own conflicting emotions. He was selfish and wanted her completely. He didn't want to share her heart. With her memory now in place, could she offer that? As careful as he'd tried to be, he'd done the one thing he was most afraid of. He'd taken a chance and lost by offering his love to someone not free to give it back. His old guards he'd thought torn down had begun to comfortably reassert themselves on his shoulders.

"That explains why the storms upset you. Do you know how long you were out there?"

She pulled her legs up onto the sofa and hugged them. "Less than two days. By daybreak, I'd already lost one oar in the storm. I believe I was hit on the head with the other oar later. After that, I don't remember much, except for waking up here."

"These men are obviously dangerous, and they want that key."

Angie got up from the sofa to look out the window. "You're sure they're gone?"

"For now, at least." He looked over her head to the beach.

"You think they could come back?"

"It's possible. We're going to have to keep an eye out until we leave tomorrow." He left her side to resume his pace.

"And what of Philip?" she asked. "Matt, suppose they did something to him? He risked his life to get me off that boat."

"You can't blame yourself. And, from what you've said, I don't think he'd want you to feel that way."

"Philip's kind of a dreamer. He's smart, but I have to admit, he's a charmer, too." She sniffed and tried to smile through her gloom. "I think he figured he could talk his way out of anything. Do you know why he made that deal with the government?" She shook her head in disbelief of her own words. "In exchange for the evidence this key would unlock, the U.S. Attorney would restore his good name. And, with that in hand, he'd planned to win me back." Tears discouraged her smile and blinded the gaze she turned on Matt. "This whole thing came about so he could win me back."

He broached the subject that was on his mind. "Are you still in love with him?"

She shook her head easily. "I never was." Her voice choked as the unwelcome tension stretched tight between them.

"He is your husband."

"Was, Matt." She met his eyes. "I was comfortable with that decision a long time ago. I was so different when I think back to when I met him, rebellious and very young, and it wasn't the way to start a marriage. But, I had to go through him to get to where I am now. There's not much I would change in my past." She drew his gaze. "Can you understand that, Matt?" She reached out and touched his arm. "What I'm feeling for you . . . what we feel for each other—"

He turned away and walked to the door. "I'm going to look around the beach."

"Matt, please," she implored. "Don't do this to us and go back in time. Don't act like you regret what we shared last night. My memory doesn't change my love or what I've said. And . . . and we can't avoid the subject."

He rubbed his hands together before he gave her a cursory glance. "I believe that's exactly what I'm going to do." He spoke matter-of-factly as he opened the door. "Like I said, I'll look around outside to see if they doubled back. You should stay inside—at least for the time being."

She watched as he left and cupped her hand to her mouth in quiet shock. *What have I done?*

Reed stood over Jill's seated figure as they waited in the little mail shack and spoke with the manager. Or at least, that's what he claimed to be. Reared back in his chair, he was busy eating an oily fried fritter from a wrinkled sheet of waxed paper. His lunch sat between two colorful boxes, filled to various depths with mail. Other boxes were scattered on the floor, apparently waiting their turn to be sorted.

"How long will we have to wait before the mail boat arrives, docks, and then takes us on?"

"As you can tell, he has much to pick up. Maybe three, maybe four hours."

At least the sing-song lilt spoken by the native islanders was a pleasure to the ear. The man of indeterminate age smiled, his dark gums illuminating the gap between his pearly white front teeth.

"I know, will it be today," he announced.

Reed frowned. He couldn't tell whether he'd just heard a question or a statement.

Jill smiled as she sipped from her bottled water. Patience was something Reed still had to acquire. She sat up in the chair and gave the man her best smile.

"We did call ahead to make arrangements to ride with the captain. You see, the situation we find ourselves in is of grave importance, a matter of life and death. We have to locate a relative who may be in danger—"

"Oh . . ." Recognition lit his eyes. "You're the ones that wish to search the isles for the young Missy?"

"That's right," Reed spoke up. "We really need your help."

"Not to worry," he said, and gave his best smile to Jill while he sat his fritter aside and searched his desk for something. "I have instructions here somewhere for you."

While he dug some more, Reed shifted his foot in anticipation. But, a look from Jill to settle down resulted in his doing just that.

"Ah . . . here it is," he said. "The captain radioed that he would change his route and pick you up on this drop at two o'clock."

Reed swung his wrist up to glance at his watch. "That's an hour from now."

"Enough time for lunch," the man said, smiling again. He reclaimed his chair and fritter. "Why don't you go over to Maybelle's." His offer was punctuated by a wave of his head. "The conch is on special today."

"Thank you," Jill said, and rose from the chair where she guided Reed to the door. "When the captain arrives, will you let him know we're at Maybelle's?"

"Most assuredly, Missy." He winked before he sank his teeth into the golden fritter.

Outside in the bright, warm sun, both Reed and Jill squinted as they adjusted their sunglasses.

"Well, we've succeeded in the first part of the trip. Now comes the hard part," he said. "Finding her on a patch of land somewhere in the ocean."

"And, we will find her," Jill said, as she looked up and down the tiny street with it's colonial-styled buildings.

"I just don't think things are supposed to end badly. We've had too many lucky breaks so far to come up empty now."

Few people were on the street. In this heat, they were probably enjoying their pleasures nearer the beach. "What do we do now?" she asked.

"What else? Eat conch fritters at Maybelle's." He linked his arm through hers. "Come on."

Angie was slicing fruit in the kitchen when Matt came through the screen door with Buster. She dropped the knife and wiped her hand, then caught his stride as he moved toward the rear of the house.

"Did you see anything?"

"No." He continued at a brisk pace to the bedroom and pushed the door open. "But, they could have seen the dinghy."

She remembered it sat near the sand dunes at the back of the house. "I forgot about it." Angie stopped at the door with Buster and watched as he sat on the edge of the bed.

He glanced her way before he pulled the lower drawer of the night stand open and fished around in it. "We have to be careful in case they come back. They didn't seem like men who make many mistakes."

"They want me." She scratched the dog's ears as she stood there. "I never meant to bring this trouble on you."

He looked up and spoke stiffly. "If I have any say, they won't get you."

"How will you stop them?"

"We'll be off the island by tomorrow evening but, if necessary, we can disappear into the sanctuary." He took a brown satchel from the drawer. A closer look, though, revealed it was a chamois bag. He worked the drawstring loose and withdrew a wooden box.

Curious, Angie absently patted the dog as she watched Matt open the box. A gun was inside. Shocked, she stepped back.

"Matt, what are you doing with a gun?"

"I'm protecting you." He lifted the gun from the box. "Just in case I didn't convince them that you haven't been here after all."

To her continued surprise, he methodically cracked the weapon open and prepared to load it, all the while barking orders. "I want you to put a bag together with some things we'll need for a hike into the woods. Get dressed, put on something that'll protect you out there, and be ready to leave at a moment's notice." He looked up from loading the gun. "You understand?"

Angie nodded as her mind raced through all he'd said, but she continued to stare at him and the gun.

"Well," he offered, "don't just stand there. Get to it."

Her reverie broken, she moved to act.

The rest of the day was an uneasy alliance for Angie and Matt. They found themselves separated, but this time by a powerful knowledge of the other. Yet, they'd come together to overcome this latest danger to their safety. She had tried to broach the subject of her memory, but he wouldn't listen, and she gave up. His anger and disappointment was still raw and needed time to heal.

She had tried to nap while he kept an outside vigil that long afternoon, but she was a tightly wound spring in a quiet house that afforded her too much time to think. She was most hurt that he had buried the memories of their lovemaking. While it was written indelibly on her mind, didn't he care at all?

She refilled Buster's water bucket, which sat next to his

food bowl. Matt had instructed her to prepare the dog to stay in the house. Angie wanted to take him along, but Matt argued that the dog could lead the men to them at a crucial time.

She heard the familiar clang of the screen door and turned her head toward it. When she saw Matt's face, she knew their fears had been realized.

"Angie," he called out. "Let's get moving."

"They came back?"

"From the south end of the island this time. We've got no more than a fifteen minute head start before they make it to the house."

With quick action, Angie stooped down to Buster, "I'm sorry, fella. We can't take you with us."

Matt left her with the dog and grabbed up the bag she'd packed and placed in the hallway. Hoisting it across his shoulder, he closed the back windows so Buster wouldn't follow them. He made a quick sweep through the house to insure the same.

"Angie." He kept a watchful eye out the south window. "Let's go, now."

"I'm coming." She squeezed the dog one more time.

"Buster will be okay," Matt said when he joined her. He ruffled the dog's coat, too. "We'll see you soon, fella."

The dog seemed to understand they were leaving him and didn't make a fuss as they pulled the front door firmly closed behind them.

Angie threw a cautious glance around as she followed Matt to the backyard. He pointed to the line of woods near the rear of the gardens.

"We need to disappear fast, so we'll cut through there," he suggested, and turned to her. "Are you with me?"

Her doubts and fears were engraved on her face and caused Matt to stop. "It's going to be okay," he said. "I didn't find you only to lose you now. So, are you with me?"

Her heart leapt at his words. Hope had found a flame. "Always," she said.

"Then, let's get out of here." He grabbed up her hand and led her to the trees.

REDEMPTION

There's a period of life when we swallow a knowledge of ourselves and it becomes either good or
sour inside.

—Pearl Bailey, 1966

CHAPTER
TWENTY-TWO

Reed turned to help Jill disembark from the boat; she was able to hop onto the sand without so much as a weave. She fished into her shoulder bag to pull out some of the flyers that carried Angie's likeness and the offer of a size-able cash award for information leading to her return.

"I'm getting better at this," she announced to Reed, who'd come up behind her. The tiny islet they were on appeared all but deserted, but a pleasant breeze whipped their clothes as they stood at the shore.

This was their second stop, and the captain, after being offered a cash incentive for his time, stopped his boat at landfalls not on his usual route so that Reed and Jill could leave the flyers and inquire about Angie.

The wiry captain pointed beyond the shore to a dirt road. "Up yonder, there's a house atop that hill. We can inquire there, leave your flyers, and move on."

Reed nodded his agreement, and watched the man start out ahead of them. Initially imbued with optimism, Reed was becoming disheartened at the lack of any sign that

Angie was out here. It became all the more real when he considered the vast scope of what he and Jill meant to accomplish.

Jill seemed to sense his mood. Falling in step with him, she spoke for his ears only. "It's early yet, Reed, and this is only our second stop. We've got at least fifteen more over the next two days. Something will break open for us."

"Damn. Magellan is looking for her, too. So, who do you think has the better resources to find her first?"

"I thought J.R. was helping."

"He is, but it'll take another day or two to corral his sources. Bureaucracy." He picked up a shell and sailed it through the air. "He'll join up with us in Bimini in two days."

As the shell's arc cut across the sky, it fell into the ocean. Simultaneous with its entry, another shape gracefully arced upward from the water and into the air. It was a dolphin.

Jill grabbed Reed's arm and pointed. "Look."

He smiled. "Yeah, the sailor's omen for a safe journey."

"See—that's the omen we needed. We're going to find Angie."

Reed believed her.

Matt knew their fifteen-minute head start was up. Only a few words had been exchanged with Angie since they'd entered the woody forest. Their focus had been attuned to negotiating the terrain and hiding evidence of their passing.

"You're sure it was them, the same men? It wasn't some other boat?" Angie had resorted to double steps and quick jogs to keep up with Matt's long, sure strides through the trees. They had left the marked trail to make tracking more difficult for their enemy.

He darted a glance to her. "Pretty sure. Try not to break

any plant limbs," he warned. "We don't want to leave obvious signs on the trail."

"Where are we going?" She picked her way through the low underbrush, the carved rubber sandals Matt had fashioned the only thing separating her and disaster.

"We'll need a place to stay tonight, and this *is* Cave Cay, remember?" He now shared a smile with Angie. "I've done some spelunking in a few that are okay to sleep in. Some even have their own running streams."

She smiled. "That's convenient."

At that moment, the rat-a-tat-tat of sporadic gunfire could be heard in the distance. Matt stopped and laid a steadying hand on Angie's arm. The gunfire repeated for two more bursts.

"They're probably spraying the house with shots," Matt said, frowning.

"Buster!" Angie's eyes grew wide. "Do you think he's been hurt?"

Matt turned from the anguish on her face and grimly narrowed his lips as he pulled her with him through the trees. "Come on, we've got to go deeper into the woods. They'll be in the sanctuary soon."

Filled with terror that the men could be on them at any moment, Angie kept a watchful eye over her shoulder as time took on the face of desperation. After traveling another half mile, she thought she might drop from the exhaustion.

"Matt," she pleaded in heavy breaths. "Can we stop for a minute."

He pulled up on his jog, and Angie crashed into him.

"Shhh . . ." he cautioned her with a finger to his lips. "I hear something."

Angie held her breath and listened. It was a grunt, intermittent at best, and much like the wild boar they'd heard a few days before.

"We've got to try avoiding the boars," Matt said. "You usually hear them first."

However, more ominous noises in the distance were getting stronger.

"Oh, hell," Angie whispered, panic running freely through her veins. "They'll find us soon."

"Not yet," Matt cautioned. He looked around the woods as he plucked two bottles of water from their bag and handed one to Angie.

"If I can lead them in a circle," he continued, "maybe we can get back to their boat before they catch us." He wiped the sweat from his forehead with the back of his hand and quickly downed three gulps. "At worst, we'll be back near the cave you fell into on your first day here."

Angie sat on the bag as she drank greedily from her bottle of water. She wiped her brow as they prepared to set off again. "Why is that cave important?"

"Just trying to think ahead. When I figure it out, I'll tell you." He helped Angie up before he replaced the bottles and hoisted the bag onto his shoulder once more.

"Are you okay?" At her nod, he smiled. "Let's move. We've got to find shelter before dark."

The tree cover in the setting sun was making it difficult to move as fast as they had been able to earlier in the day. Yet, the men had been able to keep up, causing Angie and Matt to keep on their guard.

Angie grabbed hold onto a tree as she called to Matt. "I've got to rest a minute."

He stopped beside her and dropped the bag from his shoulder. "Sure. I'm sorry I've pushed you like this, but we can't let them gain any distance on us."

She nodded, too tired to speak, and sank to the ground, resting her back against the rough bark. "Just for a minute, I promise you."

"I haven't heard our friends for a while. Do you think we lost them again?"

Angie managed to smile between her heaving breaths. "Right now, if they promised I could take a nap first, I wouldn't care if they captured me."

He shook his head. "Don't say that. Didn't you teach me not to give up? When one door closes, another opens, right?"

She held her hand out to him so he could help her stand again, grateful he was in her life and proud that she could love again. In midmotion, as her gaze strayed beyond Matt, her hand dropped like a stone.

Matt saw the change in her features and whirled to see what had frightened her.

It was grayish-black, easily over four feet long, and three feet high at the shoulders. The short, woolly hair had a clump of bristles that formed a mane along the spine. The wild boar rooted at the base of a tree to the far side of them. Matt knew its hearing and smelling was well developed, so the animal either ignored them or, knowing its superior strength, wasn't concerned with them right now. But, what about later?

He backed up the few steps to Angie, shielding her with his body.

"Matt," she whispered as she held onto him. "That animal is huge. You said they travel in groups. Are more like him around here? Will he attack us?"

"Only if they're threatened, since they're highly territorial. Or," he added, "if you enter their nesting areas. Not to worry, though," he joked. "They only occasionally kill and eat small animals."

As if to add to his point, the boar raised his head as he chewed on something. His lower teeth were turned up and protruded at least a half foot from his mouth into formidable tusks.

He reached for her hand around him. "We're not going

to make any sudden noises to alarm our friend." He pulled her up from the ground and looked up at the old tree they were under. "Angie, can you get into this tree if I boost you up to a limb?"

She followed his gaze to the tree, then to the wild boar that had returned to root in the underbrush.

"Yes. If I can shimmy up a coconut tree, surely I can do it here."

He leaned against the tree and gave Angie a leg up. She climbed from his shoulder and grasped a lower branch. Matt was able to boost her further by her feet until she caught hold of a higher branch. Soon, she was sitting in the angle formed by a tree branch, covered from view by the leaves.

"What about you?" she called down.

Matt had turned back to the boar, who now gave him his full attention. The familiar grunting began as the boar started to make a circle.

"Where's the gun?" Angie called down. "Get up here with me or protect yourself."

"We can't use it," he said, never letting his eyes leave the animal. "The noise will bring everything in this jungle right to us. And, haven't you noticed? I'm a big boy. My weight on that limb will bring us both crashing down. Just stay up there, and no matter what, keep quiet." He unsnapped one of the leather closures on his belt and released a wicked looking knife that he now weighed in his hand. "I'm going to entice it away from here."

He slowly edged away from the tree and toward the ugly, grunting beast, when he heard a new noise in the brush: trampling. He shifted his attention, until he saw the business end of a long-barreled semi-automatic gun peek from the foliage. The owner quickly followed, a smirking man with dark hair. He leveled the gun at Matt.

"Ah . . . this is too easy," he boasted in a heavy Spanish

accent. "Okay, where's the girl?" He slinked forward as he talked.

Matt willed Angie to be silent in the tree behind him. He thought quickly as he raised his hand with the knife. "I figured your friends had her by now."

"You lie. We separated to cover more ground. They're too far off. I think I'm the one to find the prize today. Where is she?"

As the man stepped closer, he unknowingly insinuated himself between Matt and the pawing boar.

In one swift move, Matt threw the knife at the boar to rile the animal. Caught off guard by Matt's actions, the man raised the gun to let off a shot, but he stumbled over the angry, charging boar. Matt ran for cover behind the tree.

The boar's tusks gored into the soft, exposed flesh at the man's leg. He let out a howl and dropped to the ground, clutching at his leg. The animal grunted in earnest as he gored defensively at the man.

Even in his sorry condition, the man was able to get one wild shot off as he fought off the heavy animal.

The explosion released a shot that whizzed through the forest canopy and found its destination in the tree Angie occupied.

The limb she clung to, weakened from the bullet, began to sway and lurch. Panicked at this turn, she grabbed a hold of the main tree trunk, when everything happened in a whir of speed.

Matt craned his neck to see her, fearing she might have been hit by the bullet, and at that same moment, the entire limb broke away from the tree.

Angie screamed as she tumbled, along with the limb, in a rolling heap onto Matt's shoulders as he stood below.

CHAPTER
TWENTY-THREE

Angie found herself landing in Matt's outstretched arms, which cushioned her fall. As they fell backward, in a tangled heap to the ground, the limb bounced heavily off Matt. He let out a pained gasp as it splintered nearby. With the thought to protect Angie from the man and wild animal nearby, he tried to raise up from the ground, but the pain was severe, and he dropped back down.

"Angie, protect yourself," he yelled, and threw an anxious glance on both of the threats to their safety. The grunting boar was running from the man who now lay quietly on the ground.

"Matt, you're hurt." Shocked to action, she crawled to his side, and saw the painful lines etched on his face. "What's wrong?"

"Get the gun out of the bag," he ordered. "And, do it quick. That gunshot will lead the other men to us."

She left him to search in their bag and found the gun in no time. "What should I do with it?"

"Put it in the pack around your waist."

"Why do you want me to keep it?"

"Protection, in case I'm not around."

When he grimaced in pain and dropped his head to the ground, she quickly knelt beside him. "Tell me what's wrong with you."

"I've got a dislocated shoulder," he whispered. "I can't move it."

"What do we do, then?"

He took in great gasps of air. "First, I want you to go over there and check the man for a pulse. See if he's still alive; hurry."

Angie looked across at the man's still form and swallowed for courage before she went to him. She held her stomach as she witnessed the tattered flesh on his legs. His shirt was torn, but she couldn't see if damage had been done to his torso. She breathed a deep breath and stooped to place her finger against his neck to find a pulse. It was there, a faint one.

"He's still alive," she called out.

"He's probably in shock from blood loss. There's nothing we can do out here. Get his gun and put it with our things."

She picked up both the knife Matt had thrown and the gun before returning to his side.

"Are you feeling any better now?" she asked. "Can you get up?"

"I can barely move." His breathing was hard between the words. "You're going to have to go on ahead to the cave without me. It's not far away."

Her eyes became wide saucers at the suggestion. "No, I won't do it." She strained to help him to a sitting position, but he roared out in pain and she stopped. "I'm not leaving you here, Matt," she announced stubbornly. "We've got to think of something."

"Getting you to safety is what's important. Leave one of the guns with me and you go on. I'll be okay."

She started to cry. "Don't ask me to do that, Matt. I can't. I won't leave you out here." She searched her head for an idea. "If we can get you to the cave, you can rest your shoulder."

"Damn, but you're a stubborn woman."

"Who is in love with a forgiving man." She kissed his lips and brow. "Now, think of something before they find us."

"You're going to have to reset my arm in the shoulder socket."

"Oh, dear. How?"

"Come to my other side and help me get closer to the tree."

Angie bit into her lip and did her best to help move him the few feet necessary. The painful struggle paid off.

"Now, I want you to leverage your foot against my armpit." At the alarm in her eyes, he said, "Don't worry, you won't hurt me. You're not that heavy, and I'll need all of your weight."

"If you say so."

"Hold my arm out, and with your back braced against the tree, push your foot and pull my arm at the same time. You have to yank it hard. I don't want to do this twice."

"You and me both," she said as she nodded. They went through the instructions one more time as she pantomimed the actions. When they were ready, she counted to three and pressed and pulled with all her might.

A dull clunk accompanied Matt's howl of pain, and let her know her effort was successful. She immediately dropped down to see if he was all right.

His eyes were closed tight as the fog of pain dissipated.

"I'm sorry I hurt you," she cried. "Can you move?"

He opened his eyes with a tired smile. "You were great. But, I can't use my shoulders and arm. They'll be sore for a while." He flexed his hand. "Roll me over so I can get up."

She helped him roll to his side and soon he was standing against the tree for support.

"What do we do about him?" She referred to Magellan's man.

"Hide him. We don't want his friends to know there's one less hunter."

Under Matt's guidance, Angie made short work of tying the unconscious man's hands with his own belt before she pushed, then dragged him into the brush. She darted concerned glances to Matt, desperately in need of rest from the shock given to his limbs. He bent over slightly while he hugged his cradled arm close to his body.

She grabbed up the strap of their bag and worked it onto her thin shoulders.

"We're losing our light fast," she said, adjusting the bag. "We need to find the cave."

"What are you doing? I can carry that," Matt said, as he came to her.

"Look at you," she said. "You can barely stand." She put her arm around his waist so he could lean on her. "I think it's about time I take care of you for a change. You haven't forgotten we've got two men on our trail, not to mention an ugly territorial pig. Of course, I'd count that pig as a friend now."

"Yes ma'am." He smiled at her offered support. "The cave's not too far."

The two of them hobbled through the woods as one shadow, far removed from the two distinct ones at their journey's start.

Matt's dream of scented candles and green grass, where he made love to Angie under the moonlight, was real enough to stir him from sleep. He slowly opened his eyes. Candles? Four flickered across from him in the breeze. The ribbon of sea air as well as the wide shaft of moonlight came from somewhere above his head. Instantly, he remembered where he was. And why.

With some difficulty, he pushed himself up from the stone floor of the above-ground open cave and looked around. He was sore all over and cringed at the pain that throbbed at his shoulder. What he wouldn't give for a shot of Demerol about now.

He turned his head and saw that Angie sat facing him. With her legs crossed, her head was dropped to her chest. He smiled. She'd fallen asleep watching over him. He had done the same with her.

"Angie." At the whisper of her name, she became instantly awake.

When she saw Matt, she smiled and leaned over to hug him. "How are you?"

"I've felt better, thank you." With his sore arm still held tight at his side, he reached out to squeeze her with his other arm. "But, I don't think I've ever been in better hands."

Angie crawled over him and reached for a wet cloth she'd placed close by. "I thought you were kidding when you said there's a stream running through here." She wiped his face. "You needed the sleep and rest, so I didn't wake you."

"How long was I out?"

She tried to sound upbeat. "No more than a couple of hours. It's been real quiet outside, too. Maybe those men didn't follow us here after all."

As she wiped his face, his eyes began to search her face, read her thoughts. Her hand ceased its motion, and she gave into the tension that had been building all day. She began to tremble.

"Matt, I don't know what I would have done without you being with me. I was so scared out there. And you, wanting me to leave you for those men to find—"

"Hey, it's okay." He drew her to his chest and massaged

her back. "They can't do much tonight, anyway," he whispered at her ear. "We'll work our way back to the beach tomorrow morning so we can meet our boat, and this will all be over."

When she shifted against his chest, he groaned in pain again.

"We need to put your arm in a sling," she said between sniffs, and sat back on her heels.

"Where did the candles come from? And, what all did you pack in that bag?"

She wiped her eyes and, seeing the amusement on his face, smiled. "Obviously I don't go camping enough. I figured candles and matches were a basic necessity." She glanced around the room. "And, they do take some of the gloom off our cave, don't you think?"

"You did good."

She smiled again, her trembles subsiding. "While I look for a sling, I'll dig something out of the bag for us to eat." As she started to move away, he stopped her.

"We should decide what we'll do next." He tried to straighten against the wall and winced again. "I've thought about it, and with my bad shoulder, our chances aren't good if we fight them both off at the same time. We have to keep them separated."

"How do we do that?"

"We create a diversion if we're confronted by both. You'll escape to a prearranged place, and I can join you later."

"Why do you keep putting yourself in danger, for me?"

"I want us both to walk off this island together." They both became silent at the import of his words. He rubbed her arm. "No matter how much I try to deny it, the future seems worthwhile again since I met you."

She gloried in this shared moment, but only briefly. "So, when do we put our plan in effect?"

He smiled at her. "We'll leave in the morning and work

our way back to the beach. That'll bring us near your cave." He watched her nod of recognition.

"You mean the one where I had a glorious adventure?"

"The same. You know how to get into it, so that'll be our escape plan." He shifted again and grimaced from the pain.

"I'm going to get you out of that shirt so we can put a sling around your neck." He drew his legs up and she knelt between them. When the shirt was unbuttoned, she slid it from one arm and managed to maneuver it around his sore one.

"What are you using for a sling?"

Angie unbuttoned her own shirt and revealed her bathing suit top. She shrugged off the shirt and reached behind her back to unsnap the bra top.

"Don't tell me," he said.

"It's elastic and we're about out of other choices."

She pulled the straps down her shoulders and slipped the article off her arms. Matt's smile widened in approval.

"Nothing here you haven't seen before, and I suspect with the pain I'll inflict, your thoughts won't stray to me for too long, anyway." She reached for her shirt again and slipped her arms into its sleeves.

"Some things aren't dulled by pain." Indeed. Matt held his breath from both the pain and pleasure he was experiencing. As she helped to draw his arm through the loop she'd made with the garment, he thought to redirect the pain and blurted out, "What's the name of your business?"

"The Angelica Gallery. I display unique, natural art pieces as jewelry. My symbol is a butterfly."

He smiled. "Ah, yeah, the butterfly—"

"On my butt." She adjusted the sling around his neck. "Actually, I got that tattoo on a dare from a very good friend. Her name's Jillian."

"The two of you together must have been a terror."

"No, but we do bring out the best in each other. That's

what good relationships should do, like me and my brother, Reed." She looked at her finished handiwork before she gazed into Matt's face again. "Like you and I."

He leaned forward and placed a kiss on her arm. "Do you know your touch makes me want you?"

At his words, she grew serious. "I've brought all this trouble on you," she said. "And, I'm beginning to realize I'm everything you aren't—impetuous, unrestrained, indiscreet . . ."

"Don't forget stubborn and nosy." He kissed her arm again.

"See? What in the world made me think we even have a chance?"

"Because we have a shared passion," he said quietly. "We love each other." He shifted from where he sat against the wall.

"Come here."

She did and bent to meet his mouth. His arm wound under her shirt and caressed her naked back.

"We're lucky," Matt said against her lips. "We've got candles and moonlight to order, just for us."

She broke away from his lips and looked up into the cave's partially open ceiling. "Look, Matt. Above us It's your blue moon."

He raised his head and saw that the bright full moon peeked down on them. "So it is," he said, and placed kisses along her mouth.

"I don't know what's in store for tomorrow," she said between nibbles to his ear.

"We know here and now, and that's all we need," he said, and kissed her. "I want to make love to you again."

Her hands dropped to his waist and she unsnapped his pants. "Raise your hips and I'll take them off," she whispered.

He complied, and soon, with Angie controlling the tempo, they kissed with a languid motion that let them ride the waves of ecstasy. After her shirt found its way off again, they took the time to explore, arouse, and pleasure each other's bodies with their hands and mouths.

Desire spiraled through Angie. She wanted more. "Matt, what about your shoulder?"

"You'll have to do the work tonight, sweetheart, that's all."

She sat astride him as his hand slid down her taut stomach to the swell of her hips. His fingers moved intimately; she groaned in pleasure as his fingers caressed the dampness there, surrendering completely to his masterful seduction. As gusts of desire shook her, she heard his voice.

"Do you want me? Tell me if you're ready."

"Yes." Her body was like liquid fire. "I want you now."

He pushed himself into her, and her flesh captured him in a time-honored ritual. They abandoned themselves to their shared ardor, a hysteria of delight, and only came up for air after the hot tide was spent.

Some time later, Angie lay on her back, pressed into Matt's side. She looked through the ceiling at the full moon and smiled. After all that had happened and was to come, she felt at peace.

"A penny for your thoughts," Matt said. He also looked to the sky.

"I was thinking about the blue moon." She raised up on her elbow and gazed at him.

"You feel it too, don't you?"

She nodded. "I feel . . . like this is a beginning of something wonderful. Even with everything facing us tomorrow, I'm . . ."

"Optimistic?" He finished for her.

"Yes, that's it. Reborn." With a contented sigh, she returned to his arm and snuggled close.

The next morning at daybreak, they prepared to leave the cave and start their hike back to the beach. If they were lucky, they could forestall a run-in with the two men, and rendezvous with their boat that afternoon.

Angie rolled her socks down before she slid her foot into her rubber beach shoes.

"How, is your shoulder?" She now helped to button Matt's shirt, which he had pulled on over the sling.

He bent forward and kissed her sweetly on the jaw before he flexed his arm. "Sore, a little tight, but better."

She started to hoist their bag onto her shoulder, when Matt slipped it away with his good arm. "I can handle this today." He took one last look around the cave before he turned to Angie. "Come on, let's get out of here."

After pushing through the opening Angie had hidden with forest debris, they took a cautious look around before they headed off.

It had been a long morning, and the sun beat down in earnest. But, Elgado could take it. What he couldn't take was poor business discipline. He couldn't understand what had happened to Manuel, Magellan's cousin. He shifted on his seat high above the trees as he looked for his quarry.

After the gunshot yesterday, he and Murphy had met up and searched the area, but had come up with nothing but a lot of ugly wild pigs. He'd considered that their prey had gotten the better of Manuel, but they couldn't find a sign of trouble. He shook his head. That man, Manuel, was a lazy bastard, and they'd only let him accompany them because the job required it. He was probably lost. Elgado laughed, and it felt good. Serves him right. If he wasn't at the boat when it was time to leave, then he could stay here.

This job had already taken more time than he'd figured was necessary. He had known within five minutes of talking with the man on the beach that they had hit pay dirt. The woman was here. Too many questions had been asked, and he was too anxious to have them leave.

He pulled a long draw from the cigarette with a finger that waved with a blunt end. From his perch high on the rock mountain, he kept an eye as sharp as an eagle's for his prey. His mistake was that he'd not killed the man right there and just gone after the woman. Low profile. He spat out some of the bitter tobacco. That was the condition of this job. So, he had to go about it slowly.

Suddenly, a shrill whistle broke the silence as a pair of binoculars sailed through the air for Elgado.

"Due north, about twenty minutes away," Murphy called up from the rock ledge below.

In one smooth move, Elgado easily caught the binoculars up in his hands and peered through them. He slowly followed the objects of his attention through the glass.

"They're moving back toward the shore," he commented.

Murphy gave off a laconic smile. "You figurin' we can head them off?"

Elgado smiled. "In a heartbeat."

CHAPTER TWENTY-FOUR

Reed sat near the wheel of the mail boat launch with the captain.

"Your lady is plumb tuckered out, I see," the captain said.

Reed looked back at Jill, who was catching some sleep huddled in a corner chair.

"Yeah, she is. But she's been a trooper. She's passed out at least 500 flyers. What about this next stop. How soon will we be back on course?"

"After I make this afternoon's pickup, we'll all stay on Bimini tonight." The wooden mailboxes, which took up most of the center of the launch, were lined with oilskin and filled with mail.

"It must be hell, getting mail only once a week over these waters," Reed observed.

"I suspect most will say it beats the alternative." The captain offered him a wicked grin. "No mail."

"I see your point," Reed said, and laughed with him.

* * *

Matt didn't let his shoulder's injury stop him from keeping a steady, fast pace to get through the forest growth and back to the beach. But, when Angie started to lag further behind, he decided they'd stop in the clearing for a few minutes.

Out of breath, she leaned forward and rested her hands on her knees.

"These clearings, with so many stone pillars. They seem familiar. Are we near home?"

Matt liked the description she'd used and smiled. "You're getting good. We're back to the marked-off sanctuary trail signs, and not so deep in the interior anymore." He looked around the area. "We'd better get moving. I don't want us to stop too long."

"What about Buster? Do you think he's all right?"

Matt frowned as his attention was drawn to the brush. He drew the gun from his waistband. "I found him in an animal shelter a few years ago. He's a survivor." He backed up, toward Angie.

"I've never had a dog before." She immediately jerked to attention when she saw Matt point the gun in the air. She turned and looked around the clearing.

"Did you see something?" she whispered. "Are the men back?"

He quietly nodded and reached down for the bag's strap. "I thought I heard something in the brush just beyond us," he whispered. "I want us to get to their boat first, so we can take it."

"I wouldn't count on that, my man." A drawling American voice came from Matt's left.

As Matt whirled with his gun pointed in that direction, a menacing click sounded by another gun came from the right.

"We meet again, pretty lady." The sinister voice near

her was precise. "Drop the gun, toss it to the ground," he ordered Matt.

Matt and Angie looked to their left and right and saw the two men, their colorings stark opposites. They stepped into the clearing from two directions.

"Who are you, and what do you want from us?" Angie looked back and forth at the faces of the two men who had terrorized her on the boat. "And, what did you do with Philip?" She backed into Matt.

"Drop the gun," the black man repeated.

Matt did. "Angie," he warned. "Don't talk to them."

The man smiled again. "You're a curious lady. Fearless, not afraid of the answers your questions bring." He strutted forward. "My name is Elgado. My friend is Murphy, and we are here to conduct business. We want the key. And, we will leave with it." He looked at Matt. "We want nothing from you, so if you interfere, you are disposable."

Murphy grinned at her. "You want to know about Philip? Last time I checked he was dead. Now, you don't want that to happen to you, do you?"

Even though Angie had suspected that was his fate, hearing it from the perpetrators tore at her heart. Matt came up to her and placed his arm around her shoulder.

"You have an injury," Elgado said. "Did you happen to run into our other friend?"

"Like Philip, your friend is dead," Angie blurted out. "And if you aren't careful, we'll send you to hell, too."

"She's got a big mouth," Murphy said, as he stepped near them.

"If you hurt her you can kiss your damn key goodbye," Matt announced in an angry voice.

"Calm down, Murphy." He gestured the gun at Angie. "Now where's the key?"

"In a safe place."

Elgado motioned to Murphy. "Check her out."

Matt was helpless as Murphy frisked Angie, though she

poked and bit at his hand at every opportunity. Matt drew her glance to tell her it would be okay. When Murphy got to her socks, he snatched them from her feet, but found nothing.

"She's not even wearing the chain," Murphy said. He next dumped their bag and found nothing there, either.

"Time is short," Elgado said. "Where is it?"

"Maybe it was lost in the jungle," Matt said. "Sorry."

Elgado looked at Angie. "Then we have no choice but to take you back to Mr. Magellan. As for your friend, he's of no use, so we may as well shoot him now."

"No," Angie screamed, and stepped in front of Matt. "I'll cooperate, but don't hurt him. Enough people have been hurt already."

"Then, tell me what I want to hear."

She looked at Matt. "It's back at the house," she answered. "I didn't wear it out here because I figured it would get lost."

"Then, lead us to it." We'll be behind you with your boyfriend in case you want to do something crazy."

"He . . . he has to lead us back because I get confused."

"All right." Elgado motioned for Matt to take the lead. "No heroics, okay?"

The group started out in double file: Angie and Matt in front, their two captors behind them.

After walking for only ten minutes, the terrain became rocky, and the waterfall crashed in the distance. The path soon gave way to a clearing marked with stones. Matt bumped into her and nodded toward the marbleized stones that formed a jagged hill. Angie darted a knowing glance to him before she stopped and turned to Elgado.

"Can I rest for a moment?"

"We've not walked that long. Keep moving."

"No," she said. "I need a rest now." With that said, she began to walk toward the hill.

"Get your butt back here," Murphy called to her. He

turned to Elgado. "I'm gonna teach that little brown bag of sass some manners once and for all."

"The hell you are." Matt tightened his hand into a fist and, rearing his good arm back, hit Murphy square in the jaw. "Run Angie," he called. "Run like hell."

The man fell backward into his partner, who pushed him away.

"Go after her," Elgado yelled. He turned to Matt and leveled the gun at his head. "And you, my friend, are dead."

Matt's attention was taken up by Angie. Her sprint to the cave that appeared to be a hill was successful. As Murphy gained on her, she stooped for a moment at the hill before she vanished from sight.

"Hey man, did you see that?" Murphy called out. "She just disappeared."

"Go in there after her," his partner yelled.

With only a little hesitation, Murphy kneeled down and, caught unawares, slipped through the opening with a loud scream.

With both of their attention drawn to the hill, Elgado's gun hand had relaxed. Matt knew this was his chance and, with a high kick, knocked the gun away.

The men circled each other and tried to weigh the other's strengths. Matt had to do something, and he had to do it fast. He had to get to Angie.

Angie thought she had prepared herself to fall into the darkly lit pool of water. She had not. Panic engulfed her as she dropped in the water and tried to get her bearings. She had to escape into a dark corner of the cave and wait for Matt. She tried not to think of the danger he could be in.

As she dragged herself to the pool's edge, a scream, followed by a loud *whoop* sounded behind her before she was knocked back in the water again. She tried crawling away from this new danger, but not before recognizing Murphy's ghost pale face in the dim room. Her fear was renewed on whether she could get away and hide.

"You bitch," he yelled. His words echoed over and over in the cavernous space. "Come here." He grabbed a piece of her soggy shirt and dragged her back to him in the water.

Angie screamed and fought him with all her might, and they both fell. When he put her neck in a chokehold, and attempted to drag her with him from the pool, she sank her teeth into his skin. Howling in pain, he released her, only to produce a gun she had not, heretofore, seen.

She had to do something, or he would shoot her. Angie screamed before she barreled into him with all her might.

The gun blast was earsplitting. For a split second, there was no sound, just the frozen aftershock from the two people in the pool. Then, an immediate rush of air, followed by high-pitched squeaks and flutters, blanketed their small air space.

Bats. Hundreds of them became dangerous, diving bodies looking for an escape. Angie kneeled in the water and, covering her head with her arms, wondered when her nightmare would end.

The gunshot was an explosive shock to Matt's senses and stole his attention from the man he fought. He paid the price as he took a punch that caused him to stagger backward.

Matt breathed hard; his shoulder felt like it was on fire as he circled the healthier man. He had to help Angie, and that meant he had to end this.

Elgado also breathed heavily, but taunted Matt. "You're injured, not at your best, are you?"

"That's okay. Without that gun, you're just right for a kicking."

Matt attacked with a ferocity that had to succeed. Careful to use only his legs and good arm, Elgado had discovered his weakness due to his injury. So, after a low kick to Elgado's abdomen, Matt turned and exposed his weak side. He couldn't have known that Elgado waited for this opening and charged, head first into the shoulder.

With a gasp, Matt dropped to the ground like a felled oak. Elgado, also injured, was bent over as he scrambled to the dirt and grabbed up the gun. He held it to Matt as he tried to rise from the ground.

"Yes," Elgado announced with pleasure, and raised the gun at an advancing Matt. "You're dead, my friend."

"I'm not your friend." He looked beyond Elgado and saw what was an unbelievable sight.

As Elgado prepared to get off a shot, a growl came from behind him. Turning to the sound, a pounce was all he saw as a ferocious animal went for his neck.

Elgado screamed, and was knocked to the ground as he tried to fight off the animal.

Matt quickly retrieved the gun that had found itself on the ground once again. With it safely in his hand, Matt called off the dog.

"Heel, fella, heel."

Buster growled as he bared his teeth at the man cowering on the ground.

Matt came around Elgado and, with the butt of the gun, knocked him out with a hard tap to the head.

"Buster, am I glad to see you," he called to the dog. "But we've got to get Angie. Come on." He tucked the gun in his waistband and headed for the cave.

CHAPTER TWENTY-FIVE

As Angie crouched in the water, the screeches from the swarm of bats soon began to subside. She peeked out from under her arm and saw that Murphy was also protecting himself with his arms. She turned to run, but he had already caught her leg and pulled her back to him.

"No, leave me alone," she screamed.

"You're more trouble than you're worth. I'm gonna make sure you pay for it, too."

He grabbed her from behind and picked her up, but she kicked and struggled in his arms. Reaching behind her with both hands, she dug her nails into his face.

A string of epithets left his lips as he turned her loose; with a wave of his knuckles, he backhanded her across the pool.

Angie hit the water hard and saw stars, but she didn't have time to register the pain. She had to find a weapon if she wanted to live. She ran her hands through the coarse silt to grab a rock, anything. He was coming at her.

"I'm gonna kill you, you hear? I don't care what Elgado says, I'm gonna kill you."

He had the gun and she believed him. As icy fear froze her veins, she ran her hands through the water again, all the time keeping her eyes on him. She came upon something hard. And sharp. Recognition flashed in her brain. Her fingers closed round the scissors she'd lost so many days ago.

When Murphy clutched her shoulder to drag her to her feet, she turned into him and pushed the scissors into his soft belly.

"Owww," he hollered, and swung her away by the arm. "What the hell did you do to me?" He looked down at his belly and saw the blood. "You stabbed me."

Fear became a potent drug when she faced Murphy's anger. He came at her. With the scissors upturned, she met him head on.

He grabbed her, but the scissors plunged into his side this time. At his deep groan, she yanked them out and pushed them again. This time, his hold on her loosened and she, in turn, released the scissors. Her heart thumped madly as she backed away, her eyes never leaving his strange gaze.

He stumbled backward before dropping to his knees. Angie continued to back away; her whimpers were pants of terror as the man finally fell forward into the water.

As the enormity of what she'd done to survive hit her, she began to shake. She tried to breathe, but her breath seemed to have solidified in her throat.

Matt! She looked up at the small opening she'd fallen through and could hear no sign from outside. She had to get to the other chamber and wait for his signal in case Elgado was waiting for her.

She tore her gaze from the man in the pool and averted her head as she felt her way into the next chamber.

"Angie, answer me. Angie, can you hear me?"

It was faint, but it was Matt's voice.

"Matt," she screamed, and the tears started to flow. "Oh, Matt. You're all right."

She rushed the rest of the way into the last chamber until his voice was louder and stronger.

"Matt, I'm okay." She looked up through the opening he had left bare from before. "What about you?"

When he finally appeared, and she saw his beautiful face, she started to cry again. "You're all right."

"Where's Murphy? I heard a gunshot—"

"I think he's dead." She turned a watchful eye toward the direction she had just left. "He's lying in the pool. Please don't make me check his pulse."

"My God, you're beautiful, Angie. Hold on, I'm going to pull you out the same way I did before."

"But your shoulder," she began.

"I'm getting you out of there if I have to use my teeth." He lowered his belt, as they had done before, and with sheer will, he pulled her from the depths of the cave.

When she finally cleared the opening, she pulled herself up and fell against him. As they rained kisses on each other, they were joined by a wet intruder.

"Buster," Angie shouted in delight. "He's okay, Matt." She ruffled the dog's fur as he licked at her face.

"He must have escaped out of the house. He showed up in the nick of time and helped save my life."

Angie laughed as she stroked the happy dog. "You're making this lifesaving bit of yours a habit, aren't you, fella?" She turned to Matt. "Did you know there are bats in that cave?"

He smiled and nodded. "Remember the acrid smell and I told you it was guano?"

Her brows narrowed a bit before she guessed the answer. "Oh, my goodness. I was sloshing around in that? No wonder I smelled awful."

"I also knew you'd never go in there again if I told you

it was a bat cave. By the way, what did you do with the chain that was around your leg? When we were leaving the house, you had it on.''

''I decided at the last minute that I would leave it for safekeeping.'' She ruffled the dog's fur at his neck and revealed his collar. The gold chain with its silver key was attached there. ''It was a little secret Buster and I shared.''

Matt laughed and drew her close in his arm. It was going to be a glorious day after all.

Early that afternoon, Angie and Matt sat on the shore, arm in arm, as Buster frolicked nearby The warm water lapped across their legs and added to their calm serenity as they waited for the boat that would take them back to the States and a new life together.

Matt rubbed his hand across her shoulder. ''I want to call on you when we return home.'' When she looked up at him, he moved his mouth over hers, relishing its softness. ''Do you mind?''

''I'd like to see you try not to.'' Her eyes held a gleam as she added, ''In fact, I think my mom and dad will love you.''

''Oh, why is that?''

''Well, my dad always thought I should marry a doctor.'' A flash of humor crossed her face. ''He's partial to them, I guess. Did I tell you he's a semi-retired cardiologist on the board at Cedars in Miami?''

''What?'' Matt's eyes twinkled suspiciously as he looked at her. ''And, what about this brother of yours, what does he do?''

Reed sat across from Jill at the back of the launch.

''I can't put off calling my parents any longer. I'll do it tonight when we arrive in Bimini.''

She nodded. "We still have this pick-up stop to check out, plus the Bimini Coast. Remember, we're not giving up hope."

"I'll find out what J.R. has in mind when we see him tonight. Maybe we'll have more success handling the search his way."

"There's nothing wrong with this idea, Reed. We have a lot of area to cover. We know Magellan doesn't have her, so we have to believe she's hiding and waiting to appear when it's safe. It's as simple as that."

Reed loved her conviction. And he particularly liked her convictions about him. "Do you think we'll ever laugh at these boat rides we've been taking?"

"Yes, when we tell Angie about them."

"I'll hold you to that," he said, smiling.

"Reed, there's something I've been meaning to ask you for the longest time." At his raised brow, she asked, "What do you do for a living?"

"That's odd. I could have sworn I told you a while back when you asked me before."

"No, you didn't."

"It's simple enough—"

"Well, that's odd."

Reed and Jill turned to the captain, who was standing near the wheel and looking toward the shore.

"What's wrong?" Reed asked.

"I had a two passenger pick-up, a man and his dog. Looks like he's had company since I've been here."

Reed joined the captain and peered out to the shore. All he could make out were two figures getting up from the surf and a dog. He stared a moment before he asked, "Where are your binoculars?"

"Right here." He passed the spyglass over to Reed. It took Reed no more than a few seconds to look through the glass before he turned, astonished by what he'd seen, to Jill.

"My God, Jill. It's her. It's Angie."

"Is that your boat coming in?"

"Yeah," Matt said, as he stood up from the shore and helped her to stand. "Looks like he has more passengers this time."

Arm in arm, they looked at the boat a few more seconds before they saw someone aboard furiously wave back in their direction.

"I wonder why they're waving like that?" Matt mused over the man's actions and only now saw that Angie seemed just as infatuated with the boat.

"Matt, the boat . . ." She started to walk into the waves.

"What are you talking about?" He went after her, and saw that the man had actually gone over the side and was now wading through the waves to meet them.

She turned to Matt, her smile wide and her eyes bright with excitement. "He's my brother. It's Reed."

"What?"

He scooped her up and waded out into the water to meet her family, his future, their destiny.

Their redemption had come full circle in that rarest of moments, once in a blue moon.

About the Author

Shirley Harrison has enjoyed writing all of her life, and is employed in the tax accounting field. She lives in the metro Atlanta area with her husband and two sons where she is an accomplished artist, a gardener, and an avid reader. You can write to her at P.O. Box 373411, Decatur, GA 30037-3411 or Email: sdh108@aol.com

Coming in November from Arabesque Books . . .

___HARVEST MOON by Rochelle Alers
1-58314-056-5 $4.99US/$6.50CAN

After Regina Cole's older husband dies, she must make arrangements
with his estranged son, Dr. Aaron Spencer. Never expecting the instant
attraction that flares between them, she must now risk everything on
their fragile trust to find a love for all time . . .

___A TEST OF TIME by Cheryl Faye Smith
1-58314-051-4 $4.99US/$6.50CAN

When Nicole Johnson married Mark Peterson, she was sure that their
deep love would last forever but when one of Mark's old flame's appears,
and threatens all of her dreams, she must confront the insecurities of
her past in order to save all they have built.

___FOR LOVE'S SAKE by Rochunda Lee
1-58314-052-2 $4.99US/$6.50CAN

Attorneys Tonya Locksley and Dexter Freeman lose themselves in desire
until Dexter's father tries to destroy the relationship. Now, Dexter must
risk both family and career to convince Tonya that she's the only woman
for him.

___A LOVE OF HER OWN by Bettye Griffin
1-58314-053-0 $4.99US/$6.50CAN

Ava Maxwell had resigned all dreams of love and family until a little boy
named Marcus and a kind man named Hilton enter her life. But her
secrets torment her and she can't help the feeling that Hilton's hiding
something as well . . .

Call toll free **1-888-345-BOOK** to order by phone or use this
coupon to order by mail.

Name _____

Address _____

City _____ State _____ Zip _____

Please send me the books I have checked above.

I am enclosing $ _____
Plus postage and handling* $ _____
Sales tax (in NY, TN, and DC) $ _____
Total amount enclosed $ _____

*Add $2.50 for the first book and $.50 for each additional book.
Send check or money order (no cash or CODs) to: **Arabesque Books,
Dept. C.O. 850 Third Avenue, 16th Floor, New York, NY 10022**
Prices and numbers subject to change without notice.
All orders subject to availabilty.
Visit our website at **www.arabesquebooks.com**.